J. T. McCarthy

The Poetry and Oratory of Ireland

J. T. McCarthy

The Poetry and Oratory of Ireland

ISBN/EAN: 9783742819765

Manufactured in Europe, USA, Canada, Australia, Japa

Cover: Foto ©Andreas Hilbeck / pixelio.de

Manufactured and distributed by brebook publishing software
(www.brebook.com)

J. T. McCarthy

The Poetry and Oratory of Ireland

THE
POETRY AND ORATORY
OF
⇥⊰❈⊱ IRELAND. ⇤⊰❈⊱

EMBRACING

MOORE'S IRISH MELODIES, THE POEMS OF CLARENCE MANGAN, THE SONGS OF
SAMUEL LOVER, THE PATRIOTIC POEMS OF DAVIS, LEVER'S MILITARY SONGS,
THE POEMS OF BANIM, FERGUSON, ALLINGHAM, D. F. M'CARTHY,
FATHER PROUT, CALLANAN, GOLDSMITH, GRIFFIN, ANSTER,
WOLF, AND NUNAN.

WITH

THE MOST BRILLIANT AND STIRRING SPEECHES OF EDMUND BURKE, HENRY
GRATTAN, JOHN PHILPOT CURRAN, RICHARD BRINSLEY SHERIDAN, ROBERT
EMMET, CHARLES PHILLIPS, RICHARD LALOR SHEIL, DANIEL
O'CONNELL, REV. DR. CAHILL, THOMAS FRANCIS MEAGHER,
THOMAS DARCY M'GEE, ARCHBISHOP M'HALE,
FATHER BURKE, REV. M. B. BUCKLEY,
MICHAEL DAVITT, A. M. SUL-
LIVAN, ETC.

COMPILED BY

J. T. McCARTHY.

EMBELLISHED WITH A FULL SET OF PORTRAITS, ENGRAVED EXPRESSLY FOR THIS WORK.

ERIN GO BRAGH

NEW YORK:
MURPHY & McCARTHY,
PUBLISHERS.

CONTENTS.

ii. CONTENTS.

CONTENTS.

CONTENTS.

PREFACE.

"Poetry," said Coleridge, "is the fragrance and the blossom of all human knowledge,—human thoughts, passions, emotions, language." The poetry of Ireland, at least its lyric poetry, is, it may be safely asserted, superior to that of other nations in the felicity of language, and variety and harmony of its numbers; moreover, its character is distinctive: the national aspiration for freedom, and the invocation of her sons to break the thrall of bondage, have been struck upon the harp-chord of Erin by nearly all her bards, and serves only to show how fertile are the resources of genius, even in treating of a single subject. But, not alone to this field is Irish poetry confined. Epic poetry is well represented; as for example, Moore's Lalla Rookh—a gem, pure in its exquisite word-painting, and harmony of metre as the pearl of that Indian ocean which is, in some part, the scene of its tragic story; and pathos, humor, and satire have all had their famous exponents in the gallery of Erin's poets. Speaking on a kindred topic, a distinguished divine (Monsignor Capel) said recently:—"The intellect of Ireland is a gulf-stream in the ocean of thought." And this opinion will be readily endorsed by all who read the poetry of Ireland; which, even after centuries of oppression, breathes the Spartan spirit of defiance of the conqueror; and, ever with the rainbow of hope in the sky of its prophetic future, heralds the day of national independence.

The selections of verse in this volume present a variety of subjects, and an array of celebrated names, which must command the attention of the most fastidious reader, and will well repay perusal. P. D. N.

MOORE'S IRISH MELODIES

GO WHERE GLORY WAITS THEE.

Air—Maid of the Valley.

GO where glory waits thee,
   But while fame elates thee,
Oh! still remember me.
When the praise thou meetest
To thine ear is sweetest,
   Oh! then remember me.
Other arms may press thee,
Dearer friends caress thee,
All the joys that bless thee,
   Sweeter far may be;
But when friends are nearest,
And when joys are dearest,
   Oh! then remember me.

When at eve thou rovest
By the star thou lovest,
   Oh! then remember me.
Think, when home returning,
Bright we've seen it burning,
   Oh! thus remember me.
Oft as summer closes,
On its lingering roses,
   Once so loved by thee,
Think of her who wove them,
Her who made thee love them,
   Oh! then remember me.

When around the dying,
Autumn leaves are lying,
   Oh! then remember me.
And, at night, when gazing,
On the gay hearth blazing,
   Oh! still remember me.
Then should music, stealing
All the soul of feeling,
To thy heart appealing,
   Draw one tear from thee;
Then let memory bring thee
Strains I used to sing thee—
   Oh! then remember me.

WAR SONG.

REMEMBER THE GLORIES OF BRIEN THE BRAVE.

Air—Molly Macalpin.

REMEMBER the glories of Brien the
      Brave,
   Though the days of the hero are o'er;
Though lost to Mononia, and cold in the
      grave,
   He returns to Kinkora no more!

That star of the field, which so often has
    pour'd
  Its beam on the battle, is set ;
But enough of its glory remains on each
    sword
  To light us to glory yet !

Mononia ! when nature embellish'd the
    tint
  Of thy fields and thy mountains so fair,
Did she ever intend that a tyrant should
    print
  The footstep of slavery there ?
No, freedom ! whose smile we shall never
    resign,
  Go, tell our invaders, the Danes,
'Tis sweeter to bleed for an age at thy
    shrine,
  Than to sleep but a moment in chains !

Forget not our wounded companions
    who stood
  In the day of distress by our side ;
While the moss of the valley grew red
    with their blood,
  They stirr'd not, but conquer'd and
    died !
The sun that now blesses our arms with
    his light,
  Saw them fall upon Ossory's plain !
Oh let him not blush, when he leaves us
    to-night,
  To find that they fell there in vain !

ERIN ! THE TEAR AND THE SMILE IN THINE EYES.

AIR—*Aileen Aroon.*

ERIN ! the tear and the smile in thine
  eyes
Blend like the rainbow that hangs in thy
  skies !
  Shining through sorrow's stream,

Saddening through pleasure's beam,
Thy sons, with doubtful gleam,
    Weep while they rise !

Erin ! thy silent tear never shall cease,
Erin ! thy languid smile ne'er shall in-
    crease,
  Till, like the rainbow's light,
  Thy various tints unite,
  And form, in Heaven's sight,
    One arch of peace !

OH BREATHE NOT HIS NAME.

AIR—*The Broken Maid.*

OH breathe not his name, let it sleep
    in the shade,
Where cold and unhonor'd his relics are
  laid ;
Sad, silent, and dark be the tears that
  we shed,
As the night-dew that falls on the grass
  o'er his head !

But the night-dew that falls, though in
    silence it weeps,
Shall brighten with verdure the grave
  where he sleeps,
And the tear that we shed, though in
  secret it rolls,
Shall long keep his memory green in our
  souls.

WHEN HE WHO ADORES THEE.

AIR—*The Fox's Sleep.*

WHEN he who adores thee has left
    but the name
  Of his fault and his sorrows behind,
Oh say wilt thou weep, when they dark-
  en the fame
  Of a life that for thee was resign'd ?
Yes, weep, and however my foes may
  condemn,
  Thy tears shall efface their decree ;

For Heaven can witness, though guilty
    to them,
  I have been but too faithful to thee !

With thee were the dreams of my earli-
    est love ;
  Every thought of my reason was thine :
In my last humble prayer to the Spirit
    above,
  Thy name shall be mingled with mine !
Oh ! blest are the lovers and friends who
    shall live
  The days of thy glory to see ;
But the next dearest blessing that Heav-
    en can give
  Is the pride of thus dying for thee !

THE HARP THAT ONCE THRO' TARA'S HALLS.

Air—*Gramachree.*

THE harp that once through Tara's
    halls
  The soul of music shed,
Now hangs as mute on Tara's walls
  As if that soul were fled.
So sleeps the pride of former days,
  So glory's thrill is o'er,
And hearts that once beat high for praise,
  Now feel that pulse no more !

No more to chiefs and ladies bright
  The harp of Tara swells ;
The chord alone that breaks at night,
  Its tale of ruin tells.
Thus Freedom now so seldom wakes,
  The only throb she gives
Is when some heart indignant breaks,
  To show that still she lives.

OH THINK NOT MY SPIRITS ARE ALWAYS AS LIGHT.

Air—*John O'Reilly the Active.*

OH think not my spirits are always as
    light
  And as free from a pang as they seem
    to you now ;

Nor expect that the heart-beaming smile
    of to-night
  Will return with to-morrow to bright-
    en my brow.
No, life is a waste of wearisome hours
  Which seldom the rose of enjoyment
    adorns ;
And the heart that is soonest awake to
    the flowers
  Is always the first to be touch'd by the
    thorns!
But send round the bowl, and be happy a
    while ;
  May we never meet worse in our pil-
    grimage here
Than the tear that enjoyment can gild
    with a smile,
  And the smile that compassion can
    turn to a tear !

The thread of our life would be dark,
    Heaven knows !
  If it were not with friendship and love
    intertwined ;
And I care not how soon I may sink to
    repose,
  When these blessings shall cease to be
    dear to my mind !
But they who have loved the fondest,
    the purest,
  Too often have wept o'er the dream
    they believed ;
And the heart that has slumber'd in
    friendship securest,
  Is happy indeed, if 'twas never de-
    ceived.
But send round the bowl, while a relic of
    truth
  Is in man or in woman, this prayer shall
    be mine—
That the sunshine of love may illumine
    our youth,
  And the moonlight of friendship con-
    sole our decline.

FLY NOT YET.

Air—*Planxty Kelly.*

FLY not yet, 'tis just the hour
    When pleasure, like the midnight
        flower
That scorns the eye of vulgar light,
Begins to bloom for sons of night,
    And maids who love the moon !
'Twas but to bless these hours of shade
That beauty and the moon were made ;
'Tis then their soft attractions glowing
Set the tides and goblets flowing.
    Oh ! stay,—Oh ! stay,—
Joy so seldom weaves a chain
Like this to-night, that oh ! 'tis pain
    To break its link so soon.

Fly not yet, the fount that play'd
In times of old through Ammon's shade,
Though icy cold by day it ran,
Yet still, like souls of mirth, began
    To burn when night was near ;
And thus should woman's heart and looks
At noon be cold as winter brooks,
Nor kindle till the night, returning,
Brings their genial hour for burning.
    Oh ! stay,—Oh ! stay,—
When did morning ever break,
And find such beaming eyes awake
    As those that sparkle here !

THO' THE LAST GLIMPSE OF ERIN WITH SORROW I SEE.

Air—*Coulin.*

THOUGH the last glimpse of Erin
    with sorrow I see,
Yet wherever thou art shall seem Erin to
    me ;
In exile thy bosom shall still be my home,
And thine eyes make my climate where-
    ever we roam.

To the gloom of some desert or cold
    rocky shore,

Where the eye of the stranger can haunt
    us no more,
I will fly with my Coulin, and think the
    rough wind
Less rude than the foes we leave frown-
    ing behind.

And I'll gaze on thy gold hair, as grace-
    ful it wreathes,
And hang o'er thy soft harp, as wildly it
    breathes ;
Nor dread that the cold-hearted Saxon
    will tear
One chord from that harp, or one lock
    from that hair.

THE MEETING OF THE WATERS.

Air—*The Old Head of Denis.*

THERE is not in the wide world a
    valley so sweet
As that vale in whose bosom the bright
        waters meet !
Oh ! the last rays of feeling and life must
        depart
Ere the bloom of that valley shall fade
        from my heart.

Yet it *was* not that nature had shed o'er
        the scene
Her purest of crystal and brightest of
        green ;
'Twas *not* the soft magic of streamlet or
        hill,
Oh ! no—it was something more exquisite
        still.

'Twas that friends, the beloved of my
        bosom, were near,
Who made every dear scene of enchant-
        ment more dear,
And who felt how the best charms of
        nature improve.
When we see them reflected from looks
        that we love.

Sweet vale of Avoca! how calm could I
    rest
In thy bosom of shade with the friends I
    love best,
Where the storms that we feel in this
    cold world should cease,
And our hearts, like thy waters, be
    mingled in peace!

RICH AND RARE WERE THE GEMS SHE WORE.

AIR—*The Summer is Coming.*

RICH and rare were the gems she
    wore,
And a bright gold ring on her wand she
    bore;
But oh! her beauty was far beyond
Her sparkling gems or snow-white wand.

"Lady! dost thou not fear to stray,
So lone and lovely through this bleak
    way?
Are Erin's sons so good or so cold,
As not to be tempted by woman or gold?"
"Sir Knight! I feel not the least alarm,
No son of Erin will offer me harm—
For though they love woman and golden
    store,
Sir Knight! they love honor and virtue
    more."

On she went, and her maiden smile
In safety lighted her round the Green
    Isle.
And blest forever is she who relied
Upon Erin's honor, and Erin's pride!

AS A BEAM O'ER THE FACE OF THE WATERS MAY GLOW

AIR—*The Young Man's Dream.*

AS a beam o'er the face of the waters
    may glow,
While the tide runs in darkness and cold-
    ness below,

So the cheek may be tinged with a warm
    sunny smile,
Though the cold heart to ruin runs dark-
    ly the while.

One fatal remembrance, one sorrow that
    throws
Its bleak shade alike o'er our joys and
    our woes,
To which life nothing brighter or darker
    can bring,
For which joy has no balm and affliction
    no string!

Oh! this thought in the midst of enjoy-
    ment will stay,
Like a dead leafless branch in the sum-
    mer's bright ray;
The beams of the warm sun play round
    it in vain,
It may smile in his light, but it blooms
    not again!

ST. SENANUS AND THE LADY.

AIR—*The Brown Thorn.*

ST. SENANUS.

"OH! haste and leave this sacred
    isle,
Unholy bark, ere morning smile:
For on thy deck, though dark it be,
    A female form I see;
And I have sworn this sainted sod
Shall ne'er by woman's feet be trod!"

THE LADY.

"O father, send not hence my bark,
Through wintry winds and billows dark;
I come with humble heart to share
    Thy morn and evening prayer;
Nor mine the feet, O holy saint,
The brightness of thy sod to taint."

The lady's prayer Senanus spurn'd ;
The winds blew fresh, the bark return'd.
But legends hint, that had the maid
    Till morning's ight delay'd,
And given the saint one rosy smile,
She ne'er had left his lonely isle.

HOW DEAR TO ME THE HOUR.

Air—*The Twisting of the Rope.*

HOW dear to me the hour when day-
    light dies,
    And sunbeams melt along the silent
       sea,
For then sweet dreams of other days
    arise,
    And memory breathes her vesper sigh
       to thee.

And as I watch the line of light that plays
    Along the smooth wave towards the
       burning west,
I long to tread the golden path of rays,
    And think 'twould lead to some bright
       isle of rest !

TAKE BACK THE VIRGIN PAGE.

WRITTEN ON RETURNING A BLANK BOOK.

Air—*Dermott.*

TAKE back the virgin page,
    White and unwritten still ;
Some hand more calm and sage
    The leaf must fill.
Thoughts come, as pure as light,
    Pure as even *you* require ;
But oh ! each word I write,
    Love turns to fire.

Yet let me keep the book ;
    Oft shall my heart renew,
When on its leaves I look,
    Dear thoughts of you !

Like you, 'tis far and bright ;
    Like you, too bright and fair
To let wild passion write
    One wrong wish there !

Haply, when from those eyes
    Far, far away I roam,
Should calmer thoughts arise
    Toward you and home ;
Fancy may trace some line,
    Worthy those eyes to meet,
Thoughts that not burn, but shine,
    Pure, calm, and sweet !

And as the records are
    Which wandering seamen keep,
Led by their hidden star
    Through winters deep ;
So may the words I write
    Tell through what storms I stray,
You still the unseen light
    Guiding my way !

THE LEGACY.

Air—*Unknown.*

WHEN in death I shall calm recline,
    Oh bear my heart to my mis-
       tress dear ;
Tell her it lived upon smiles and wine
    Of the brightest hue, while it linger'd
       here.

Bid her not shed one tear of sorrow
    To sully a heart so brilliant and light ;
But balmy drops of the red grape bor-
       row,
    To bathe the relic from morn till
       night.

When the light of my song is o'er,
    Then take my harp to your ancient
       hall ;
Hang it up at that friendly door,
    Where weary travellers love to call.

Scarce could love me were they living
  now ;
But my loneliness hath darker ills—
  Such dun duns as Conscience, Thought
    & Co.,
Awful Gorgons ! worse than tailors' bills
  Twenty golden years ago !

Did I paint a fifth of what I feel,
  Oh, how plaintive you would ween I
    was !
But I won't, albeit I have a deal,
  More to wail about than Kerner has !
Kerner's tears are wept for wither'd
  flowers.
  Mine for wither'd hopes ; my scroll of
    woe
Dates, alas ! from youth's deserted bow-
  ers,
  Twenty golden years ago !

Yet, may Deutschland's bardlings flourish
  long ;

Me, I tweak no beak among them ;—
  hawks
Must not pounce on hawks : besides, in
  song
I could once beat all of them by chalks.
Though you find me as I near my goal,
  Sentimentalizing like Rousseau,
Oh ! I had a grand Byronian soul
  Twenty golden years ago !

Tick-tick, tick-tick !—not a sound save
  Time's.
  And the wind-gust as it drives the
    rain—
Tortured torturer of reluctant rhymes,
  Go to bed, and rest thine aching brain !
Sleep !—no more the dupe of hopes or
  schemes ;
  Soon thou sleepest where the thistles
    blow—
Curious anticlimax to thy dreams
  Twenty golden years ago !

THE POEMS OF SAMUEL LOVER.

THE ANGEL'S WHISPER.

A BABY was sleeping,
Its mother was weeping,
For her husband was far on the wild
    raging sea;
And the tempest was swelling
Round the fisherman's dwelling,
And she cried, "Dermot, darling, oh
   come back to me!"

Her beads while she number'd,
The baby still slumber'd,
And smiled in her face as she bended
   her knee;
"Oh blest be that warning,
My child, thy sleep adorning,
For I know that the angels are whisper-
   ing with thee.

"And while they are keeping
Bright watch o'er thy sleeping,
Oh, pray to them softly, my baby, with
   me!
And say thou wouldst rather
They'd watch o'er thy father!—
For I know that the angels are whisper-
   ing with thee."

The dawn of the morning
Saw Dermot returning,
And the wife wept with joy her babe's
   father to see;
And closely caressing
Her child, with a blessing,
Said, "I knew that the angels were
   whispering with thee."

THE FAIRY BOY.

A MOTHER came when stars were
   paling,
Wailing round a lonely spring;
Thus she cried, while tears were falling,
   Calling on the Fairy King:
"Why, with spells my child caressing,
   Courting him with fairy joy,
Why destroy a mother's blessing,—
   Wherefore steal my baby-boy?

"O'er the mountain, through the wild-
   wood,
Where his childhood loved to play,
Where the flowers are freshly springing,
   There I wander day by day;
There I wander, growing fonder
   Of the child that made my joy,
On the echoes wildly calling
   To restore my fairy boy.

SAMUEL LOVER.

" But in vain my plaintive calling,—
Tears are falling all in vain,—
He now sports with fairy pleasure,
He's the treasure of their train !
Fare thee well ! my child, forever,
In this world I've lost my joy,
But in the *next* we ne'er shall sever,
There I'll find my angel boy."

TRUE LOVE CAN NE'ER FORGET.

" TRUE love can ne'er forget;
Fondly as when we met,
Dearest, I love thee yet,
My darling one ! "
Thus sung a minstrel gray
His sweet impassion'd lay,
Down by the Ocean's spray,
At set of sun.
But wither'd was the minstrel's sight,
Morn to him was dark as night,
Yet his heart was full of light,
And thus the lay begun :
" True love can ne'er forget;
Fondly as when we met,
Dearest, I love thee yet,
My darling one ! "

" Long years are past and o'er,
Since from this fatal shore
Cold hearts and cold winds bore
My love from me."
Scarcely the minstrel spoke,
When forth, with flashing stroke,
A boat's light oar the silence broke,
Over the sea.
Soon upon her native strand
Doth a lovely lady land,
While the minstrel's love-taught hand
Did o'er his wild harp run :
" True love can ne'er forget;
Fondly as when we met,
Dearest, I love thee yet,
My darling one ! "

Where the minstrel sat alone,
There that lady fair had gone,
Within his hand she placed her own.

The bard dropp'd on his knee;
From his lips soft blessings came,
He kiss'd her hand with truest flame,
In trembling tone she named—*her*
name,
Though her he could not see;
But oh !—the touch the bard could
tell
Of that dear hand, remember'd well.
Ah !—by many a secret spell
Can true love find his own ;
For true love can ne'er forget ;
Fondly as when they met,
He loved his lady yet,
His darling one !

NYMPH OF NIAGARA.

NYMPH OF NIAGARA ! Sprite of
the mist !
With a wild magic my brow thou hast
kiss'd ;
I am thy slave, and my mistress art thou,
For thy wild kiss of magic is yet on my
brow.

I feel it as first when I knelt before thee,
With thy emerald robe flowing brightly
and free,
Fringed with the spray-pearls, and floating in mist—
Thus 'twas my brow with wild magic
you kiss'd.

Thine am I still ;—and I'll never forget
The moment the spell on my spirit was
set ;—
Thy chain but a foam-wreath—yet
stronger by far
Than the manacle, steel-wrought, for
captive of war ;

For the steel it will rust, and the war
will be o'er,
And the manacled captive be free as
before ;

While the foam-wreath will bind me
  forever to thee!—
I love the enslavement—and would not
  be free!

Nymph of Niagara! play with the
  breeze,
Sport with the fauns 'mid the old forest trees;
Blush into rainbows at kiss of the sun,
From the gleam of his dawn till his
  bright course be run;

I'll not be jealous—for pure is thy
  sporting,
Heaven-born is all that around thee is
  courting—
Still will I love thee, sweet Sprite of
  the mist,
As first when my brow with wild magic
  you kiss'd!

HOW TO ASK AND HAVE.

"Oh, 'tis time I should talk to
  your mother,
  Sweet Mary," says I:
"Oh, don't talk to my mother," says
  Mary,
  Beginning to cry:
"For my mother says men are deceivers,
  And never, I know, will consent;
She says girls in a hurry who marry
  At leisure repent."

"Then, suppose I would talk to your
  father,
  Sweet Mary," says I;
"Oh, don't talk to my father," says
  Mary,
  Beginning to cry:
"For my father, he loves me so dearly,
  He'll never consent I should go—
If you talk to my father," says Mary,
  "He'll surely say 'No.'"

"Then how shall I get you, my jewel?
  Sweet Mary," says I;

"If your father and mother's so cruel,
  Most surely I'll die!"
"Oh, never say die, dear," says Mary;
  "A way now to save you, I see:
Since my parents are both so contrary—
  You'd better ask me."

THE LAND OF THE WEST.

Oh! come to the West, love,—oh,
  come there with me;
'Tis a sweet land of verdure that springs
  from the sea,
Where fair plenty smiles from her emerald throne;
Oh, come to the West, and I'll make thee
  my own!
I'll guard thee, I'll tend thee, I'll love
  thee the best,
And you'll say there's no land like the
  land of the West.

The South has its roses and bright skies
  of blue,
But ours are more sweet with love's own
  changeful hue—
Half sunshine, half tears,—like the girl
  I love best,
Oh! what is the South to the beautiful
  West!
Then come to the West, and the rose on
  thy mouth
Will be sweeter to me than the flowers
  of the South!

The North has its snow-towers of daz-
  zling array,
All sparkling with gems in the ne'er-
  setting day,
There the Storm-King may dwell in the
  halls he loves best,
But the soft-breathing Zephyr he plays
  in the West.
Then come there with me, where no
  cold wind doth blow,
And thy neck will seem fairer to me
  than the snow!

What will you do, love, when waves
 divide us,
And friends may chide us
 For being fond ? "
" Though waves divide us, and friends
 be chiding,
In faith abiding,
 I'll still be true !
And I'll pray for thee on the stormy
 ocean,
In deep devotion—
 That's what I'll do ! "

" What would you do, love, if distant tid-
 ings
Thy fond confidings
 Should undermine ?—
And I, abiding 'neath sultry skies,
Should think other eyes
 Were as bright as thine ? "
" Oh, name it not !—though guilt and
 shame

Were on thy name,
 I'd still be true :
But that heart of thine—should another
 share it—
I could not bear it !
 What would I do ? "

" What would you do, love, when home
 returning,
With hopes high-burning,
 With wealth for you,
If my bark, which bounded o'er foreign
 foam,
Should be lost near home—
 Ah ! what would you do ? "
" So thou wert spared—I'd bless the
 morrow
In want and sorrow,
 That left me you ;
And I'd welcome thee from the wasting
 billow,
This heart thy pillow—
 That's what I'd do ! "

THE POEMS

OF

THOMAS DAVIS,

National Ballads and Songs.

THE MEN OF TIPPERARY.

Air—*Original.*

I.

LET Britain boast her British hosts,
 About them all right little care
 we ;
Not British seas nor British coasts
 Can match the man of Tipperary !

II.

Tall is his form, his heart is warm,
 His spirit light as any fairy ;
His wrath is fearful as the storm
 That sweeps The Hills of Tipperary !

III.

Lead him to fight for native land,
 His is no courage cold and wary ;
The troops live not on earth would
 stand
 The headlong Charge of Tipperary !

IV.

Yet meet him in his cabin rude,
 Or dancing with his dark-haired
 Mary,
You'd swear they knew no other mood
 But Mirth and Love in Tipperary !

V.

You're free to share his scanty meal,
 His plighted word he'll never vary—
In vain they tried with gold and steel
 To shake The Faith of Tipperary !

VI.

Soft is his *cailín's* sunny eye,
 Her mien is mild, her step is airy,
Her heart is fond, her soul is high—
 Oh ! she's the pride of Tipperary !

VII.

Let Britain brag her motley rag :
 We'll lift the Green more proud and
 airy :
Be mine the lot to bear that flag.
 And head The Men of Tipperary '

THOMAS DAVIS.

VIII.

Though Britain boasts her British
    hosts,
    About them all right little care we;
Give us, to guard our native coasts,
    The Matchless Men of Tipperary!

THE RIVERS.

Air—*Kathleen O'More.*

I.

THERE'S a far-famed Blackwater
    that runs to Loch Neagh,
There's a fairer Blackwater that runs to
    the sea,
    The glory of Ulster,
    The beauty of Munster,
        These twin rivers be.

II.

From the banks of that river Benburb's'
    towers arise;
This stream shines as bright as a tear
    from sweet eyes;
    This, fond as a young bride;
    That, with focman's blood dyed—
        Both dearly we prize.

III.

Deep sunk in that bed is the sword of
    Monroe,
Since, 'twixt it and Donagh, he met
    Owen Roe,
    And Charlemont's cannon
    Slew many a man on
        These meadows below.

IV.

The shrines of Armagh gleam far over
    yon lea,
Nor afar is Dungannon that nursed lib-
    erty,
    And yonder Red Hugh
    Marshal Bagenal o'erthrew
        On Béal-an-atha-Buidhe.

V.

But far kinder the woodlands of rich
    Convamore,
And more gorgeous the turrets of saint-
    ly Lismore;
    There the stream, like a maiden
    With love overladen,
        Pants wild on each shore.

VI.

Its rocks rise like statues, tall, stately,
    and fair,
And the trees, and the flowers, and
    the mountains, and air,
    With Wonder's soul near you,
    To share with, and cheer you,
        Make Paradise there.

VII.

I would rove by that stream, ere my
    flag I unrolled;
I would fly to these banks, my betrothed
    to enfold—
    The pride of our sire-land,
    The Eden of Ireland,
        More precious than gold.

VIII.

May their borders be free from oppres-
    sion and blight;
May their daughters and sons ever fond-
    ly unite—
    The glory of Ulster,
    The beauty of Munster,
        Our strength and delight.

GLENGARIFF.

Air—*O'Sullivan's March.*

I.

I WANDERED at eve by Glengar-
    iff's sweet water,

Half in the shade, and half in the
　　moon,
And thought of the time when the Sac-
　　sanach slaughter
Reddened the night and darkened the
　　noon ;
Mo nuar ! mo nuar ! mo nuar ! I said—
　　When I think, in this valley and
　　sky—
　　Where true lovers and poets should
　　sigh—
Of the time when its chieftain O'Sullivan
　　fled.

II.

Then my mind went along with O'Sullivan
　　marching
　　Over Musk'ry's moors and Ormond's
　　plain,
His *curachs* the waves of the Shannon
　　o'erarching,
　　And his pathway mile-marked with
　　the slain :
Mo nuar ! mo nuar ! mo nuar ! I said—
　　Yet 'twas better far from you to go,
　　And to battle with torrent and foe,
Than linger as slaves where your sweet
　　waters spread.

III.

But my fancy burst on, like a clan o'er
　　the border,
　　To times that seemed almost at hand,
When grasping her banner, old Erin's
　　Lamh Laidir
　　Alone shall rule over the rescued land ;
O baotho ! O baotho ! O baotho ! I said—
　　Be our marching as steady and
　　strong,
　　　And freemen our valleys shall
　　　throng,
When the last of our foemen is vanquished
　　and fled.

THE WEST'S ASLEEP.

Air—*The Brink of the White Rocks.*

I.

WHEN all besides a vigil keep,
　　The West's asleep, the West's
　　asleep—
Alas ! and well may Erin weep,
When Connaught lies in slumber deep.
There lake and plain smile fair and free,
'Mid rocks—their guardian chivalry—
Sing oh ! let man learn liberty
From crashing wind and lashing sea.

II.

That chainless wave and lovely land
Freedom and Nationhood demand—
Be sure, the great God never planned,
For slumbering slaves, a home so grand.
And, long, a brave and haughty race
Honored and sentinelled the place—
Sing oh ! not even their sons' disgrace
Can quite destroy their glory's trace.

III.

For often, in O'Connor's van,
To triumph dashed each Connaught
　　clan—
And fleet as deer the Normans ran
Through Corlieu's Pass and Ardrahan.
And later times saw deeds as brave ;
And glory guards Clanricard's grave—
Sing oh ! they died their land to save,
At Aughrim's slopes and Shannon's wave.

IV.

And if, when all a vigil keep,
The West's asleep, the West's asleep—
Alas ! and well may Erin weep,
That Connaught lies in slumber deep.
But—hark !—some voice like thunder
　　spake,
" *The West's awake, the West's awake*"—
" Sing oh ! hurra ! let England quake,
We'll watch till death for Erin's sake !"

AILLEEN.

'TIS not for love of gold I go,
    'Tis not for love of fame ;
Though fortune should her smile bestow
    And I may win a name,
             Ailleen,
    And I may win a name.

And yet it is for gold I go,
    And yet it is for fame,
That they may deck another brow,
    And bless another name,
             Ailleen,
    And bless another name.

For this—*but* this, I go ; for this
    I lose thy love awhile,
And all the soft and quiet bliss
    Of thy young, faithful smile,
             Ailleen,
    Of thy young, faithful smile.

I go to brave a world I hate,
    And woo it o'er and o'er,
And tempt a wave, and try a fate
    Upon a stranger shore,
             Ailleen,
    Upon a stranger shore.

Oh ! when the bays are all my own,
    I know a heart will care !
Oh ! when the gold is wooed and won,
    I know a brow shall wear,
             Ailleen,
    I know a brow shall wear !

And when, with both return'd again,
    My native land to see,
I know a smile will meet me there,
    And a hand will welcome me,
             Ailleen,
    And a hand will welcome me.

SOGGARTH AROON.

AM I the slave they say.
    Soggarth aroon ?
Since you did show the way,
    Soggarth aroon,
Their slave no more to be;
While they would work with me
Ould Ireland's slavery,
    Soggarth aroon ?

Why not her poorest man,
    Soggarth aroon,
Try and do all he can,
    Soggarth aroon,
Her commands to fulfil
Of his own heart and will,
Side by side with you still,
    Soggarth aroon ?

Loyal and brave to you,
    Soggarth aroon,
Yet be no slave to you,
    Soggarth aroon,—
Nor, out of fear to you,
Stand up so near to you—
Och ! out of fear to *you !*
    Soggarth aroon !

Who in the winter's night,
  Soggarth aroon,
When the cowld blast did bite
  Soggarth aroon,
Came to my cabin-door,
And on my earthen-flure
Knelt by me, sick and poor,
  Soggarth aroon ?

Who, on the marriage-day,
  Soggarth aroon,
Made the poor cabin gay,
  Soggarth aroon—
And did both laugh and sing,
Making our hearts to ring,
At the poor christening,
  Soggarth aroon?

Who, as friend only met,
  Soggarth aroon,
Never did flout me yet,
  Soggarth aroon ?
And when my hearth was dim,
Gave, while his eye did brim,
What I should give to him,
  Soggarth aroon ?

Och ! you, and only you,
  Soggarth aroon !
And for this I was true to you,
  Soggarth aroon ;
In love they'll never shake,
When for ould Ireland's sake,
We a true part did take,
  Soggarth aroon !

THE FETCH.

THE mother died when the child was
    born,
  And left me her baby to keep ;
I rock'd its cradle the night and morn,
  Or, silent, hung o'er it to weep.

'Twas a sickly child through its infancy,
  Its cheeks were so ashy pale ;

Till it broke from my arms to walk in
    glee,
  Out in the sharp, fresh gale.

And then my little girl grew strong,
  And laugh'd the hours away ;
Or sung me the merry lark's mountain
    song,
  Which he taught her at break of day.

When she wreathed her hair in thicket
    bowers,
  With the hedge-rose and hare-bell blue,
I call'd her my May, in her crown of
    flowers
  And her smile so soft and new.

And the rose, I thought, never shamed
    her cheek,
  But rosy and rosier made it ;
And her eye of blue did more brightly
    break,
  Thro' the blue-bell that strove to shade
    it

One evening I left her asleep in her
    smiles,
  And walk'd through the mountains
    lonely ;
I was far from my darling, ah ! many
    long miles,
  And I thought of her, and her only !

She darken'd my path like a troubled
    dream,
  In that solitude far and drear ;
I spoke to my child ! but she did not
    seem
  To hearken with human ear.

She only look'd with a dead, dead eye,
  And a wan, wan cheek of sorrow,
I knew her Fetch ! she was call'd to die,
  And she died upon the morrow.

THE IRISH MAIDEN'S SONG.

YOU know it, now—it is betray'd
   This moment—in mine eye—
And in my young cheek's crimson shade,
   And in my whisper'd sigh ;
You know it, now—yet listen, now—
   Though ne'er was love more true,
My plight and troth, and virgin vow,
   Still, still I keep from you,
           Ever—

Ever, until a proof you give
   How oft you've heard me say
I would not e'en his empress live,
   Who idles life away
Without one effort for the land,
   In which my fathers' graves
Were hollow'd by a despot hand—
   To darkly close on slaves——
           Never !

See ! round yourself the shackles hang,
   Yet come you to Love's bowers,
That only he may soothe their pang,
   Or hide their links in flowers ;—
But try all things to snap them, first,
   And should all fail, when tried,
The fated chain you cannot burst
   My twining arms shall hide——
           Ever !

THE RECONCILIATION.

THE old man he knelt at the altar
   His enemy's hand to take,
And at first his weak voice did falter,
   And his feeble limbs did shake ;
For his only brave boy, his glory,
   Had been stretch'd at the old man's
      feet,
A corpse, all so haggard and gory,
   By the hand which he now must greet.

And soon the old man stopp'd speaking
   And rage which had not gone by,
From under his brows came breaking
   Up into his enemy's eye—
And now his limbs were not shaking,
   But his clench'd hands his bosom
      cross'd,
And he look'd a fierce wish to be taking
   Revenge for the boy he had lost !

But the old man he look'd around him,
   And thought of the place he was in,
And thought of the promise which bound
   him,
   And thought that revenge was sin—
And then, crying tears, like a woman,
   "Your hand !" he said—"aye, *that*
      hand !
And I do forgive you, foeman,
   For the sake of our bleeding land !"

POEMS

— OF —

SAMUEL FERGUSON.

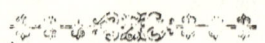

DEIRDRA'S FAREWELL TO ALBA.

OLD IRISH ROMANCE.

FAREWELL to fair Alba, high house
of the sun,
Farewell to the mountain, the cliff, and
the dun ;
Dun Sweeny, adieu ! for my love cannot
stay,
And tarry I may not when love cries
away.

Glen Vashan ! Glen Vashan ! where roe-
bucks run free,
Where my love used to feast on the red
deer with me,
Where rock'd on thy waters while stormy
winds blew,
My love used to slumber—Glen Vashan,
adieu !

Glendaro ! Glendaro ! where birchen
boughs weep
Honey dew at high noon o'er the nightingale's sleep,
Where my love used to lead me to hear
the cuckoo
'Mong the high hazel bushes—Glenda
adieu !

Glen Urchy ! Glen Urchy ! where loudly and long

My love used to wake up the woods with
his song,
While the son of the rock, from the
depths of the dell,
Laugh'd sweetly in answer—Glen Urchy,
farewell !

Glen Etive ! Glen Etive ! where dappled
does roam,
Where I leave the green sheeling I first
call'd a home ;
Where with me and my true love delighted
to dwell,
The sun made his mansion—Glen Etive,
farewell !

Farewell to Inch Draynach, adieu to the
roar
Of the blue billows bursting in light on
the shore ;
Dun Fiagh, farewell ! for my love cannot
stay,
And tarry I may not when love cries
away.

DEIRDRA'S LAMENT FOR THE SONS OF USNACH.

OLD IRISH ROMANCE.

THE lions of the hill are gone,
And I am left alone—alone :
Dig the grave both wide and deep,
For I am sick, and fain would sleep !

SAMUEL FERGUSON.

The falcons of the wood are flown,
And I am left alone—alone :
Dig the grave both deep and wide,
And let us slumber side by side.

The dragons of the rock are sleeping,
Sleep that wakes not for our weeping :
Dig the grave, and make it ready ;
Lay me on my true-love's body.

Lay their spears and bucklers bright
By the warriors' sides aright ;
Many a day the three before me
On their linked bucklers bore me.

Lay upon the low grave floor,
'Neath each head, the blue claymore ;
Many a time the noble three
Redden'd these blue blades for me.

Lay the collars, as is meet,
Of their greyhounds at their feet ;
Many a time for me have they
Brought the tall red deer to bay.

In the falcon's jesses throw
Hook and arrow, line and bow ;
Never again by stream or plain
Shall the gentle woodsmen go.

Sweet companions ye were ever—
Harsh to me, your sister, never ;
Woods and wilds and misty valleys
Were, with you, as good's a palace.

Oh ! to hear my true love singing,
Sweet as sound of trumpets ringing ·
Like the sway of ocean swelling
Roll'd his deep voice round our dwelling.

Oh ! to hear the echoes pealing
Round our green and fairy sheeling,
When the three, with soaring chorus,
Pass'd the silent skylark o'er us.

Echo, now sleep, morn and even—
Lark alone enchant the heaven !—
Ardan's lips are scant of breath,
Neesa's tongue is cold in death.

Stag, exult on glen and mountain—
Salmon, leap from loch to fountain—
Heron, in the free air warm ye—
Usnach's sons no more will harm ye !

Erin's stay no more you are,
Rulers of the ridge of war ;
Never more 'twill be your fate
To keep the beam of battle straight !

Woe is me ! by fraud and wrong,
Traitors false and tyrants strong,
Fell Clan Usnach, bought and sold,
For Barach's feast and Conor's gold !

Woe to Eman, roof and wall !—
Woe to Red Branch, hearth and hall !—
Tenfold woe and black dishonor
To the foul and false Clan Conor !

Dig the grave both wide and deep,
Sick I am, and fain would sleep !
Dig the grave and make it ready,
Lay me on my true love's body !

THE DOWNFALL OF THE GAEL.

O'GNIVE, BARD OF O'NEILL.

MY heart is in woe,
    And my soul deep in trouble,—
  For the mighty are low,
And abased are the noble :

  The sons of the Gael
Are in exile and mourning,
  Worn, weary, and pale,
As spent pilgrims returning ;

  Or men who, in flight
From the field of disaster,
  Beseech the black night
On their flight to fall faster ;

  Or seamen aghast
When their planks gape asunder,
  And the waves fierce and fast
Tumble through in hoarse thunder ;

Or men whom we see
That have got their death-omen—
Such wretches are we
In the chains of our foemen!

Our courage is fear,
Our nobility vileness,
Our hope is despair,
And our comeliness foulness.

Their is mist on our heads,
And a cloud chill and hoary
Of black sorrow, sheds
An eclipse on our glory.

From Boyne to the Linn
Has the mandate been given,
That the children of Finn
From their country be driven.

That the sons of the king—
Oh, the treason and malice!—
Shall no more ride the ring
In their own native valleys;

No more shall repair
Where the hill foxes tarry,
Nor forth to the air
Fling the hawk at her quarry,

For the plain shall be broke
By the share of the stranger,
And the stone-mason's stroke
Tell the woods of their danger;

The green hills and shore
Be with white keeps disfigured,
And the Mote of Rathmore
Be the Saxon churl's haggard!

The land of the lakes
Shall no more know the prospect
Of valleys and brakes—
So transform'd is her aspect!

The Gael cannot tell,
In the uprooted wildwood
And red ridgy dell,
The old nurse of his childhood:

The nurse of his youth
Is in doubt as she views him,
If the wan wretch, in truth,
Be the child of her bosom.

We starve by the board,
And we thirst amid wassail—
For the guest is the lord,
And the host is the vassal!

Through the woods let us roam,
Through the wastes wild and barren;
We are strangers at home!
We are exiles in Erin!

And Erin's a bark
O'er the wide waters driven!
And the tempest howls dark,
And her side planks are riven!

And in billows of might
Swell the Saxon before her,—
Unite, oh, unite!
Or the billows burst o'er her!

O'BYRNE'S BARD TO THE CLANS OF WICKLOW.

GOD be with the Irish host,
Never be their battle lost!
For, in battle, never yet
Have they basely earn'd defeat.

Host of armor red and bright,
May ye fight a valiant fight!
For the green spot of the earth,
For the land that gave you birth.

Who in Erin's cause would stand,
Brothers of the avenging band,
He must wed immortal quarrel,
Pain and sweat and bloody peril.

On the mountain bare and steep,
Snatching short but pleasant sleep,
Then, ere sunrise, from his eyrie,
Swooping on the Saxon quarry.

'Tis time to make our flight
When neighbor steals on neighbor thus,
And stabbers strike by night.

" And black and bloody the revenge
For this dark midnight's sake
The kindred of my murder'd friends
On thine and thee will take,
Unless thou rise and fly betimes,
Unless thou fly with me,
Sweet Una, from this land of crimes
To peace beyond the sea.

" For trustful pillows wait us there,
And loyal friends beside,
Where the broad lands of my father
are,
Upon the banks of Clyde.
In five days hence a ship will be
Bound for that happy home;
Till then we'll make our sanctuary
In sea-cave's sparry dome.
Then busk thee, Una Phelimy,
And o'er the waters come ! "

 * * * *

The midnight moon is wading deep,
The land sends off the gale,
The boat beneath the sheltering steep
Hangs on a seaward sail ;
And, leaning o'er the weather rail,
The lovers, hand in hand,
Take their last look of Innisfail—
" Farewell, doom'd Ireland ! "

" And art thou doomed to discord still ?
And shall thy sons ne'er cease

To search and struggle for thine ill,
Ne'er share thy good in peace ?
Already do thy mountains feel
Avenging Heaven's ire ;
Hark—hark—this is no thunder peal,
That was no lightning fire ! "

It was no fire from heaven he saw,
For, far from hill and dell,
O'er Gobbin's brow the mountain flaw
Bears musket-shot and yell,
And shouts of brutal glee, that tell
A foul and fearful tale,
While over blast and breaker swell
Thin shrieks and woman's wail.

Now fill they far the upper sky,
Now down 'mid air they go,
The frantic scream, the piteous cry,
The groan of rage and woe ;
And wilder in their agony
And shriller still they grow—
Now cease they, choking suddenly,
The waves boom on below.

" A bloody and a black revenge !
Oh, Una, bless'd are we
Who this sore-troubled land can change
For peace beyond the sea ;
But for the manly hearts and true
That Antrim still retain,
Or be their banner green or blue,
For all that there remain,
God grant them quiet freedom too,
And blithe homes soon again ! "

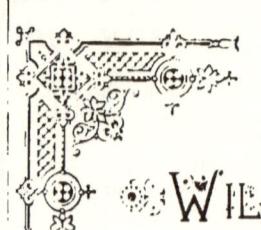

POEMS

— OF —

WILLIAM ALLINGHAM

THE WINDING BANKS OF ERNE;

OR, THE EMIGRANT'S ADIEU TO BALLY-
SHANNON.

(A LOCAL BALLAD.)

ADIEU to Ballyshannon! where I
was bred and born;
Go where I may, I'll think of you, as
sure as night and morn,
The kindly spot, the friendly town,
where every one is known,
And not a face in all the place but part-
ly seems my own:
There's not a house or window, there's not
a field or hill,
But, east or west, in foreign lands, I'll
recollect them still.
I leave my warm heart with you, though
my back I'm forced to turn—
So adieu to Ballyshannon, and the winding banks of Erne!

No more on pleasant evenings we'll
saunter down the Mall,
When the trout is rising to the fly, the
salmon to the fall.
The boat comes straining on her net, and
heavily she creeps:
Cast off, cast off!—she feels the oars,
and to her berth she sweeps;
Now fore and aft keep hauling, and
gathering up the clue.
Till a silver wave of salmon rolls in
among the crew.

Then they may sit, with pipes a-lit, and
many a joke and " yarn;"—
Adieu to Ballyshannon, and the winding
banks of Erne !

The music of the waterfall, the mirror of
the tide,
When all the green-hill'd harbor is full
from side to side—
From Portnasun to Bullicbawns, and
round the Abbey Bay,
From rocky Inis Saimer to Coolnargit
sand-hills gray;
While far upon the southern line, to
guard it like a wall.
The Leitrim mountains, clothed in blue,
gaze calmly over all,
And watch the ship sail up or down, the
red flag at her stern ;—
Adieu to these, adieu to all the winding
banks of Erne !

Farewell to you, Kildoney lads, and
them that pull an oar,
A lug-sail set, or haul a net, from the
Point to Mullaghmore ;
From Killybegs to bold Slieve-League,
that ocean-mountain steep,
Six hundred yards in air aloft, six hun-
dred in the deep;
From Dooran to the Fairy Bridge, and
round by Tullen strand,
Level and long, and white with waves,
where gull and curlew stand;
Head out to sea when on your lee the
breakers you discern !—
Adieu to all the billowy coast, and wind-
ing banks of Erne !

Farewell Coolmore,—Bundoran! and
    your summer crowds that run
From inland homes to see with joy the
    Atlantic-setting sun :
To breathe the buoyant salted air, and
    sport among the waves;
To gather shells on sandy beach, and
    tempt the gloomy caves :
To watch the flowing, ebbing tide, the
    boats, the crabs, the fish ;
Young men and maids to meet and
    smile, and form a tender wish ;
The sick and old in search of health, for
    all things have their turn—
And I must quit my native shore, and the
    winding banks of Erne !

Farewell to every white cascade from
    the Harbor to Belleek,
And every pool where fins may rest, and
    ivy-shaded creek ;
The sloping fields, the lofty rocks, where
    ash and holly grow,
The one split yew-tree gazing on the
    curving flood below ;
The Lough, that winds through islands
    under Turaw mountain green ;
And Castle Caldwell's stretching woods,
    with tranquil bays between ;
And Breesie Hill, and many a pond
    among the heath and fern,—
For I must say adieu—adieu to the
    winding banks of Erne !

The thrush will call through Camlin
    groves the livelong summer day ;
The waters run by mossy cliff, and bank
    with wild-flowers gay ;
The girls will bring their work and sing
    beneath a twisted thorn,
Or stray with sweethearts down the path
    among the growing corn ;
Along the river side they go, where I
    have often been,—
Oh, never shall I see again the days
    that I have seen !
A thousand chances are to one I never
    may return.—

Adieu to Ballyshannon, and the winding
    banks of Erne !

Adieu to evening dances, when merry
    neighbors meet,
And the fiddle says to boys and girls,
    " Get up and shake your feet !"
To "shanachus" and wise old talk of
    Erin's days gone by—
Who trench'd the rath on such a hill, and
    where the bones may lie
Of saint, or king, or warrior chief ; with
    tales of fairy power,
And tender ditties sweetly sung to pass
    the twilight hour.
The mournful song of exile is now for
    me to learn—
Adieu, my dear companions on the wind-
    ing banks of Erne !

Now measure from the Commons down
    to each end of the Purt,
Round the Abbey, Moy, and Knather,—
    I wish no one any hurt ;
The Main Street, Back Street, College
    Lane, the Mall, and Portnasun,
If any foes of mine are there, I pardon
    every one.
I hope that man and womankind will do
    the same by me ;
For my heart is sore and heavy at
    voyaging the sea.
My loving friends I'll bear in mind, and
    often fondly turn .
To think of Ballyshannon, and the wind-
    ing banks of Erne.

If ever I'm a money'd man, I mean,
    please God, to cast
My golden anchor in the place where
    youthful years were pass'd :
Though heads that now are black and
    brown must meanwhile gather
    gray,
New faces rise by every hearth, and old
    ones drop away—
Yet dearer still that Irish hill than all the
    world beside ;

It's home, sweet home, where'er I roam,
    through lands and waters wide,
And if the Lord allows me, I surely will
    return
To my native Ballyshannon, and the
    winding banks of Erne.

THE ABBOT OF INNISFALLEN

(A KILLARNEY LEGEND.)

THE Abbot of Innisfallen
    Awoke ere dawn of day;
Under the dewy green leaves
Went he forth to pray.

The lake around his island
    Lay smooth and dark and deep;
And wrapt in a misty stillness,
    The mountains were all asleep.

Low kneel'd the Abbot Cormac,
    When the dawn was dim and gray:
The prayers of his holy office
    He faithfully 'gan say.

Low kneel'd the Abbot Cormac,
    When the dawn was waxing red;
And for his sins' forgiveness
    A solemn prayer he said:

Low kneel'd that holy Abbot,
    When the dawn was waxing clear;
And he pray'd with loving-kindness
    For his convent-brethren dear.

Low kneel'd that blessèd Abbot,
    When the dawn was waxing bright;
He pray'd a great prayer for Ireland,
    He pray'd with all his might.

Low kneel'd that good old Father,
    While the sun began to dart;
He pray'd a prayer for all mankind,
    He pray'd it from his heart.

The Abbot of Innisfallen
    Arose upon his feet;

He heard a small bird singing,
    And oh, but it sung sweet!

He heard a white bird singing well
    Within a holly-tree;
A song so sweet and happy
    Never before heard he.

It sung upon a hazel,
    It sung upon a thorn;
He had never heard such music
    Since the hour that he was born.

It sung upon a sycamore,
    It sung upon a brier;
To follow the song and hearken
    This Abbot could never tire.

Till at last he well bethought him
    He might no longer stay;
So he bless'd the little white singing bird,
    And gladly went his way.

But, when he came to his Abbey-walls,
    He found a wondrous change;
He saw no friendly faces there,
    For every face was strange.

The strange men spoke unto him;
    And he heard from all and each
The foreign tongue of the Sassenach,
    Not wholesome Irish speech.

Then the oldest monk came forward,
    In Irish tongue spake he:
"Thou wearest the holy Augustine's
    dress,
    And who hath given it to thee?"

"I wear the holy Augustine's dress,
    And Cormac is my name,
The Abbot of this good Abbey
    By grace of God I am.

"I went forth to pray, at break of day;
    And when my prayers were said,
I hearken'd awhile to a little bird,
    That sung above my head."

POEMS

—OF—

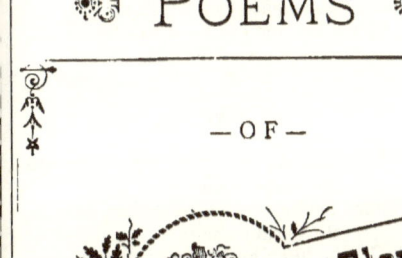

LEGENDS AND LYRICS.

THE PILLAR TOWERS OF IRELAND.

I.

THE pillar towers of Ireland, how
   wondrously they stand
By the lakes and rushing rivers through
   the valleys of our land ;
In mystic file, through the isle, they lift
   their heads sublime,
These gray old pillar temples—these
   conquerors of time !

II.

Beside these gray old pillars, how perishing and weak
The Roman's arch of triumph, and the
   temple of the Greek,
And the gold domes of Byzantium, and
   the pointed Gothic spires,
All are gone, one by one, but the temples
   of our sires !

III.

The column, with its capital, is level
   with the dust,
And the proud halls of the mighty, and
   the calm homes of the just ;
For the proudest works of man, as certainly but slower,
Pass like the grass at the sharp scythe
   of the mower !

IV.

But the grass grows again when in majesty and mirth,
On the wing of the Spring, comes the
   goddess of the Earth :
But for man in this world no spring-tide
   o'er returns
To the labors of his hands or the ashes
   of his urns !

V.

To favorites hath Time—the pyramids
   of Nile,
And the old mystic temples of our own
   dear isle ;
As the breeze o'er the seas, where the
   halcyon has its nest,
Thus Time o'er Egypt's tombs and the
   temples of the West !

VI.

The names of their founders have vanished
    in the gloom,
Like the dry branch in the fire or the
    body in the tomb ;
But to-day, in the ray, their shadows still
    they cast—
These temples are forgotten gods—these
    relics of the past !

VII.

Around these walls have wandered the
    Briton and the Dane—
The captives of Armorica, the cavaliers
    of Spain—
Phœnician and Milesian, and the plunder-
    ing Norman Peers—
And the swordsmen of brave Brian, and
    the chiefs of later years !

VIII.

How many different rites have these gray
    old temples known !
To the mind what dreams are written in
    these chronicles of stone !
What terror and what error, what gleams
    of love and truth,
Have flashed from these walls since the
    world was in its youth !

IX.

Here blazed the sacred fire, and when the
    sun was gone,
As a star from afar to the traveller it
    shone ;
And the warm blood of the victim have
    these gray old temples drunk,
And the death-song of the Druid and the
    matin of the Monk.

X.

Here was placed the holy chalice that held
    the sacred wine,
And the gold cross from the altar, and the
    relics from the shrine,

And the mitre, shining brighter with its
    diamonds than the East,
And the crozier of the Pontiff and the
    vestments of the Priest !

XI.

Where blazed the sacred fire, rung out
    the vesper-bell,—
Where the fugitive found shelter, became
    the hermit's cell;
And hope hung out its symbol to the in-
    nocent and good,
For the Cross o'er the moss of the pointed
    summit stood !

XII.

There may it stand forever, while this
    symbol doth impart
To the mind one glorious vision, or one
    proud throb to the heart ;
While the beast needeth rest may these
    gray old temples last,
Bright prophets of the future, as preach-
    ers of the past !

———

THE LAY MISSIONER.

HAD I a wish—'twere this: that
    Heaven would make
My heart as strong to imitate as love,
That half its weakness it could leave,
    and take
Some spirit's strength, by which to soar
    above ;
A lordly eagle mated with a dove—
Strong will and warm affection, these be
    mine :
Without the one no dreams has fancy
    wove,
Without the other soon these dreams de-
    cline,
Weak children of the heart, which fade
    away and pine !

For a Son of this World, and an heir to
the King
Who rules over man, is this beautiful
Spring.

III.

O Kathleen, methought, when the bright
babe was born,
More lovely than morning appeared the
bright morn ;
The birds sang more sweetly, the grass
greener grew,
And with buds and with blossoms the old
trees looked new ;
And methought when the Priest of the
Universe came—
The Sun, in his vestments of glory and
flame—
He was seen the warm rain-drops of
April to fling
On the brow of the babe, and baptize
him The Spring !

IV.

O Kathleen, dear Kathleen ! what treas-
ures are piled
In the mines of the Past for this wonder-
ful Child !
The lore of the sages, the lays of the
bards,
Like a primer, the eye of this infant re-
gards ;
All the dearly-bought knowledge that
cost life and limb,
Without price, without peril. are offered
to him ;
And the blithe bee of Progress conceal-
eth its sting !
As it offers its sweets to this beautiful
Spring !

V.

O Kathleen, they tell us of wonderful
things,
Of speed that surpasseth the fairy's
fleet wings ;

How the lands of the world in commun-
ion are brought,
And the slow march of speech is as rap-
id as thought.
Think, think what an heir-loom the
great world will be,
With this wonderful wire 'neath the
Earth and the Sea ;
When the snows and the sunshine to-
gether shall bring
All the wealth of the world to the feet of
the Spring.

VI.

O Kathleen, but think of the birth-gifts
of love,
That THE MASTER who lives in the
GREAT HOUSE above,
Prepares for the poor child that's born
on His land—
Dear God ! they're the sweet flowers
that fall from Thy hand—
The crocus, the primrose, the violet given
Awhile, to make Earth the reflection of
Heaven ;
The brightness and lightness that round
the world wing
Are Thine, and are ours, too, through
thee, happy Spring !

VII.

O Kathleen, dear Kathleen ! that dream
is gone by,
And I wake once again, but, thank God !
thou art by ;
And the land that we love looks as
bright in the beam,
Just as if my sweet dream was not all
out a dream :
The spring-tide of Nature its blessing
imparts—
Let the spring-tide of Hope send its
pulse through our hearts ;
Let us feel 'tis a mother, to whose
breast we cling,
And a brother we hail, when we welcome
the Spring.

THE POEMS OF FRANCIS MAHONY.

VERT-VERT, THE PARROT.

FROM THE FRENCH OF THE JESUIT

GRESSET.

His Original Innocence.

ALAS! what evils I discern in
    Too great an aptitude for learning!
And fain would all the ills unravel
That aye ensue from foreign travel;
Far happier is the man who tarries
Quiet within his household "Lares:"
Read, and you'll find how virtue vanishes,
How foreign vice all goodness banishes,
And how abroad young heads will grow
        dizzy,
Proved in the underwritten Odyssey.

In old Nevers, so famous for its
Dark narrow streets, and Gothic turrets,
Close on the brink of Loire's young flood,
Flourished a convent sisterhood
Of *Ursulines.* Now in this order
A parrot lived as parlor-boarder;
Brought in his childhood from the *An-
        tilles,*
And sheltered under convent mantles:
Green were his feathers, green his pin-
        ions,

And greener still were his opinions;
For vice had not yet sought to pervert
This bird, who had been christened *Vert-
        Vert,*
Nor could the wicked world defile him,
Safe from its snares in this asylum.
Fresh, in his teens, frank, gay, and
        gracious,
And, to crown all, somewhat loquacious;
If we examine close, not one, or he,
Had a vocation for a nunnery.

The convent's kindness need I mention?
Need I detail each fond attention,
Or count the tit-bits which *in Lent* he
Swallowed remorseless and in plenty?
Plump was his carcass; no, not higher
Fed was their confessor, the friar;
And some even say that our young Hec-
        tor
Was far more loved than the "Director."
Dear to each novice and each nun—
He was the life and soul of fun;
Though, to be sure, some hags censor-
        ious
Would sometimes find him too uproarious.
What did the parrot care for those old
Dames, while he had for him the house-
        hold?
He had not yet made his "profession,"

REV. FRANCIS MAHONEY (Father Prout).

Nor come to years called "of discretion;"
Therefore, unblamed, he ogled, flirted,
And romped like any unconverted;
Nay sometimes, too, by the Lord Harry !
He'd pull their caps and " scapulary."
But what in all his tricks seemed oddest,
Was that at times he'd turn so modest,
That to all bystanders the wight
Appeared a finished hypocrite.
In accent he did not resemble
Kean, though he had the tones of Kemble;
But fain to do the sisters' biddings,
He left the stage to Mrs. Siddons.
Poet, historian, judge, financier,
Four problems at a time he'd answer
He had a faculty like Cæsar's.
Lord Althorp, baffling all his teazers,
Could not surpass Vert-Vert in puzzling,
" Goodrich " to him was but a gosling.

Placed when at table near some vestal,
His fare, be sure, was of the best all,—
For every sister would endeavor
To keep for him some sweet *hors d'œuvre*.
Kindly at heart, in spite of vows and
Cloisters, a nun is worth a thousand !
And aye, if Heaven would only lend her,
I'd have a nun for a nurse tender !

Then, when the shades of night would
    come on,
And to their cells the sisters summon,
Happy the favored one whose grotto
This sultan of a bird would trot to :
Mostly the young ones' cells he toyed in
(The aged sisterhood avoiding),
Sure among all to find kind offices,—
Still he was partial to the novices,
And in *their* cells our anchorite
Mostly cast anchor for the night ;
Perched on the box that held the relics,
    he
Slept without notion of indelicacy.
Rare was his luck ; nor did he spoil it
By flying from the morning toilet ;
Not that I can admit the fitness
Of (at the toilet) a male witness ;
But that I scruple in this history
To shroud a single fact in mystery.

Quick at all arts, our bird was rich at
That best accomplishment, called chit-
    chat ;
For, though brought up within the clois-
    ter,
His beak was not closed like an oyster,
But, trippingly, without a stutter,
The longest sentences would utter ;
Pious withal, and moralizing
His conversation was surprising ;
None of your equivoques, no slander—
To such vile tastes he scorned to pander ;
But his tongue ran most smooth and nice
    on
"Deo sit laus" and " Kyrie eleison ;"
The maxims he gave with best emphasis
Were Suarez's or Thomas à Kempis's ;
In Christmas carols he was famous,
" Orate, fratres," and OREMUS ;"
If in good humor, he was wont
To give a stave from " *Think well on't ;*"
Or, by particular desire, he
Would chant the hymn of " Dies iræ."
Then in the choir he would amaze all
By copying the tone so nasal
In which the sainted sisters chanted—
(At least that pious nun my aunt did).

Hys fatall Renowne.

The public soon began to ferret
The hidden nest of so much merit,
And, spite of all the nuns' endeavors,
The fame of Vert-Vert filled all Nevers ;
Nay, from Moulines folks came to stare at
The wondrous talent of this parrot ;
And to fresh visitors *ad libitum*
Sister Sophie had to exhibit him.
Drest in her tidiest robes, the virgin,
Forth from the convent cells emerging,
Brings the bright bird, and for his plum-
    age
First challenges unstinted homage ;
Then to his eloquence adverts,—
"What preacher's can surpass Vert-
    Vert's ?
Truly in oratory few men,
Equal this learned catechumen ;

Fraught with the convent's choicest les-
sons,
And stuffed with piety's quintessence ;
A bird most quick of apprehension,
With gifts and graces hard to mention :
Say in what pulpit can you meet
A Chrysostom half so discreet,
Who'd follow in his ghostly mission
So close the 'fathers and tradition ?' "
Silent meantime, the feathered hermit
Waits for the sister's gracious permit,
When, at a signal from his mentor,
Quick on a course of speech he'll enter ;
Not that he cares for human glory,
Bent but to save his auditory ;
Hence he pours forth with so much unc-
tion
That all his hearers feel compunction.

Thus for a time did Vert-Vert dwell
Safe in his holy citadelle ;
Scholared like any well-bred abbé,
And loved by many a cloistered Hebé ;
You'd swear that he had crossed the
same bridge
As any youth brought up in Cambridge.
Other monks starve themselves ; but his
skin
Was sleek like that of a Franciscan,
And far more clean ; for this grave Solon
Bathed every day in *eau de Cologne.*
Thus he indulged each guiltless gambol,
Blessed had he ne'er been doomed to
ramble !

For in his life there came a crisis
Such as for all great men arises,—
Such as what NAP to Russia led,
Such as the "FLIGHT" of Mahomed ;
O town of Nantz ! yes, to thy bosom
We let him go, alas ! to lose him !
Edicts, O town famed for *revoking,*
Still was Vert-Vert's loss more provoking !
Dark be the day when our bright Don
went
From this to a far-distant convent !
Two words comprise that awful era
Words big with fate and woe—"IL IRA ! "

Yes, " he shall go ; " but, sisters ! mourn
ye
The dismal fruits of that sad journey.—
Ills on which Nantz's nuns ne'er reckoned,
When for the beauteous bird they
beckoned.

Fame, O Vert-Vert ! in evil humor,
One day to Nantz had brought the rumor
Of thy accomplishments,—" acumen,"
" *Nous* " and " *esprit,*" quite super-
human :
All these reports but served to enhance
Thy merits with the nuns of Nantz.
How did a matter so unsuited
For convent ears get hither bruited ?
Some may inquire. But " nuns are
knowing,"
" *And first to hear what gossip's going.*"
Forthwith they taxed their wits to elicit
From the famed bird a friendly visit.
Girls' wishes run in a brisk current,
But a nun's fancy is a torrent ;
To get this bird they'd pawn the
missal ;
Quick they indite a long epistle,
Careful with softest things to fill it,
And then with musk perfume the billet ;
Thus, to obtain their darling purpose,
They send a writ of *habeas corpus.*

Off goes the post. When will the answer
Free them from doubt's corroding cancer ?
Nothing can equal their anxiety,
Except, of course, their well-known
piety.
Things at Nevers meantime went harder
Than well would suit such pious ardor ;
It was no easy job to coax
This parrot from the Nevers folks.
What, take their toy from convent belles ?
Make Russia yield the Dardanelles !
Filch his good rifle from a " Suliote,"
Or drag her " Romeo " from a " Juliet " !
Make an attempt to take Gibraltar,
Or try the old corn laws to alter !
This seemed to them and eke to us
" Most wasteful and ridiculous."

SCENE AT GOUGANE BARRE.

THE

POEMS

— OF —

J. J. CALLANAN.

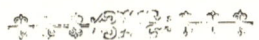

THE REVENGE OF DONAL COMM.

'TIS midnight, and November's gale
Sweeps hoarsely down Glengar-
av's vale,
Through the thick rain its fitful tone
Shrieks like a troubled spirit's moan,
The Moon that from her cloud at eve
Look'd down on Ocean's gentle heave,
And bright on lake and mountain shone,
Now wet and darkling journeys on ;
From the veil'd heaven there breaks no
ray
To guide the traveller on his way,
Save when the lightning gilds awhile
The craggy peak of Sliav-na-goil,
Or its far-streaming flashes fall
Upon Glengarav's mountain wall,
And kindles with its angry streak
The rocky zone it may not break.
At times is heard the distant roar
Of billows warring 'gainst the shore ;
And rushing from their native hills,
The voices of a thousand rills
Come shouting down the mountain's side,
When the deep thunder's peal hath died.
How fair at sunset to the view
On its loved rock the Arbutus grew !
How motionless the heather lay
In the deep gorge of that wild bay !
Through the tall forest not a breeze
Disturb'd the silence of the trees ;

O'er the calm scene their foliage red
A venerable glory shed,
And sad and sombre beauty gave
To the wild hill and peaceful wave.

To-morrow's early dawn will find
That beauty scatter'd on the wind ;
To-morrow's sun will journey on
And see the forest's glory gone—
The Arbutus shiver'd on the rock
Beneath the tempest's angry shock,
The monarch Oak all scathed and riven
By the red arrowy bolt of heaven ;
While not a leaf remains behind,
Save some lone mourner of its kind,
Wither'd and drooping on its bough,
Like him who treads that valley now.

Alone he treads—still on the blast
The sheeted rain is driving fast,
And louder peals the thunder's crash,
Louder the ocean's distant dash—
Amid the elemental strife
He walks as wreckless, as if life
Were but a debt he'd freely pay
To the next flash that cross'd his way :
Yet is there something in his air
Of purpose firm that mocks despair ;
What that, and whither he would go
Through storm and darkness, none may
know ;
But his unerring steps can tell,
There's not a deer in that wild dell
Can track its mazy depths so well.

He gains the shore—his whistle shrill
Is answer'd—ready at his will;
In a small cove his pinnace lay—
"Weigh quick, my lads, I cross the bay."
No question ask they, but a cheer
Proclaims their bosoms know not fear.
Sons of the mountain and the wave,
They shrink not from a billowy grave.
Those hearts have oft braved death before,
'Mid Erin's rocks and Biscay's roar;
Each lightly holds the life he draws,
If it but serve his Chieftain's cause;
And thinks his toil full well he pays,
If he bestow one word of praise.

At length they've clear'd the narrow bay—
Up with the sails, away! away!
O'er the broad surge she flies as fleet
As on the tempest's wing the sleet.
And fearless as the sea-bird's motion
Across his own wild fields of ocean,
Though winds may wave and seas o'erwhelm,
There is a hand upon that helm
That can control its trembling power,
And quits it not in peril's hour;
Full frequently from sea to sky
That Chieftain looks with anxious eye,
But naught can be distinguish'd there
More desperate than his heart's despair.

On yonder shore what means that light
That flings its murky flame through night?
Along the margin of the ocean
It moves with slow and measured motion.
Another follows, and behind
Are torches flickering in the wind.
Hark! heard you on the dying gale
From yonder cliffs the voice of wail?
'Twas but the tempest's moaning sigh,
Or the wild sea-bird's lonely cry.
Hush! there again—I know it well,
It is the sad Ululla's swell,
That mingles with the death-bell's toll
Its grief for some departed soul.

Inver-na-mare, thy rugged shore
Is alter'd since the days of yore,
Where once ascending from the town
A narrow path look'd fearful down,
O'er the bleak cliffs which wildly gave
Their rocky bosom to the wave.
A beauteous and unrivall'd sweep
Of beach extends along the deep;
Above is seen a sloping plain,
With princely house and fair domain,
Where erst the deer from covert dark
Gazed wildly on the anchor'd bark,
Or listen'd the deep copse among
To hear the Spanish seaman's song
Come sweetly floating up the bay,
With the last purple gleam of day.—
All changed, even yon projecting steep
That darkly bends above the deep,
And mantles with its joyless shade
The waste that man and time have made.
There, 'mid its tall and circling wood,
In olden times an abbey stood:
It stands no more—no more at even
The vesper hymn ascends to Heaven;
No more the sound of Matin bell
Calls forth each father from his cell,
Or breaks upon the sleeping ear
Of Leim-a-tagart's mountaineer,
And bids him on his purpose pause,
Ere yet the foraying brand he draws.

Where are they now? Go climb that height,
Whose depth of shade yields scanty light.
Where the dark alders droop their head
O'er Ard-na-mrahar's countless dead,
And nettle tall and hemlock waves
In rank luxuriance o'er the graves:
There fragments of the sculptured stone,
Still sadly speak of grandeur gone.
And point the spot, where dark and deep
The fathers and their abbey sleep.
That train hath reach'd the abbey ground,
The flickering lights are ranged around,
    And resting on the bier,
Amid the attendants' broken sighs,
And pall'd with black, the coffin lies;
    The Monks are kneeling near.

The abbot stands above the dead,
With gray and venerable head,
   And sallow cheek and pale.
The Miserere hymn ascends,
And its deep solemn sadness blends
   With the hoarse and moaning gale.
The last " Amen" was breathed by all,
And now they had removed the pall,
   And up the coffin rear'd ;
When a stern " Hold !" was heard aloud,
And wildly bursting through the crowd,
   A frantic form appear'd.

He paused awhile and gasp'd for breath :
His look had less of life than death,
He seem'd as from the grave—
So all unearthly was his tread ;
And high above his stately head
   A sable plume did wave.
Clansmen and fathers look'd aghast :
But when the first surprise was past,
   Yet louder rose their grief ;
For when he stood above the dead,
And took the bonnet from his head,
   All knew Ivera's Chief ;
No length of time could e'er erase,
Once seen, that Chieftain's form and face.
Calmly he stood amid their gaze,
While the red torches' shifting blaze,
As strong it flicker'd in the breeze,
That wildly raved among the trees,
Its fitful light upon him threw,
And Donal Comm stood full to view.
His form was tall, but not the height
Which seems unwieldly to the sight ;
His mantle, as it backward flow'd,
An ample breadth of bosom show'd ;
His sabre's girdle round his waist
A golden buckle tightly braced ;
A close-set trews display'd a frame
You could not all distinctly name
If it had more of strength or grace ;
But when the light fell on his face,
The dullest eye beheld a man
Fit to be Chieftain of his clan.

His cheek, though pale, retain'd the hue
Which from Iberian blood it drew ;
His sharp and well-form'd features bore

Strong semblance to his sires of yore ;
Calm, grave, and dignified, his eye
Had an expression proud and high,
And in its darkness dwelt a flame
Which not even grief like his could tame ;
Above his bent brow's sad repose,
A high heroic forehead rose,—
But o'er its calm you mark'd the cloud
That wrapp'd his spirit in its shroud ;
His clustering locks of sable hue,
Upon the tempest wildly flew.
Unreck'd by him the storm may blow ;
His feelings are with her below.

" Remove the lid," at length he cried.
None stirr'd, they thought it strange ; beside,
Her kinsman mutter'd something—
" Haste,
I have not breath or time to waste
In parley now—Ivera's chief
May be permitted one, last, brief
Farewell with her he loved, and then,
Eva is yours and earth's again."
At length, reluctant they obey'd :
Slowly he turn'd aside his head,
And press'd his hand against his brow—
'Tis done at last, he knows not how ;
But when he heard one piercing shriek,
A deadlier paleness spread his cheek ;
Sidelong he look'd, and fearfully,
Dreading the sight he yet would see ;
Trembled his knees, his eye grew dim,
His stricken brain began to swim ;
He stagger'd back against a yew
That o'er the bier its branches threw ;
Upon his brows the dews of death
Collected, and his quick low breath
Seem'd but the last and feeble strife,
Ere yet it yield, of parting life.
There lay his bride—death hath not quite
O'ershadow'd all her beauty's light ;
Still on her brow and on her cheek
It linger'd, like the sun's last streak
On Sliav-na-goila's head of snow
When all the vales are dark below—
Her lids in languid stillness lay
Like lilies o'er a stream-parch'd way,
Which kiss no more the wave of light

That flash'd beneath them purely bright;
Above her forehead, fair and young,
Her dark-brown tresses clustering hung,
Like summer clouds, that still shine on
When he who gilds their folds is gone.
Her features breathed a sad sweet tone
Caught ere the spirit left her throne,
Like that the night-wind often makes
When some forsaken lyre it wakes,
And minds us of the master hand
That once could all its voice command.

"Cold be the hand, and curst the blow,"
Her kinsman cried, "that laid thee
    low ;—
Curst be the steel that pierced thy heart."
Forth sprang that Chief with sudden
    start,
Tore off the scarf that veil'd her breast—
That dark deep wound can tell the rest.
He gazed a moment, then his brand
Flash'd out so sudden in his hand,
His boldest clansmen backward reel'd—
Trembling, the aged abbot kneel'd.
"Is this a time for grief," he cried,
"And thou thus low, my murder'd bride ?
Fool ! to such boyish feelings bow,
Far other task hath Donal now ;
Hear me, ye thunder upon high !
And thou, bless'd ocean, hear my cry !
Hear me ! sole resting friend, my sword,
And thou, dark wound, attest my word !
No food, no rest shall Donal know,
Until he lay thy murderer low—
Until each sever'd quivering limb
In its own lustful blood shall swim.
When my heart gains this poor relief,
Then, Eva, wilt thou bless thy chief.
Bless him !—no, no, that word is o'er,
My sweet one ! thou can'st bless no more ;
No more, returning from the strife
Where Donal fought to guard thy life
And free his native land, shalt thou
Wipe the red war drops from his brow,
And hush his toils and cares to rest
Upon thy fond and faithful breast."
He gazed a moment on her face,
And stoop'd to take the last embrace,
And as his lips to hers he prest,

The coffin shook beneath his breast,
That heaved convulsive as 'twould break;
Then in a tone subdued and meek,
"Take her," he said, and calmly rose,
And through the friends that round him
    close.
Unheeding what their love would say,
All silently he urged his way ;
Then wildly rushing down the steep
He plunged amid the breaker's sweep.

Awfully the thunder
    Is shouting through the night,
And o'er the heaven convulsed and riven
    The lightning-streams are bright.
Beneath their fitful flashing,
    As from hill to hill they leap,
In ridgy brightness dashing
    Comes on loud ocean's sweep.

Fearfully the tempest
    Sings out his battle-song,
His war is with the unflinching rocks,
    And the forests tall and strong ;
His war is with the stately bark ;
    But ere the strife be o'er,
Full many a pine, on land and brine,
    Shall rise to heaven no more.

The storm shall sink in slumber,
    The lightning fold its wing,
And the morning star shall gleam afar,
    In the beauty of its king ;
But there are eyes shall sleep in death
    Before they meet its ray ;
Avenger ! on thine errand speed,
    Haste, Donal, on thy way !

Carriganassig, from thy walls
    No longer now the warder calls ;
No more is heard o'er goblets bright
    Thy shout of revelry at night ;
No more the bugle's merry sound
Wakes all thy mountain echoes round,
When for the foray, or the chase,
At morn rush'd forth thy hardy race
And northward as it died away
Roused the wild deer of Kaoim-an-é.

THOUGH DARK FATE HATH REFT ME.

THOUGH dark Fate hath reft me
　　Of all that was sweet,
And widely we sever,
　　Too widely to meet—
Oh, yet while one life pulse
　　Remains in this heart,
'Twill remember thee, Mary,
　　Wherever thou art.

How sad were the glances
　　At parting we threw !

No word was there spoken
　　But the stifled adieu ;
My lips o'er thy cold cheek
　　All raptureless pass'd—
'Twas the first time I press'd it—
　　It must be the last.

But why should I dwell thus
　　On scenes that but pain,
Or think on thee, Mary,
　　When thinking is vain ?
Thy name to this bosom
　　Now sounds like a knell :
My fond one, my dear one,
　　Forever—farewell !

THE

POEMS

OF

OLIVER GOLDSMITH.

THE DESERTED VILLAGE.

SWEET Auburn! loveliest of the plain,
Where health and plenty cheer'd
the laboring swain,
Where smiling Spring its earliest visit
paid,
And parting Summer's lingering blooms
delay'd;
Dear lovely bowers of innocence and
ease,
Seats of my youth, when every sport
could please—
How often have I loiter'd o'er thy green,
Where humble happiness endear'd each
scene!
How often have I paused on every
charm—
The shelter'd cot, the cultivated farm,
The never-failing brook, the busy mill,
The decent church that topt the neighbor-
ing hill,
The hawthorn bush, with seats beneath
the shade,
For talking age and whispering lovers
made!
How often have I bless'd the coming day
When toil remitting lent its turn to play,
And all the village train, from labor free,
Led up their sports beneath the spread-
ing tree;

While many a pastime circled in the
shade,
The young contending as the old sur-
vey'd;
And many a gambol frolick'd o'er the
ground,
And sleights of art and feats of strength
went round,
And still, as each repeated pleasure tired,
Succeeding sports the mirthful band in-
spired;
The dancing pair that simply sought re-
nown
By holding out to tire each other down;
The swain mistrustless of his smutted
face,
While secret laughter titter'd round the
place;
The bashful virgin's sidelong looks of
love,
The matron's glance that would those
looks reprove!
These were thy charms, sweet village!
sports like these,
With sweet succession, taught even toil to
please;
These round thy bowers their cheerful in-
fluence shed;
These were thy charms—but all these
charms are fled.

OLIVER GOLDSMITH (from a portrait by Sir Joshua Reynolds).

Sweet smiling village, loveliest of the lawn,
Thy sports are fled, and all thy charms withdrawn;
Amidst thy bowers the tyrant's hand is seen,
And desolation saddens all thy green:
One only master grasps the whole domain,
And half a tillage stints thy smiling plain.
No more thy glassy brook reflects the day,
But choked with sedges works its weary way;
Along thy glades, a solitary guest,
The hollow-sounding bittern guards its nest:
Amidst thy desert walks the lapwing flies,
And tires their echoes with unvaried cries:
Sunk are thy bowers in shapeless ruin all,
And the long grass o'ertops the mouldering wall;
And, trembling, shrinking from the spoiler's hand,
Far, far away, thy children leave the land.

Ill fares the land, to hastening ills a prey,
Where wealth accumulates and men decay:
Princes and lords may flourish or may fade—
A breath can make them, as a breath has made;
But a bold peasantry, their country's pride,
When once destroy'd can never be supplied.

A time there was, ere England's griefs began,
When every rood of ground maintain'd its man:
For him light labor spread her wholesome store,
Just gave what life required, but gave no more:

His best companions, innocence and health,
And his best riches, ignorance of wealth.

But times are alter'd; trade's unfeeling train
Usurp the land, and dispossess the swain:
Along the lawn, where scatter'd hamlets rose,
Unwieldy wealth and cumbrous pomp repose;
And every want to luxury allied,
And every pang that folly pays to pride.
Those gentle hours that plenty bade to bloom,
Those calm desires that ask'd but little room,
Those healthful sports that graced the peaceful scene,
Lived in each look, and brighten'd all the green;—
These, far departing, seek a kinder shore,
And rural mirth and manners are no more.

Sweet Auburn! parent of the blissful hour,
Thy glades forlorn confess the tyrant's power.
Here, as I take my solitary rounds,
Amidst thy tangling walks and ruin'd grounds,
And, many a year elapsed, return to view
Where once the cottage stood, the hawthorn grew—
Remembrance wakes with all her busy train,
Swells at my breast, and turns the past to pain.

In all my wanderings round this world of care,
In all my griefs—and God has given my share—
I still had hopes, my latest hours to crown,
Amidst these humble bowers to lay me down;
To husband out life's taper at the close,

And keep the flame from wasting, by re-
pose.
I still had hopes, for pride attends us still,
Amidst the swains to show my book-
learn'd skill—
Around my fire an evening group to
draw,
And tell of all I felt, and all I saw :
And, as a hare, whom hounds and horns
pursue,
Pants to the place from whence at first he
flew,
I still had hopes, my long vexations past,
Here to return—and die at home at last.

O bless'd retirement, friend to life's de-
cline,
Retreats from care, that never must be
mine.—
How blest is he who crowns, in shades
like these,
A youth of labor with an age of ease ;
Who quits the world where strong temp-
tations try—
And, since 'tis hard to combat, learns to
fly !
For him no wretches, born to work and
weep,
Explore the mine, or tempt the dangerous
deep :
No surly porter stands, in guilty state,
To spurn imploring famine from the gate ;
But on he moves to meet his latter end,
Angels around befriending virtue's
friend—
Sinks to the grave with unperceived de-
cay,
While resignation gently slopes the
way—
And, all his prospects brightening to the
last,
His heaven commences ere the world be
pass'd.

Sweet was the sound, when oft at evening's close
Up yonder hill the village murmur rose.

There, as I pass'd with careless steps and
slow,
The mingling notes came soften'd from
below :
The swain responsive as the milkmaid
sung,
The sober herd that low'd to meet their
young,
The noisy geese that gabbled o'er the
pool,
The playful children just let loose from
school,
The watchdog's voice that bay'd the
whispering wind
And the loud laugh that spoke the va-
cant mind—
These all in sweet confusion sought the
shade,
And fill'd each pause the nightingale had
made.
But now the sounds of population fail,
No cheerful murmurs fluctuate in the
gale,
No busy steps the grass-grown footway
tread,
For all the blooming flush of life is fled—
All but yon widow'd, solitary thing,
That feebly bends beside the plashy
spring :
She, wretched matron—forced in age,
for bread,
To strip the brook with mantling cresses
spread,
To pick her wintry fagot from the
thorn,
To seek her nightly shed, and weep till
morn—
She only left of all the harmless train,
The sad historian of the pensive plain !

Near yonder copse, where once the
garden smiled,
And still where many a garden flower
grows wild—
There, where a few torn shrubs the place
disclose,
The village preacher's modest mansion
rose.

A man he was to all the country dear,
And passing rich with forty pounds a
  year.
Remote from towns he ran his godly
  race,
Nor e'er had changed, nor wish'd to
  change, his place ;
Unpractised he to fawn, or seek for
  power,
By doctrines fashion'd to the varying
  hour ;
Far other aims his heart had learn'd to
  prize—
More bent to raise the wretched than to
  rise.
His house was known to all the vagrant
  train ;
He chid their wanderings, but relieved
  their pain :
The long-remember'd beggar was his
  guest,
Whose beard descending swept his aged
  breast ;
The ruin'd spendthrift, now no longer
  proud,
Claim'd kindred there, and had his claims
  allow'd ;
The broken soldier, kindly bade to stay,
Sat by his fire, and talk'd the night
  away—
Wept o'er his wounds, or, tales of sorrow
  done,
Shoulder'd his crutch and show'd how
  fields were won.
Pleased with his guests, the good man
  learn'd to glow,
And quite forgot their vices in their
  woe ;
Careless their merits or their faults to
  scan,
His pity gave ere charity began.

  Thus to relieve the wretched was his
    pride,
And his failings lean'd to virtue's side—
But in his duty prompt at every call,
He watch'd and wept, he pray'd and
  felt for all ;

And, as a bird each fond endearment
  tries
To tempt its new-fledged offspring to the
  skies,
He tried each art, reproved each dull
  delay,
Allured to brighter worlds, and led the
  way.

  Beside the bed where parting life was
    laid,
And sorrow, guilt, and pain by turns dis-
  may'd,
The reverend champion stood. At his
  control
Despair and anguish fled the struggling
  soul ;
Comfort came down the trembling wretch
  to raise,
And even his last faltering accents whisper'd praise.

  At church, with meek and unaffected
    grace,
His looks adorn'd the venerable place ;
Truth from his lips prevail'd with double
  sway,
And fools, who came to scoff, remain'd to
  pray.
The service pass'd, around the pious man
With ready zeal each honest rustic ran ;
Even children follow'd, with endearing
  wile,
And pluck'd his gown, to share the good
  man's smile :
His ready smile a parent's warmth ex-
  press'd,
Their welfare pleased him, and their
  cares distress'd.
To them his heart, his love, his griefs
  were given,
But all his serious thoughts had rest in
  heaven :
As some tall cliff, that lifts its awful form,
Swells from the vale, and midway leaves
  the storm,
Though round its breast the rolling clouds
  are spread,
Eternal sunshine settles on its head.

Beside yon straggling fence that skirts
the way
With blossom'd furze unprofitably gay—
There, in his noisy mansion, skill'd to
rule,
The village master taught his little school.
A man severe he was, and stern to view;
I knew him well, and every truant knew:
Well had the boding tremblers learn'd to
trace
The day's disasters in his morning face;
Full well they laugh'd with counterfeited
glee
At all his jokes—for many a joke had he;
Full well the busy whisper, circling round,
Convey'd the dismal tidings when he
frown'd.
Yet he was kind; or if severe in aught,
The love he bore to learning was in fault.
The village all declared how much he
knew—
'Twas certain he could write, and cipher
too;
Lands he could measure, terms and tides
presage,
And even the story ran that he could
gauge.
In arguing, too, the parson ow'd his skill,
For even though vanquish'd, he could
argue still;
While words of learnéd length and
thundering sound
Amazed the gazing rustics ranged
around—
And still they gazed, and still the wonder
grew
That one small head could carry all he
knew.

But pass'd is all his fame; the very
spot
Where many a time he triumph'd is forgot.
Near yonder thorn, that lifts its head on
high,
Where once the sign-post caught the
passing eye,
Low lies that house where nutbrown
draughts inspired,

Where graybeard mirth and smiling toil
retired,
Where village statesmen talk'd with looks
profound,
And news much older than their ale went
round.
Imagination fondly stoops to trace
The parlor splendors of that festive place;
The whitewash'd wall, the nicely sanded
floor,
The varnish'd clock that click'd behind
the door;
The chest contrived a double debt to pay,
A bed by night, a chest of drawers by
day;
The pictures placed for ornament and
use,
The twelve good rules, the royal game of
goose;
The hearth, except when Winter chill'd
the day,
With aspen boughs and flowers and fen-
nel gay;
While broken teacups, wisely kept for
show,
Ranged o'er the chimney, glisten'd in a
row.

Vain transitory splendors! could not
all
Reprieve the tottering mansion from its
fall?
Obscure it sinks; nor shall it more 'im-
part
An hour's importance to the poor man's
heart:
Thither no more the peasant shall repair
To sweet oblivion of his daily care;
No more the farmer's news, the barber's
tale,
No more the woodman's ballad shall pre-
vail;
No more the smith his dusky brow shall
clear,
Relax his ponderous strength and lean to
hear;
The host himself no longer shall be found

THE

POEMS

— OF —

John Philpot Curran.

OH! SLEEP.

OH! sleep, awhile thy power suspend-
      ing,
   Weigh not my eyelids down;
For memory, see! with eve attending,
   Claims a moment for her own.
I know her by her robe of mourning,
   I know her by her faded light,
When faithful, with the gloom returning,
   She comes to bid a sad good-night.

Oh! let me here, with bosom swelling,
   While she sighs o'er the time that's
      past—
Oh! let me weep, while she is telling
   Of joys that pine, and pangs that I et.
And now, oh! sleep, while grief is stream-
      ing,
   Let thy balm sweet peace restore,
While fearful hope, through tears is
      beaming,
   Soothe to rest, that wakes no more.

THE DESERTER'S LAMENTA-
TION.

IF, sadly thinking,
   With spirits sinking,
Could more than drinking

Our griefs compose—
A cure for sorrow,
From grief I'd borrow,
And hope to-morrow
   Might end my woes.

But since in wailing
There's naught availing,
For death unfailing
   Will strike the blow;
Then for that reason,
And for a season,
Let us be merry
   Before we go!

A way-worn ranger,
To joy a stranger,
Through every danger
   My course I've run:
Now death befriending,
His last aid lending,
My griefs are ending,
   My woes are done.

No more a rover,
Or hapless lover,
Those cares are over—
   My cup runs low;
Then, for that reason,
And for the season,
Let us be merry
   Before we go.

THE MONKS OF THE ORDER OF ST. PATRICK,

COMMONLY CALLED

THE MONKS OF THE SCREW.

WHEN St. Patrick this order estab-
      lish'd,
   He call'd us the "Monks of the
      Screw;"
Good rules he reveal'd to our Abbot,
   To guide us in what we should do ;
But first he replenish'd our fountain
   With liquor the best in the sky ;
And he said, on the word of a saint,
   That the fountain should never run
      dry.

Each year, when your octaves approach,
   In full chapter convened let me find
      you :
And when to the Convent you come,
   Leave your favorite temptation behind
      you.
And be not a glass in your Convent,
   Unless on a festival, found ;
And, this rule to enforce, I ordain it
   One festival all the year round.

My brethren, be chaste, till you're tempt-
      ed ;
   While sober, be grave and discreet ;
And humble your bodies with fasting,
   As oft as you've nothing to eat.
Yet, in honor of fasting, one lean face
   Among you I'd always require ;
If the Abbot should please, he may wear it,
   If not, let it come to the Prior.

Come, let each take his chalice, my
      brethren,
   And with due devotion prepare,
With hands and with voices uplifted,
   Our hymn to conclude with a prayer.
May this chapter oft joyously meet,
And this glad libation renew,
To the Saint, and the Founder, and Ab-
      bot,
   And Prior, and Monks of the Screw !

THE GREEN SPOT THAT BLOOMS O'ER THE DESERT OF LIFE,

O'ER the desert of life, where you
      vainly pursued
   Those phantoms of hope, which their
      promise disown,
Have you e'er met some spirit, divinely
      endued,
   That so kindly could say, you don't
      suffer alone ?
And, however your fate may have smiled,
      or have frown'd,
   Will she deign, still, to share as the
      friend or the wife ?
Then make her the pulse of your heart ;
      for you've found
   The green spot that blooms o'er the
      desert of life.

Does she love to recall the past moments,
      so dear,
   When the sweet pledge of faith was
      confidingly given,
When the lip spoke the voice of affection
      sincere,
   And the vow was exchanged, and re-
      corded in heaven ?
Does she wish to re-bind, what already
      was bound,
   And draw closer the claim of the friend
      and the wife ?
Then make her the pulse of your heart :
      for you've found
   The green spot that blooms o'er the
      desert of life.

GERALD GRIFFIN.

THE POEMS OF GERALD GRIFFIN.

THE BRIDAL OF MALAHIDE.

AN IRISH LEGEND.

THE joy-bells are ringing
  In gay Malahide,
The fresh wind is singing
  Along the sea-side;
The maids are assembling
  With garlands of flowers,
And the harpstrings are trembling
  In all the glad bowers.

Swell, swell the gay measure!
  Roll trumpet and drum!
'Mid greetings of pleasure
  In splendor they come!
The chancel is ready,
  The portal stands wide
For the lord and the lady,
  The bridegroom and bride.

What years, ere the latter,
  Of earthly delight
The future shall scatter
  O'er them in its flight!
What blissful caresses
  Shall Fortune bestow,
Ere those dark-flowing tresses
  Fall white as the snow!

Before the high altar
  Young Maud stands array'd;
With accents that falter
  Her promise is made—
From father and mother
  Forever to part,
For him and no other
  To treasure her heart.

The words are repeated,
  The bridal is done,
The rite is completed—
  The two, they are one;
The vow, it is spoken
  All pure from the heart,
That must not be broken
  Till life shall depart.

Hark! 'mid the gay clangor
  That compass'd their car,
Loud accents, in anger,
  Come mingling afar!
The foe's on the border,
  His weapons resound
Where the lines in disorder
  Unguarded are found.

As wakes the good shepherd,
  The watchful and bold,
When the ounce or the leopard

Is seen in the fold ;
So rises already
  The chief in his mail,
While the new-married lady
  Looks fainting and pale.

" Son, husband, and brother,
  Arise to the strife,
For sister and mother,
  For children and wife !
O'er hill and o'er hollow,
  O'er mountain and plain,
Up, true men, and follow !—
  Let dastards remain !"

Farrah ! to the battle !
  They form into line—
The shields, how they rattle !
  The spears, how they shine !
Soon, soon shall the foeman
  His treachery rue—
On, burgher and yeoman,
  To die, or to do !

The eve is declining
  In lone Malahide,
The maidens are twining
  Gay wreaths for the bride ;
She marks them unheeding—
  Her heart is afar,
Where the clansmen are bleeding
  For her in the war.

Hark ! loud from the mountain,
  'Tis Victory's cry !
O'er woodland and fountain
  It rings to the sky !
The foe has retreated !
  He flies to the shore ;
The spoiler's defeated—
  The combat is o'er !

With foreheads unruffled
  The conquerors come—
But why have they muffled
  The lance and the drum ?
What form do they carry
  Aloft on his shield ?

And where does he tarry,
  The lord of the field ?

Ye saw him at morning,
  How gallant and gay !
In bridal adorning,
  The star of the day :
Now weep for the lover—
  His triumph is sped,
His hope, it is over !
  The chieftain is dead.

But, oh for the maiden
  Who mourns for that chief,
With heart overladen
  And rending with grief !
She sinks on the meadow—
  In one morning-tide,
A wife and a widow,
  A maid and a bride !

Ye maidens attending,
  Forbear to condole !
Your comfort is rending
  The depths of her soul.
True—true, 'twas a story
  For ages of pride ;
He died in his glory—
  But, oh, he *has* died !

The war-cloak she raises
  All mournfully now,
And steadfastly gazes
  Upon the cold brow.
That glance may forever
  Unalter'd remain,
But the bridegroom will never
  Return it again.

The dead-bells are tolling
  In sad Malahide,
The death-wail is rolling
  Along the sea-side ;
The crowds, heavy hearted,
  Withdraw from the green,
For the sun had departed
  That brighten'd the scene !

Even yet in that valley,
  Though years have roll'd by,
When through the wild sally
  The sea-breezes sigh,
The peasant, with sorrow,
  Beholds in the shade,
The tomb where the morrow
  Saw Hussy convey'd.

How scant was the warning,
  How briefly reveal'd,
Before on that morning
  Death's chalice was fill'd!
The hero who drunk it
  There moulders in gloom,
And the form of Maud Plunket
  Weeps over his tomb.

The stranger who wanders
  Along the lone vale,
Still sighs while he ponders
  On that heavy tale:
"Thus passes each pleasure
  That earth can supply—
Thus joy has its measure—
  We live but to die!"

HARK! HARK! THE SOFT BUGLE.

HARK! hark! the soft bugle sounds
    over the wood,
  And thrills in the silence of even,
Till faint, and more faint, in the far solitude,
  It dies on the portals of heaven!
But echo springs up, from her home in
    the rock,
  And seizes the perishing strain;
And sends the gay challenge, with
    shadowy mock,
From mountain to mountain again!
          And again!
From mountain to mountain again.

Oh, thus let my love, like a sound of
    delight,

Be around thee while shines the glad
    day,
And leave thee, unpain'd, in the silence
    of night,
  And die like sweet music away.
While hope, with her warm light, thy
    glancing eye fills,
  Oh, say—"Like that echoing strain,
Though the sound of his love has died
    over the hills,
  It will waken in heaven again."
          And again!
  It will waken in heaven again.

A SOLDIER—A SOLDIER TO-NIGHT IS OUR GUEST.

FAN, fan the gay hearth, and fling
    back the barr'd door,
Strew, strew the fresh rushes around on
    our floor,
And blithe be the welcome in every
    breast—
For a soldier—a soldier to-night is our
    guest.

All honor to him who, when danger afar
Had lighted for ruin his ominous star,
Left pleasure, and country, and kindred
    behind,
And sped to the shock on the wings of
    the wind.

If you value the blessings that shine at
    our hearth—
The wife's smiling welcome, the infant's
    sweet mirth—
While they charm us at eve, let us think
    upon those
Who have bought with their blood our
    domestic repose.

Then share with the soldier your hearth
    and your home,
And warm be your greeting whene'er he
    shall come;

Let love light a welcome in every
        breast—
For a soldier—a soldier to-night is our
        guest.

AILEEN AROON.

WHEN like the early rose,
        Aileen aroon!
Beauty in childhood blows.
        Aileen aroon!
When like a diadem,
Buds blush around the stem,
Which is the fairest gem?
        Aileen aroon!

Is it the laughing eye?
        Aileen aroon!
Is it the timid sigh?
        Aileen aroon!
Is it the tender tone,
Soft as the string'd harp's moan?
Oh, it is truth alone,
        Aileen aroon!

When, like the rising day,
        Aileen aroon!
Love sends his early ray,
        Aileen aroon!
What makes his dawning glow
Changeless through joy or woe?
Only the constant know,
        Aileen aroon!

I know a valley fair,
        Aileen aroon!
I knew a cottage there,
        Aileen aroon!
Far in that valley's shade
I knew a gentle maid,
Flower of the hazel glade,
        Aileen aroon!

Who in the song so sweet,
        Aileen aroon!
Who in the dance so sweet,
        Aileen aroon!

Dear were her charms to me,
Dearer her laughter free,
Dearest her constancy,
        Aileen aroon!

Were she no longer true,
What should her lover do?
        Aileen aroon!
Fly with his broken chain
Far o'er the sounding main,
Never to love again,
        Aileen aroon!

Youth must with time decay,
        Aileen aroon!
Beauty must fade away,
        Aileen aroon!
Castles are sack'd in war,
Chieftains are scatter'd far,
Truth is a fixéd star,
        Aileen aroon!

KNOW YE NOT THAT LOVELY RIVER?

AIR—"*Roy's wife of Aldivalloch.*"

KNOW ye not that lovely river?
        Know ye not that smiling river?
            Whose gentle flood,
            By cliff and wood,
With wildering sound goes winding ever.
Oh! often yet with feeling strong,
On that dear stream my memory ponders,
    And still I prize its murmuring song,
For by my childhood's home it wanders.
            Know ye not, &c.

There's music in each wind that flows
    Within our native woodland breathing;
There's beauty in each flower that blows
    Around our native woodland wreathing.
The memory of the brightest joys
    In childhood's happy morn that found
        us,

THE

POEMS

◄OF►

JOHN ANSTER.

DIRGE SONG.

FROM THE IRISH.

LIKE the oak of the vale was thy
    strength and thy height,
Thy foot like the erne of the mountain in
    flight :
Thy arm was the tempest of Loda's fierce
    breath,
Thy blade, like the blue mist of Lego,
    was death !

Alas, how soon the thin cold cloud
The hero's bloody limbs must shroud !
I see thy father, full of days ;
For thy return behold him gaze ;
The hand, that rests upon the spear,
Trembles in feebleness and fear—
He shudders, and his bald, gray brow
Is shaking, like the aspen bough ;
He gazes, till his dim eyes fail
With gazing on the fancied sail :
Anxious he looks—what sudden
    streak
Flits, like a sunbeam, o'er his cheek !
" Joy, joy, my child, it *is* the bark,
That bounds on yonder billow dark !"
His child looks forth with straining
    eye,
And sees—the light cloud sailing
    by :

His gray head shakes ; how sad,
    how weak
That sigh ! how sorrowful that cheek !

His bride from her slumbers will waken
    and weep,
But when shall the hero arouse him from
    sleep ?
The yell of the stag-hound—the clash of
    the spear,
May ring o'er his tomb—but the dead
    cannot hear.
Once he wielded the sword, once he
    cheer'd to the hound,
But his pleasures are past, and his slum-
    ber is sound :
Await not his coming, ye sons of the
    chase,
Day dawns ! but it nerves not the dead
    for the race ;
Await not his coming, ye sons of the
    spear,
The war-song ye sing—but the dead
    will not hear.

Oh ! blessing be with him who sleeps in
    the grave,
The leader of Lochlin ! the young and the
    brave !
On earth didst thou scatter the strength
    of our foes,

Then blessing be thine, in thy cloud of
    repose !
Like the oak of the vale was thy strength
    and thy might,
Thy foot, like the erne of the mountain
    in flight ;
Thy arm was the tempest of Loda's fierce
    breath,
Thy blade, like the blue mist of Lego,
    was death.

THE HARP.

CLARA, hast thou not often seen, and
        smiled,
            A rosy child,
Deeming that none were near,
Touch with a trembling hand
        Some fine-toned instrument ;
Then gaze, with sparkling eye, as on her
    ear
The murmurs died, like gales, that having
    fann'd
        Soft summer flowers, sink spent.
Half fearing, still she lingers,
        Till o'er the strings again she
            flings,
Less tremblingly, her fingers !—
        But if a stranger eye
        The timid sport should spy,
        Oh ! then, with pulses wild,
        This rosy child
        Will throb, and fly,
Turn pale and tremble, tremble and turn
    red,
And in thy bosom hide her head.

Even thus the harp to me
        Hath been a plaything strange,
A thing of fear, of wonder, and of glee ;
    Yet would I not exchange
This light harp's simple gear for all that
    man holds dear ;
And should the stranger's ear its tones
    regardless hear,
        It still is sweet to *thee !*

THE EVERLASTING ROSE.

EMBLEM of hope ! enchanted flower,
        Still breathe around thy faint per-
            fume,
Still smile amid the wintry hour,
    And boast, even now, a spring-tide
        bloom :
Thine is, methinks, a pleasant dream,
    Lone lingerer in the icy vale,
Of smiles that hail'd the morning beam,
    And sighs more sweet for evening's
        gale !

Still are thy green leaves whispering
    Low sounds to fancy's ear, that tell
Of mornings when the wild-bee's wing
    Shook dew-drops from thy sparkling
        cell !
With thee the graceful lily vied,
    As summer breezes waved her head ;
And now the snow-drop at thy side
    Meekly contrasts thy cheerful red.

Well dost thou know each varying voice
    That wakes the seasons, sad or gay ;
The summer thrush bids thee rejoice,
    And wintry robin's dearer lay.
Sweet flower ! how happy dost thou
    seem,
    'Mid parching heat, 'mid nipping frost !
While gathering beauty from each beam,
    No hue, no grace, of thine is lost !

Thus hope, 'mid life's severest days,
    Still soothes, still smiles away despair ;
Alike she lives in pleasure's rays,
    And cold affliction's winter air :
Charmer alike in lordly bower
    And in the hermit's cell, she glows ;
The poet's and the lover's flower,
    The bosom's everlasting rose !

IF I MIGHT CHOOSE.

IF I might choose where my tired limbs
        shall lie

When my task here is done, the oak's
  green crest
  Shall rise above my grave—a little
    mound,
Raised in some cheerful village cemetery.
  And I could wish, that, with unceasing
    sound,
A lonely mountain rill was murmuring
  by—
  In music—through the long soft twi-
    light hours.
And let the hand of her, whom I love best,
  Plant round the bright green grave
    those fragrant flowers
In whose deep bells the wild-bee loves to
  rest ;
  And should the robin from some neigh-
    boring tree
Pour his enchanted song—oh ! softly
  tread,
For sure, if aught of earth can soothe the
  dead,
  He still must love that pensive melody!

OH! IF, AS ARABS FANCY.

OH ! if, as Arabs fancy, the traces
  on thy brow
Were symbols of thy future state, and I
  could read them now,

Almost without a fear would I explore
  the mystic chart,
Believing that the world were weak to
  darken such a heart.

As yet to thy untroubled soul, as yet to
  thy young eyes,
The skies above are very heaven—the
  earth is paradise ;
The birds that glance in joyous air—the
  flowers that happiest be,
They toil not, neither do they spin, are
  they not types of thee ?

And yet, and yet—beloved child—to
  thy enchanted sight,
Blest as the present is, the days to come
  seem yet more bright,
For thine is hope, and thine is love, and
  thine the glorious power
That gives to hope its fairy light, to love
  its richest dower.

For me that twilight time is past—those
  sunrise colors gone—
The prophecies of childhood—and the
  promises of dawn ;
And yet what is, though scarcely heard,
  will speak of what has been,
While love assumes a gentler tone, and
  hope a calmer mien.

THE POEMS OF REV. CHARLES WOLFE.

The Rev. Charles Wolfe, a minister of the Established Church, was a native of Dublin. It is to be regretted that he died in the prime of manhood, for a youth of such promise gave hope of a distinguished future. He furnished another evidence to the truth of that apothegm of the ancients –" Whom the gods love die young." His lines, entitled as above, at first appeared anonymously, and created such general admiration, that, along with several speculations as to their authorship, not a few absolute claims were made for that honor by impudent aspirants for fame. Medwin, in his "Conversations of Lord Byron," asserts his belief among the speculators that they were *written by the noble poet*, though all he establishes is the fact that they were *admired and read* by him. Though the extract is longer than is desirable to be given in a work like the present, yet it is so pregnant with evidence of the high worth at which Wolfe was rated among the highest, that I cannot resist giving it, as a tribute due to his memory.

"The conversation turned after dinner on the lyrical poetry of the day, and a question arose as to which was the most perfect ode that had been produced. Shelley contended for Coleridge's on Switzerland, beginning ' Ye clouds,' &c., &c.; others named some of Moore's Irish Melodies, and Campbell's Hohenlinden; and, had Lord Byron not been present, his own Invocation to Manfred, or Ode to Napoleon, or on Prometheus, might have been cited.

"' Like Gray,' said he, ' Campbell smells too much of the oil; he is never satisfied with what he does; his finest things have been spoiled by over-polish—the sharpness of the outline is worn off. Like paintings, poems may be too highly finished. The great art is effect, no matter how produced.

"I will show you an ode you have never seen, that I consider little inferior to the best which the present prolific age has brought forth.' With this he left the table, almost before the cloth was removed, and returned with a magazine, from which he read the following lines on Sir John Moore's burial, which perhaps require no apology for finding a place here."

Here follow the stanzas, after which Medwin continues— "The feeling with which he recited these admirable stanzas I shall never forget. After he had come to an end he repeated the third, and said it was perfect, particularly the lines—

"' But he lay like a warrior taking his rest,
With his martial cloak around him.'

"' I should have taken,' said Shelley, ' the whole for a rough sketch of Campbell's.'
"' No,' replied Lord Byron; ' Campbell would have claimed it, if it had been his.'
"' I afterward had reason to think that the ode was Lord Byron's; that he was piqued at none of his own being mentioned; and, after he had praised the verses so highly, could not own them. No other reason can be assigned for his not acknowledging himself the author, particularly as he was a great admirer of General Moore."

Here we have Coleridge, Campbell, and Moore among the hypothetical authors; Byron and Shelley, as admirers and conjecturers; and, after all, it was a young Irishman who produced this poem. Such literary honor is worth recording, not only for the sake of the memory of the departed poet, but for the fame of the land that gave him birth.—S. LOVER.

GO, FORGET ME.

GO, forget me—why should sorrow
  O'er that brow a shadow fling?
Go, forget me—and to-morrow
  Brightly smile, and sweetly sing.
Smile—though I shall not be near thee:
Sing—though I shall never hear thee:
  May thy soul with pleasure shine,
  Lasting as the gloom of mine.

Like the sun, thy presence glowing,
  Clothes the meanest things in light,
And when thou, like him, art going,
  Loveliest objects fade in night.
All things look'd so bright about thee,
That they nothing seem without thee;
  By that pure and lucid mind
  Earthly things were too refined.

Go, thou vision wildly gleaming,
Softly on my soul that fell;
Go, for me no longer beaming—
Hope and Beauty! fare ye well!
Go, and all that once delighted
Take, and leave me all benighted;
Glory's burning, generous swell,
Fancy and the Poet's shell.

THE BURIAL OF SIR JOHN MOORE.

NOT a drum was heard, not a funeral-note,
As his corse to the rampart we hurried;
Not a soldier discharged his farewell shot
O'er the grave where our hero we buried.

We buried him darkly at dead of night,
The sods with our bayonets turning,
By the struggling moonbeam's misty light,
And the lantern dimly burning.

No useless coffin enclosed his breast,
Not in sheet or in shroud we wound him;
But he lay like a warrior taking his rest,
With his martial cloak around him.

Few and short were the prayers we said,
And we spoke not a word of sorrow;
But we steadfastly gazed on the face that was dead,
And we bitterly thought of the morrow.

We thought, as we hollow'd his narrow bed,
And smooth'd down his lonely pillow,
That the foe and stranger would tread o'er his head,
And we far away on the billow!

Lightly they'll talk of the spirit that's gone,
And o'er his cold ashes upbraid him,—
But little he'll reck, if they let him sleep on
In the grave where a Briton has laid him.

But half of our heavy task was done,
When the clock struck the hour for retiring;
And we heard the distant and random gun
That the foe was sullenly firing.

Slowly and sadly we laid him down,
From the field of his fame, fresh and gory;
We carved not a line, we raised not a stone—
But we left him alone in his glory!

THE CHAINS OF SPAIN ARE BREAKING.

THE chains of Spain are breaking!
Let Gaul despair, and fly;
Her wrathful trumpet's speaking,
Let tyrants hear, and die.

Her standard, o'er us arching,
Is burning red and far;
The soul of Spain is marching,
In thunders to the war—

Look around your lovely Spain,
And say, shall Gaul remain?—
Behold yon burning valley;
Behold yon naked plain—
Let us hear their drum—
Let them come, let them come!
For vengeance and freedom rally,
And, Spaniards! onward for Spain.

Remember! remember Barossa;
Remember Napoleon's chain—
Remember your own Saragossa,

And strike for the cause of Spain—
Remember your own Saragossa,
    And onward! onward! for Spain.

———

OH! SAY NOT THAT MY HEART IS COLD.

OH! say not that my heart is cold
    To aught that once could warm it;
That nature's form, so dear of old,
    No more has power to charm it;
Or that the ungenerous world can chill,
One glow of fond emotion,
For those, who made it dearer still,
    And shared my wild devotion.

Still oft those solemn scenes I view,
    In rapt and dreamy sadness;
Oft look on those, who loved them too,
    With fancy's idle gladness;
Again I long'd to view the light,
    In nature's features glowing;
Again to tread the mountain's height,
    And taste the soul's o'erflowing.

Stern duty rose, and frowning flung
    Her leaden chain around me;
With iron look, and sullen tongue,
    He mutter'd, as he bound me—
"The mountain breeze, the boundless heaven,
    Unfit for toil the creature;
These for the free, alone, are given—
    But, what have slaves with nature?"

———

GONE FROM HER CHEEK.

GONE from her cheek is the summer bloom,
And her cheek has lost its faint perfume,
And the gloss has dropp'd from her raven hair,
And her forehead is pale, though no longer fair;

And the spirit, that set in her soft, blue eye,
    Is sunk in cold mortality;
And the smile that play'd on her lip is fled,
And every grace has left the dead.

Like slaves, they obey'd her in height of power,
But left her, all, in her winter-hour;
And the crowds that swore for her love to die,
Shrunk from the tone of her parting sigh—
    And this is man's fidelity!

'Tis woman alone, with a firmer heart,
Can see all those idols of life depart;
And love the more, and soothe, and bless
    Man in his utter wretchedness.

———

OH, MY LOVE HAS AN EYE OF THE SOFTEST BLUE.

OH, my love has an eye of the softest blue,
    Yet it was not that that won me;
But a little bright drop from her soul was there,
    'Tis that that has undone me.

I might have pass'd that lovely cheek,
    Nor perchance my heart have left me;
But the sensitive blush that came trembling there,
    Of my heart it forever bereft me.

I might have forgotten that red, red lip,
    Yet how from that thought to sever?
But there was a smile from the sunshine within,
    And that smile I'll remember forever.

Think not 'tis nothing but lifeless clay,
    The elegant form that haunts me;

And thou shouldst smile no more.
And I on thee should look my last,
'Tis the gracefully elegant mind that
    moves
In every step, that enchants me.

Let me not hear the nightingale sing,
    Though I once in its notes delighted;
The feeling and mind that comes whis-
        pering forth
Has left me no music beside it.

Who could blame had I loved that face,
    Ere my eye could twice explore her;
Yet it is for the fairy intelligence there,
    And her warm, warm heart, I adore
        her.

———

IF I HAD THOUGHT THOU COULDST HAVE DIED.

IF I had thought thou couldst have
    died,
    I might not weep for thee;
But I forgot, when by thy side,
    That thou couldst mortal be.
It never through my mind had pass'd
    The time would e'er be o'er,

And still upon that face I look,
    And think 'twill smile again;
And still the thought I will not brook,
    That I must look in vain.
But when I speak, thou dost not say
    What thou ne'er leftst unsaid,
And now I feel, as well I may,
    Sweet Mary! thou art dead.

If thou wouldst stay e'en as thou art,
    All cold, and all screne,
I still might press thy silent heart;
    And where thy smiles have been!
While e'en thy child bleak corse I have,
    Thou seemest still mine own,
But there I lay thee in thy grave—
    And I am now alone.

I do not think, where'er thou art,
    Thou hast forgotten me;
And I, perhaps, may soothe this heart
    In thinking too of thee;
Yet there was round thee such a dawn
    Of light ne'er seen before,
As fancy never could have drawn,
    And never can restore.

THE

— OF —

❧ P. D. NUNAN. ❧

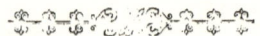

EILEEN O'DONOHUE.

THERE'S a lonely road in Lisnalee,
  And a huckster's house hard by ;
On the landscape drear grows not a tree,
  Nor flower to cheer the eye.

But a light in the cabin window burns,
  When the long winter nights begin,
And each youth to the welcome beacon turns,
  To game at the humble inn.

For a pack of cards is in the box,
  At Peggy O'Shea's *shebeen ;*
And something else that's sure to coax—
  'Tis duty-free *potheen.*

And of all the boys who " cut for deal,"
  And gambled there till day,
The lightest of heart and likewise heel,
  Was reckless Daniel Ray.

But Fortune one night Dan Ray forsook,
  And he being run to earth,
And every *brown** from his pocket shook,
  Sat silently by the hearth.

Silent he sat till one there spoke,
  Who played at the gaming board,
His tale was meant for a half-sad joke,
  But Dan swallowed every word :

" Dan Ray, if to play you want a stake,
  List to a tale that's true :—
Last night at Laurel Hill was a wake,
  And to-day a funeral too :

* A penny.

" The Flower of Laurel Hill is dead,
  Eileen O'Donohue !—
As she kneaded some dough to make cake bread,
  The cock flapped his wings and crew :

" Eileen heeded not that warning crow,
  But made her cake in haste,
And, as she sang, put a morsel of dough
  Into her mouth to taste.

" A gulp of that convulsed throat is heard—
  Her breath to carry it fails—
She struggled—she sank, and ne'er more stirr'd,
  Nor woke at her mother's wails !

" There's a ring of gold on her finger white,
  On her neck a string of pearl ;
For gems were poor Eileen's delight,
  And they're buried with the girl.

" Go seek her tomb in the churchyard gray—
  She's buried in old Kilmeen."
A mocking smile on his lip did play,
  As he quaff'd his glass of *potheen.*

One minute brooded Daniel Ray,
  Then bright his dark brow grew,—
" Fill me a noggin, Peggy O'Shea,
  And lend me a crowbar too.

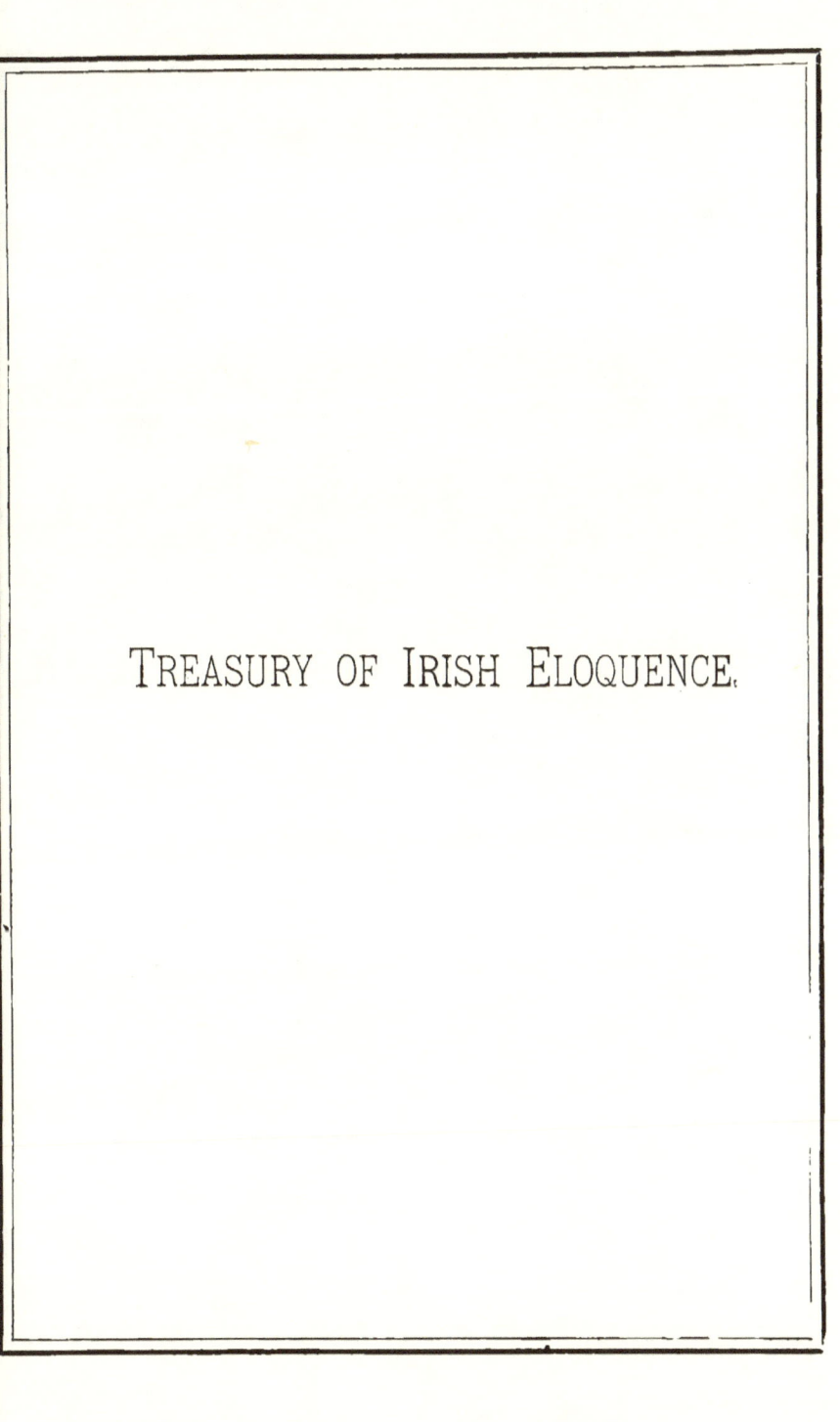

Treasury of Irish Eloquence.

REV. DR. CAHILL, D.D.

THE

TREASURY

OF

IRISH ELOQUENCE,

BEING A COMPENDIUM OF

Irish Oratory and Literature.

COMPILED WITH ANNOTATIONS FROM THOMAS DAVIS, DR. McNEVIN, DR. MADDEN,

AND OTHERS.

EMBRACING THE MOST BRILLIANT AND STIRRING SPEECHES OF

*EDMUND BURKE, HENRY GRATTAN, JOHN PHILPOT CURRAN, RICH
ARD BRINSLEY SHERIDAN, ROBERT EMMETT, CHARLES PHILLIPS,
RICHARD LALOR SHIEL, DANIEL O'CONNELL, REV. DR.
CAHILL, THOS. FRANCIS MEAGHER, THOMAS D'ARCY
MAGEE, ARCHBISHOP McHALE, FATHER
BURKE, REV. MICHAEL B. BUCK
LEY, MICHAEL DAVITT,
A. M. SULLIVAN.*

With a Preface by P. D. Nunan.

EMBELLISHED WITH A FULL SET OF PORTRAITS ENGRAVED BY KILBURN.

NEW YORK:

MURPHY & McCARTHY,

PUBLISHERS.

PREFACE.

Eloquence is aptly defined as the clothing of one's thoughts in the most appropriate and effective language calculated to convince the reason or stir the emotions. Eloquence, then, like poetry and the sister arts, is an intellectual gift of the highest order, and requires in its possessor for effective use in public speaking, essentials not employed in the latter. The orator, in all ages, has been the leader in great movements, the pioneer of reforms, and the champion of the people. Indeed, we may go further and say, the orator is the high-priest of the temple of Liberty; for his voice is the tocsin which summons her worshippers, and its echoes have often penetrated even the prison walls, and revived within the breast of the drooping captive that spirit which can never die, since it is of the human soul an immortal aspiration.

> "Eternal Spirit of the chainless mind!
> Brightest in dungeons — Liberty thou art;
> For then thy habitation is the heart!"

By some divine provision of Providence, as the occasion arose, whether in early or modern times—in every political convulsion that has agitated the world—the epoch gave birth to the orator of his race to oppose the oppression of tyrannical rule, or plead the public cause, in the struggle for needed reforms. It was when the ambition of Philip of Macedon led him to attempt to enslave the Athenians, that the figure of Demosthenes, conspicuous for all time on the pedestal of Fame, arose in their midst, and by the potency of his native eloquence aroused that latent fire of patriotism, which prompts even the weakest nation to repel the invader and defend its altars. So too, Rome, when treason was in her ruler and corruption in her senate, gave to the world a Cicero, whose philippics are handed down amongst the treasures of classical literature.

Oratory, then, has had at all times for its highest inspiration, patriotism; and for its favorite theme, the wrongs of oppressed races trampled under the heel of crowned despotism. No nation, perhaps, would be less proud than Ireland undoubtedly is, of the rich heritage which her orators have left her in their public utterances; which are, for the most part, powerful protests against tyrannical oppression, scathing denunciations of wrong, and unflinching assertion of the principles of Truth and Justice; *magna est veritas et prevalebit:* the principle, if not the award (save in a most stinted measure) of Justice, has at length been conceded, or rather wrung from, the alien government of that down-trodden country; proving the adage, that Truth *will* ultimately prevail.

The orators of Ireland form a galaxy of genius scarcely excelled in the intellectual firmament by any other nation. True, there are comparatively few now living who have stood amidst the multitude to hear the great tribune O'Connell, and whose hearts were swayed by the varying emotions conjured up by the magic of that voice, even as a waving field of corn bows at the breath of the west wind. It is not given to any of us to have listened in rapt attention to the thrilling tones of Grattan, inveighing against the destruction of the Constitution of '82, and the Act of Union, against cut-throat Castlereagh, and the traitors who bartered away their country's liberty for a mess of pottage; or again, to have heard the silver tongue of Curran in defence of the United Irishmen, before a perjured judge and packed juries. Their lips and those of their contemporaries and disciples are sealed forever. But their voices are not stilled. They speak to us from the shelves of every library, where taste and culture combine in the selection of all that is beautiful in literature.

The speeches of Grattan are elaborate compositions, not mere extempore utterances; and hence, may be regarded as models of forensic rhetoric. So, too, Curran's speeches, and also Shiel's, afford a rare treat to the reader, enriched as they are with a wealth of learned allusion, apt simile, and sparkling wit. Amongst the pulpit orators of Ireland, the illustrious Father Burke towers pre-eminent as a preacher and scholar. His discourses are each a grand superstructure raised by the chain of logical sequence on a sacred text or historical contention; and with him may be ranked (since the fame of both is world-wide) Dr. Cahill, distinguished alike as a preacher and scientist.

This volume presents to the reader all that is most excellent — almost every gem — in the rich mine of Irish oratorical literature. Its title, "The Treasury of Irish Eloquence," aptly describes its contents; but it is, in truth, more than a treasury: such a book is a *treasure*, in the full sense of the word; for it affords at all times to the mind of the attentive reader a rare intellectual treat. If he be an Irishman, and has never had the advantage of reading his country's history, he will gather many facts of the throes of her agony, when the heroic efforts of her sons for freedom in '98 proved futile, and she sank again bleeding under the scourge of her relentless foe. These facts, and others of prior and subsequent periods, he will learn — not in the dry language of history, but from the burning words of her brilliant orators at the bar and in the senate.

To the student, the debater, or the aspirant for honors on the platform or the pulpit, the selections here given are all that is most excellent in composition, copious and elegant in diction, and effective in delivery; and many of them are worthy to be committed wholly or in part to memory.

P. D. N.

Boston, Mass., October 1st, 1885.

CONTENTS.

CONTENTS. xi

xii   CONTENTS.

ADDRESSES, LECTURES AND SERMONS.

BY

REV. D. W. CAHILL.

[1]

REV. DR. CAHILL'S ADDRESS,

———

MR. CHAIRMAN AND BELOVED FELLOW-COUNTRYMEN, — I do believe there is no nation in the world able to shout with the Irish. Our countryman, Dean Swift, counselled the Irish people, in his day, not to make speeches at public meetings, for fear of the Attorney General. " Do not speak," said he, " when you meet, as the law may punish you: but there is no law against shouting, — hence, groan and shout." And from that day to this, we can groan and shout better than any people in the whole world. Till I came here on this evening, I thought I could never forgive either Lord J. Russell or Lord Palmerston; but the speakers who have preceded me have inflicted such a castigation on them, that, with your kind permission, I will forgive them, — not in this world, — but in the next. For this purpose, I must have the key of the Kingdom of Heaven, and also the key of the other place, in order that, when I first let them out, I can next let them in.

Mr. Chairman, you have exaggerated my small services in reference to the public letters which I have written. Whatever merit I may have, consisted in my knowing well the history of Ireland. The history of other countries is learned from the cool pen of the historian, but that of Ireland is learned from the crimsoned tombs of the dead. The history of other nations is collected from the growing population and successful commerce, but the sad story of Ireland is gathered from the deserted village, the crowded poorhouse, and the mournful swelling canvas of the emigrant ship. You gave me too much credit for those slender productions of mine, and perhaps you are not aware that it was on the graves of the starved and shroudless victims of English misrule I stood when I indited the epistles. I dated them from the grave-pits of Sligo and the fever-sheds of Skibbereen. If I seemed to weep, it was because I followed to coffinless tombs tens of thousands of my poor, persecuted fellow-countrymen; and if my descriptions appeared tinged with red, it was because I dipped my pen in their fresh bleeding graves in order to give suitable coloring to the terrific page on which a cruel fate has traced the destinies of Ireland. It was not my mind but my bosom that dictated; it was not my pen but my heart that wrote the record.

And where is the Irishman who would not feel an involuntary impulse of national pride in asserting the invincible genius of our own creed while he gazes on the crumbling walls of our ancient churches, which, even in their old age, lift their hoary heads as faithful witnesses of the past struggles of our faith, and still stand in their massive frame-work, resisting to the last the power of the despoiler, and scarcely yielding to the inevitable stroke of time? And where is the heart so cold, that would not pour forth a boiling torrent of national anger at seeing the children of forty generations consigned to a premature grave, or banished by cruel laws to seek amongst the strangers the protection they are refused at home?

Nature does not deny a home to the untutored savage that wanders naked over her boundless domain; even the maternal genius of the inhospitable forest gives a welcome asylum to her young; she brings them forth from her bare womb, suckles them on her stormy bosom, and feeds them at her desert streams. She teaches them to kneel beneath the dark canopy with which she shrouds the majesty of her inaccessible rocks; she warns them to flee from danger in the moaning voice of the unchained tempests, and she clothes her kingdom in verdure and sunlight to cheer them in their trackless home. Well has the divine heart of Campbell given a preference to the savage beast over the ill-fated lot of the exiled Irishman, in these immortal lines which express the history of our nation: —

> " Where is my cabin door fast by the wildwood,
>   Where is my sire that wept for its fall?
> Where is the mother that watched o'er my childhood?
>   Where is my bosom friend, dearer than all?

familiar with their hard trials, and feel intensely their dire fate; and, in the midst of all their misfortunes, they never lose the native affections of their warm Irish hearts.

About the year 1849 I went on board an emigrant ship at the custom-house in Dublin in order to see the accommodation of the poor emigrants. While walking on the deck, I saw a decent poor man from the County Meath, with the ugliest dog I ever beheld in his arms. He seemed to be keeping up a kind of private conversation with this dog, and occasionally he kissed him so affectionately, that I was led to speak to him, and made some inquiry about him. He told me that the dog's name was Brandy, that he and his mother were in his family for several years, and that he was the same age as his youngest child. He continued to say, that on the day he was ejected, and his house thrown down, Brandy's house was thrown down too; in fact, that the poor dog was exterminated as well as himself. That he took pity on him, brought him to Dublin, paid fifteen shillings for his passage to America, and that he would support him with his children as long as he lived. While we were speaking, the dog began to bark; on which I inquired what he was barking at. "Oh! sir," said he, "he knows we are talking about the _andlord. He knows his name as well as I do, and the creature always cries and roars when he hears his name mentioned."

Oh, many a trial the poor Irish have endured during the last six years! Many a volume could be filled with the cruel persecution of the faithful Irish. From Galway to America, the track of the ship is marked by the whitened bones of the murdered Irish that lie along the bottom of the abysses of the moaning ocean. And yet those that have reached the friendly shore still drag a heavy chain which binds them to their native land; still they long to see their own beloved hills, and lay their bones with the ancient dead of their Faith and their kindred. And if death summons them beyond the Mississippi, or amidst the snows of Canada, or the pestilence of Mexico, they turn their fading eyes towards the day-star that rises over Ireland, and their last prayer is offered to Heaven for the ι.oerty of their country — the last sigh to God is made for the freedom of her altars.

REV. DR. CAHILL'S ADDRESS TO THE CATHOLICS OF GLASGOW.

—

MR. CHAIRMAN, LADIES AND GENTLEMEN, — I am laboring on the present occasion under a deficiency, for which I am convinced you will pardon me, namely, I am afraid you will not understand me in consequence of my Irish accent. I now beg to tell you, with the deepest feeling of a lasting gratitude, that, although I have received many marks of public favor heretofore in Ireland and in England, I have never found myself placed in a position of such exalted distinction as on the present occasion. Surrounded as I am, not by hundreds but by thousands of gentlemen and ladies, by priests and people, I return my homage for your advocacy, on this evening, of a great principle in thus honoring the individual who now addresses you.

Your eloquent and valued address, written on satin in golden letters, shall be preserved by me as long as I live; it is a model of exquisite taste, and conveys impressions of affection which I shall carefully bind up with the most cherished feelings of my life; but there is an eloquence of soul which the golden ink could not express; and that silent thrilling language must be read in the merry faces, the sparkling looks, and ardent bosoms which reveal to my inmost heart the sincerity and the intensity of your feeling towards me.

In associating me in the most remote connection with the great O'Connell, you do me an honor which would raise even a great man to imperishable fame; as you illume me with a ray from that immortal name which sheds unfading lustre on the records of Ireland's saddest and brightest history, and which will live in the burning affections of the remotest posterity of a grateful country. I am

Rev. Dr. Cahill's Lecture.

DELIVERED AT THE ACADEMY OF MUSIC, NEW YORK, MARCH 17TH,
1860. — "THE FIDELITY OF IRELAND IN DEFENCE OF HER
LIBERTIES AND HER ANCIENT RELIGION."

———

LADIES AND GENTLEMEN, — I assure you, though I have
had the pleasure of meeting you here before, I never was so
completely overpowered in my life as upon the present occasion. I have made a bow to you as gracefully as I could,
endeavoring to acknowledge the compliment you have paid
me, but that was with the front of my head. As there are a great
many of my friends at my back, and as I am not able to make a bow
with the back of my head, permit me to turn about and make a bow
to the ladies and gentlemen behind me. I am endeavoring to take
in breath to give myself voice to fill this most extensive hall. Since
I have had the pleasure of being here with you, I have addressed
large assemblies in the city of New York and elsewhere; but
whether it is the height of the hall, or whether it is my excitement,
I think this is the largest assembly I have ever seen in the whole
course of my life. I never shall forget the compliment paid to me
to come here this day. It is not so much the delight of meeting
you here as the delight I experienced in witnessing your glorious
procession. I came from the city of Troy yesterday. (A voice —
Where were you?) I like to see you all up to concert pitch, and I
would be a bad performer, indeed, if we don't have abundance of
melody this evening. I little thought of the glorious satisfaction
that awaited me in looking at your procession. I assure you I never
felt more proud of Irishmen than on this day. I have been told that
if I had been present at the Cathedral this morning I would have

learned eloquence from the most beautiful and polished discourse of the gentleman who preached there to-day. I am sorry I could not be there. It is a loss I shall regret as long as I live.

When I went out to look at the procession I was delighted to see the number of banners, the cap of liberty over the harp of Ireland; and what I was very glad to see was the American flag side by side with every banner as it passed my hotel. The stars and stripes went, if I may use the phrase, hand in hand with the harp of Ireland. How I longed to be a great man, as I saw every one uncover his head as he passed the statue of Washington. I was delighted to see such worship, if I may so speak, offered to the memory of the dead. Thousands of men taking off their hats and bending themselves in humble posture as they passed by the "Father of his Country." I was delighted to see one man drive six horses, but my astonishment was drowned when eight horses came afterwards, to see the crowded reins in the hands of the skilful driver. Then I beheld the men clad in armor passing along, and I saw the forest of steel lifted above the harp of Ireland. A suggestive idea presented itself to my mind as I saw brave men, in regular military step, with their muskets lifted, their bayonets fixed, and there, going before, beside, and after, the glorious harp of Ireland.

I saw the cavalry, the soldiers mounted on their beautiful horses, and they held their swords so much to my taste, and they moved so regular, and the whole procession was so orderly. There were Ireland and America joined in the two emblems, the Irish harp and the American stripes and stars. But I was greatly astonished when I saw a man driving twelve horses. The horses seemed to go by the same kind of sense as if they were twelve human beings. When I saw the driver with the bundle of reins in his hand, and the horses moving with such regularity and precision, I said, I would like to know the name of that driver. That man must be from Tipperary, and his name O'Connell, for that is just the way O'Connell used to drive a coach and four through every act of Parliament.

So you see I have been looking sharply; and my weakness was such, if you so call it, that, as the whole scene passed before me, and my heart upon Ireland, tears, Irish tears, stood in my eyes. Perhaps these tears made the men look bigger and finer, but I thought they were the finest men I ever saw. I have seen the

The Immaculate Conception,

A Sermon Delivered by Rev. Dr. Cahill, in St. James' Cathedral, Brooklyn, on Sunday, March 25, 1860, for the Benefit
of the Sisters of Mercy.

DEAREST BRETHREN, — Mankind since the beginning of the
world never saw such a day as the anniversary we are now
met to celebrate. This is the 25th of March, the date of the
Annunciation of the Blessed Virgin, the festival being put off
till to-morrow, but we meet to celebrate it on this day for a purpose
of my own, and I again repeat that up to that period and perhaps
since, mankind never did or never will behold such a day as the anniversary we now celebrate. God the Father, in a week painted the
skies — a great work. He took out His imperial compasses, and He
swept the wide arch of the Universe and within the circle He put all
things that the eye can behold. He painted the gorgeous and glorious colors that we see above us. But the day that the Second
Person of the Trinity, the Son of God, deigned to unite Himself
with our nature — to descend as it were from His throne to unite
Himself with man, to elevate man to Heaven, above the angels —
the day that He did this is without exception the greatest and the
most glorious that mankind ever met to celebrate.

You are aware that when Adam fell the gates of Heaven were
bolted against him and his posterity. But yesterday a heap of clay,
to-day an organized being with an immortal soul, who could have
ever supposed he could rebel against God, his Father — his Creator?
Who could have supposed that he would have been so mad as to
forfeit for an apple his glorious privileges? The day Heaven was
bolted against him his race was excluded, the earth on which he stood

was cursed, God withdrew his immediate patronage from him, and the darkness of night settled down like a cloud over the whole earth. But see how great is the justice of God, how impenetrable His ways, how unsearchable His judgments, what may be called His just vengeance after thousands of years, during which the earth was covered with pitch darkness and man excluded, only to be saved by a belief in a future day of hope. It is on this day that Heaven begins to be reconciled to man, and the Second Person of the Trinity begins to be united with our nature. Think till fancy is exhausted, and who could have supposed that a rebel could be so lifted. The Son of God, long before the foundation of the world was laid, long before the Heaven of the angels was formed, long before a single creature was created, long before Adam was made, addressed His Father and said: Father, it is written in the head of the book that You could not be pleased with the blood of goats and oxen. It is written in the head of the book, in the very first of Our transactions, that these sacrifices could not please You, and behold I come to offer myself. Man will fall — I know it, because I see into futurity. I know that Adam will fall and I know that he can never redeem himself. How could darkness produce light? How could crime produce virtue? How can the rebel who is finite, pay off a debt which is infinite? How can finity pay infinity? Therefore, Father, do You recollect it was entered into the book of Our transactions — it was not even at the end of the first page, but it was in the beginning of the first page — what St. Paul calls the masterpiece of the power and wisdom of God. Man cannot pay You, therefore I stand before You in My bare head, and I say, pour upon My head the vials of Your wrath. Under the imputability of sin here I come as the only mode of compensation, and pour upon Me the vials of Your reddest wrath.

Four thousand years elapsed before that eternal promise was fulfilled, but as sure as God lives that promise was to be fulfilled, and therefore this is the day — the 25th of March — when the Angel Gabriel announced to Mary that this great compact was to be realized, and that God was to be united with man. And He stood before the throne of God as a criminal to pay the infinite debt which Adam incurred by his transgression. This is decidedly the most important fact that ever the Church of God could celebrate. I have, therefore, taken advantage of this festival to discuss for you one of the most

The Last Judgment,

A Sermon Delivered by Very Rev. D. W. Cahill, D.D., in
St. Peter's Church, Barclay Street, New York, on Sunday
Evening, November 29, 1863.

———

DEAREST BRETHREN, — God's word contains no subject
that is presented in such majestic grandeur, such withering
terror, and yet such infinite joy, as the Gospel of this day
which I have just read for you. One does not know what
fact on this awful day is most wonderful; whether we consider the
end of time, the destruction of the world, the multitudinous congre-
gation of all men, the fate of the damned, and the glories of the
blessed — yet incomprehensible as are all these considerations, they
all fade, when compared with the majesty of God on that day, sitting
in imperial triumph on the clouds, surrounded by the whole Court
of Angels and Saints. It is the great day reserved in Heaven for
celebrating the triumph of virtue over vice, the dominion of the
Saviour over the power of Satan — the most awful hour Eternity ever
saw. It is the mightiest moment in the life of God; it is the end of
Christ's mission on earth; the consummation of all the mysteries
God ever published; the final sentence of the wicked, when God
and those they love are separated forever. In a word, the Gospel
of this day presents in one large view everthing glorious in Heaven,
terrible in Hell, awful in Eternity, and great in God. It is a picture
worthy of God, representing at once Earth, Hell, Heaven, with their
unnumbered populations. No serious man can behold it without
thrilling astonishment; no Christian, however perfect, can look on
it without terror; no sinner can believe it without amendment. As
time once began, so time now ends. Only one condition of things

now remains, namely, Eternity. Time is past on this day; a mere second of existence in the life of God.

How wonderful is human language : though creatures of a moment, we can discuss things eternal; though mere worms, we can paint things omnipotent : like the broken fragment of a mirror, reflecting the whole firmament, in our slender phrase we can describe the infinitude of God. In all past scenes up to the present moment, everything on earth was finite, limited. It was man who was the actor, and time was the condition of things. God is the actor on this day, and Eternity is the condition. It is all infinity. This day is the day of Christ. He summons all the dead : He commands all Hell : He is accompanied by all Heaven. No tongue can, of course, tell this scene. The soul's silent contemplation can best behold any part of it. What brush, or what artist, could paint the sun in its meridian glory? One glance at his burnished flood of gold will exhibit him best. And who can describe the Redeemer on His own day of power and glory? St. Luke but faintly tells it when he says : " The powers of Heaven shall be moved, and then they shall see the Son of Man coming in a cloud, in great power and majesty."

When the day of general judgment will come, no mortal can tell : the highest Archangel round God's throne cannot know it : it is among the eternal secrets of His own mind. It is a future free act of His independent will ; and no creature can unlock the depths of God's liberty. We resemble Him in our spiritual essence to a small extent : we know the past and the present, in our own limited circle of time. The angelic essence knows the past and the present in a wider circle of knowledge : but no creature, however exalted, can know the future, unless God reveals it. Futurity can have no real existence, since it has not as yet commenced to exist. It is solely confined to the mind of God, the internal mind of God : and is therefore essentially beyond the reach of the highest creature. We only know that the terrible day of judgment will certainly arrive in some future revolving century. The same Almighty word that called all things into being has spoken it : the same unerring testimony that built Nature has described its future wreck. The feelings, the maddening agonies, the very words of the burning inhabitants are minutely detailed by the language of Christ Himself. The world, therefore, destroyed by future fire under the anger of God, is as

REV. DR. CAHILL. 75

DR. CAHILL TO FIVE PROTESTANT CLERGYMEN.

LETTERKENNY, May 30th, 1853.

REVEREND SIR, — We, the undersigned, having heard you deliver a controversial lecture this evening in the chapel of Letterkenny, feel it our solemn duty, as ministers of God and embassadors of Christ, to protest against the doctrines set forth by you, as unscriptural and contrary to the teaching of the Catholic Church. We would therefore take the liberty of inviting you to a public discussion, to be carried on in a kind and Christian spirit, in which we call upon you to prove that the doctrines contained in the twelve supplementary articles of the creed of Pope Pius IV. were ever propounded and set forth in the Christian Church as a creed before the year 1564.

Secondly — We invite you to bring on the platform your rule of faith, and give us your Church's authorized interpretation of the sixth, ninth, and tenth chapters of St. Paul to the Hebrews — or, if you prefer it, your Church's *authorized* exposition of the simplest portions of the Holy Writ — the Lord's prayer.

Thirdly — We invite you and any number of your brother priests to meet an equal number of clergy of the Church of England, to prove the assertions you used in endeavoring to establish the unscriptural doctrine of the sacrifice of the Mass. Trusting you will receive the invitation in the same spirit in which it is dictated, we remain yours faithfully in Christ,

> F. GOOLD, Archdeacon of Raphoe.
> J. IRWIN, Rector of Aughaninshin.
> R. SMITH, Curate of Cornwall.
> J. W. IRWIN, Curate of Raymohy.
> J. LINSKEA, Glenalla.

REVEREND SIRS, — I have the honor to acknowledge the receipt of your polite note, dictated in a spirit of great courtesy, and having stamped on it the clear impress of the distinguished character of the gentlemen whose names it bears. I shall then at once proceed to give a hasty reply to those passages in your respected communication which demand commentary from me.

Firstly, then, I solemnly deny, and conscientiously protest against your unauthorized assumption of calling yourselves "the ministers of God and embassadors of Christ;" and I complain loudly of your most unjustifiable intrusion in designating your modern local conventicle by the name of the "Catholic Church." Gentlemen, I assure you I do not mean, even remotely, to utter one offensive sentiment to you personally by telling you that you are libelling God and calumniating the Apostles in using this language. You are, on the contrary, the ecclesiastical ministers of the British Parliament, you are the clerical embassadors of the Queen of England, and you are the rebel children of the most terrific apostasy the world ever saw. The Thirty-nine articles of your creed (which learned Protestants call contradictory and incongruous) are the *accidental result* of a majority of voices in the British senate-house of that day. This act of Parliament forms the preface of your Book of Common Prayer, and the decisions of that Parliamentary session are unavowedly the very basis and the theological title of the Anglican creed, as expressed in these Articles. In point of fact, and according to the language of the English Parliament, that creed should be appropriately called a "bill," like any other Parliamentary bill passed by a majority in that house. Beyond all doubt, its proper name should be "the Protestant Religion Bill," or some other such designation, proceeding, as it does, professedly, and originating officially from the decision of the senate-house, and from the authority of the Crown. The authority does not even pretend to be derived from Christ, as it acknowledges itself to be fallible, and, of course, progressive and human.

And the Prime Minister of England can lay aside any of your present opinions when he thinks fit, as was recently proved in the case of the Rev. Mr. Gorham; and the Queen can annul the united doctrinal decision of your national convocation at her pleasure. Argue this case as you will, and call this authority by whatever name you please, there it is, the supreme arbiter of your Church, the essential sanction and source of your faith. Thus, in point of fact, you pray to God as the Premier likes; and you believe in God as the Queen pleases; and you multiply or diminish the articles of your "Religion Bill" as the Parliament decides. You are, therefore, judicially and officially, the very creatures of the State; and you wear your surplices and preach by precisely the same authority mented by your attendance at my lectures on the Holy Sacrifice of the Mass, and I have felt rather honored by the united note of the five Protestant clergymen, transmitted to me through the courtesy of the Protestant Archdeacon of Raphoe, and the brother-in-law of our late Viceroy. I have not, I hope, in any words which escaped me at that lecture, uttered any sentiment which could offend; and I here disclaim again intending to say one word in this note (beyond my own professional duty) to give the smallest uneasiness to gentlemen towards whom I feel much personal respect, and to whom I beg unfeignedly to offer the expression of high and distinguished consideration.

I have the honor to be, Rev. Sirs, your obedient servant,

D. W. CAHILL, D. D.

P. S. — As you have gratuitously originated this correspondence, you can have no claim on me for its continuance; and, therefore, I respectfully decline taking any further notice of any letters which you may do me the honor to send me in future.

LETTER OF THE REV. DR. CAHILL TO THE RIGHT HON. THE EARL OF DERBY.

NEW BRIGHTON, Saturday, October 21, 1852.

MY LORD EARL, — Some few months ago our gracious Queen, in a speech from the throne, very emphatically announced her royal determination to uphold the principles of the Protestant Church, and she called on her servants there assembled, in her presence, to assist her in maintaining the liberties of the Protestant Constitution. There must be, my Lord, in the royal mind some hidden fear of this Church being in danger, in order to account for the large space which this idea has taken up in the royal oration. If this declaration had been made by your Lordship, or by any one of the present Ministry, it would still command an important attention; but when it proceeds from the head of your Church — from the œcumenical source of all Protestant truth, it comes before the world invested with all the realities of Parliamentary gravity and English history. For the first time in my life, I do agree with the sentiments deduced from a royal speech; and I do, therefore, believe that your Church is in imminent danger at the present moment; and I believe, moreover, that neither her most gracious Majesty, with all her royal power, my Lord John Russell, with the base Whigs, nor your Lordship, with the most judicious combination of Whig and Tory which your skill in Parliamentary chemistry can produce, will be able to stay much longer the downfall of an institution which is a libel on God's Gospel, a fortress for public injustice, and the scandalous disturber of our national peace. The danger to be apprehended, however, will not proceed, in the first instance, from an external enemy; it will come from her long

REV. MICHAEL B. BUCKLEY.

SERMONS AND LECTURES.

BY

REV. MICHAEL BERNARD BUCKLEY.

[ ]

SERMON.

PANEGYRIC OF SAINT FINBAR, PATRON SAINT OF THE DIOCESE OF CORK.*

[Rev. Michael Bernard Buckley, the eloquent preacher, and graduate of Maynooth College, Dublin, from whose numerous lectures in the United States, in 1870, and elsewhere, we take the following, was born in Cork, March 9th, 1831, and died in the same city, May 17th, 1872.]

" The wise man shall seek out the wisdom of all the ancients, and will be occupied in the prophets . . . he will give his heart to resort early to the Lord that made him, and he will pray in the sight of the Most High. He will pour forth the words of his wisdom as showers, and in his prayer he will confess to the Lord. . . . He shall shew forth the discipline he hath learned, and shall glory in the law of the covenant of the Lord. Many shall praise his wisdom and it shall never be forgotten. The memory of him shall not depart away, and his name shall be in request from generation to generation. Nations shall declare his wisdom, and the Church shall shew forth his praise." — ECCLESIASTICUS, xxxix. 1, and following verses.

DEARLY BELOVED BRETHREN, — We are assembled here to-night to celebrate the memory of a great and glorious Saint of the Church of God, of whose character and history those words of divine wisdom appear to me to afford a most perfect and apposite delineation. Throughout the entire course of the narrative which I shall deliver to you of his life, you cannot but perceive the faithful aptitude of the description; you cannot fail to observe how diligently he sought out the wisdom of the ancients, and how he was occupied in the prophets — how he gave his heart to resort early to the Lord that made him, and how he prayed in the sight of the Most High — how he poured forth the words of his wisdom in showers — how he showed forth the discipline he had

* Preached in the Church of St. Finbar, Cork, September 27, 1863.

learned, and gloried in the law of the covenant of the Lord. And
you will also see with what prophetic truth the posthumous fame of
the Saint has been described by the Wise Man when he says, "Many
shall praise his wisdom, and it shall never be forgotten — the memory
of him shall not depart away, and his name shall be in request from
generation to generation. Nations shall declare his wisdom, and
the Church shall shew forth his praise." I come not to describe to
you to-night the life and actions of any great hero of this world. I
do not seek to awaken your admiration by describing the exploits of
some famous general, or the diplomatic tactics of some celebrated
statesman. Mine is no story of blood-red battlefields and glorious
victories; my hero shone neither on the field nor in the cabinet; he
was not the inventor of a new philosophy, but the obsequious disciple
of an old one. We have not heard that he was eloquent, nor does
it appear that he was distinguished as a writer; he was not noble nor
was he wealthy; his birth was probably obscure, and his life was
certainly secluded, and yet, strange as it may appear after the lapse
of twelve hundred years, his memory is green in the souls of his
posterity, as the grass that still blooms on the "lone little island"
which in early life his sainted footsteps trod. "The just man," says
the Sacred Scripture, "shall be in eternal remembrance," and so it
was with St. Finbar. His was the heroism of justice, of virtue, of
wisdom; his battles were those which he fought against the world,
the flesh, and the devil; his victories were those which he gained
over that triple alliance of his enemies; his philosophy was that of
Jesus the Son of God; his eloquence was the simple but moving
eloquence of the Gospel, by which he exhorted to virtue and deterred
from vice; his only writing was that by which he unconsciously
inscribed his name on the memories of men; Christianity was his
most excellent patent of nobility; and his only wealth and inheritance
were the grace of the Almighty during life, and after death that
glory which he now enjoys, and which was entailed on him from his
Eternal Father, who has said, "They who instruct others unto justice
shall shine like stars for all eternity." We all desire to know something of the great men of olden times, and we are justified in praising
them by the example of the Sacred Scriptures; but, to us citizens of
Cork, and much more to us members of this Parish, it must be
particularly interesting to know something of the life of the great

pride, to cherish this inestimable boon, and to show forth in our lives that we are worthy disciples in the school of faith established here by our holy Patron. And, on this night, when the most adorable Body and Blood of our Divine Redeemer are exposed for the special veneration of the faithful, I think I cannot do better than ask you to cherish in your hearts an ardent love for that most holy sacrament as the best means of enlivening your faith and meriting the patronage and intercession of the holy St. Finbar. "What is man, O Lord: that thou art mindful of him, or the son of man that thou shouldst visit him?" What have we done, O Lord! that Thou shouldst descend from Thy throne of glory and visit the poorest of Thy servants? Thou art here in the midst of us, as Thou wert on the night of the Last Supper amongst the Apostles — so near that we may behold Thee—so condescending that we may converse with Thee like friends — so generous that we may ask of Thee what we please, and be sure to obtain it — so loving and tender that our bosoms may melt in the contemplation of Thy sweetness — and yet so exalted, so glorious, so powerful, that we may exhaust the language of praise and adoration, and still be at loss for epithets worthy of Thy greatness. There is the great Lord, my brethren, looking down on us to-night — the same who, on the last day, will appear in the clouds of heaven to judge us. Oh! let us propitiate Him now in the day of His mercy, for on that day His justice alone shall prevail; and believe me there is no safer way to avert the terrors of Jehosophat than to keep the lamp of faith forever brightly burning in your bosoms — not that cold faith by which we merely believe in God, but that faith which worketh by charity, and which is so strongly recommended by Christ and His Apostles. Grant us, therefore, O Lord, the grace to believe in Thee, to hope in Thee, to love Thee, that when that last hour of earthly existence shall have passed away, we may experience in our souls the happy transition of faith into vision, and of hope into possession, charity alone remaining. And do thou, O holy St. Finbar, intercede, we beseech thee, to God for us, that as it is to thy Apostolate our city is indebted for the blessings of Christian faith, we may so shape our conduct, and direct our lives, that following faithfully the beacon of that faith enkindled by thee before us, we may reach in safety the heaven of eternal bliss, to enjoy with thee the blessed society of God and his angels, forever, and forever. Amen.

Sermon on the Profession of a Nun.

"Hearken, O daughter, and see : and incline thine ear and forget thy people and thy father's house, and the king shall greatly admire thy beauty, for he is the Lord thy God." — Ps. xliv. 12.

DEARLY BELOVED SISTER, — On this day, — certainly the most important of your life, — when, after the most mature deliberations, you have consecrated for the rest of your days your whole being to the service of God, it is of advantage to you that you should hear some words, under the auspices of religion, that may strengthen you for the accomplishment of the work you have so nobly begun. Into the retreat which you have chosen for your future years you will carry all the infirmity of your nature, and for you, as well as for us in the world, life will be ever a warfare. It is well, then, that you should have ever before your eyes a model which may show you not only the possibility of proceeding in your adopted course, but which may also illustrate the ease with which all its difficulties can be surmounted. When we undertake some new and previously unattempted task, we are apt to lose courage, and sometimes to despair of success ; but when we try what some other wayfarer on life's journey has ventured and achieved, we are stimulated by his example, and go on bravely to the end. Thus I would propose to you, dear sister, the life and character of the Blessed Virgin Mary, as the great standard which you should follow ; for she is the brightest model of innocence, self-sacrifice, and religious consecration ever presented by God to an admiring world. I do not wish you to imagine that in following this standard you can ever attain to anything like the purity and holiness of Mary, for none other, save her, ever was or will be " full of grace." But by imitating her virtues you can arrive at a height of sanctity you will do more for Him here than you would do abroad. You have come, not to repose, but to labor; not to do your own will, but the will of Him who has this day made you especially His own. You have heard His voice in your ear and in your heart, inviting you to become His child, and you have not hesitated to come. You have never once looked back. "Hearken, O daughter, and see, and forget thy people and thy father's house, and the King shall greatly desire thy beauty, for He is the Lord thy God." Oh! the glory of our religion, that every day presents to our eyes so many miracles of grace, fortifying weak mortals with the strength of giants, clothing tender woman in a panoply of might, so that her worth is estimated by more than all the treasures of earth. "Who shall find a valiant woman? Far and from the uttermost coasts is the price of her." Proceed, then, dear sister, in your hallowed course — follow the blessed light of heaven that illumes your pathway. Mary is looking down on you this moment from the heights of Heaven, and in you she is well pleased. Could you but behold the gentle eyes of that tenderest and sweetest of mothers, how much would the fervor of your devotions be intensified, and the strength of your resolutions increased! May she be your powerful mediatrix before the eternal Throne; that acting all your life with the docility and innocence of a child, you may adorn your soul with those beautifying graces which may make you worthy to be eternally saved by your Eternal Father, the King who shall desire thy beauty, thy Lord and thy God.

SERMON ON THE BLESSED VIRGIN MARY.

"Comfortress of the afflicted, pray for us."

DEARLY BELOVED BRETHREN, — There is no sorrow like that which the heart endures in secret; of which we ourselves alone are conscious, and which oppresses us with gloom and dejection, while the world thinks us light-hearted and gay. We mix amongst our friends, and, while they see the faint smile that lights our cheek at the passing jest, they little dream of the misery, the untold agony, that wrings our bosoms, and brings us well nigh to the confines of despair. Oh! at such a moment how we long to find some sympathizing friend — some tender-hearted bosom to which we may freely disclose the sad story of our wrongs — the bitter catalogue of our afflictions. And when, at length, the melancholy tale is told, and the patient listener turns to console us, how sweetly the words of solace fall upon our ear; how the heart expands with love, with gratitude, with courage, and the tears, which, but a few moments before, were the silent interpreters of unutterable woe, are suddenly converted, by the magic touch of sympathy, into the exponents of equally unalterable joy. But where shall we find this sweet consoler, this gentle confidant, this tender heart, before which we may bare our own, and to which we may impart the last secret of our sorrows? Alas! for the perversity of human nature, such friendship is rare, very rare, in this cold, heartless world. Self-love predominates over every generous impulse of nature, and it has almost passed into a proverb, that hearts which have confided most have been most frequently betrayed. But there is at least one human being to whom we are invited to recur in all our tribulations, into whose sacred bosom no profane thought of self-love ever presumed to

LECTURE ON THE NATIONAL MUSIC OF IRELAND.*

IN Ireland, from time immemorial, music and poetry have been so much cultivated conjointly by the same class of men, and not, as in other countries, each by a different order of votaries, that, as far as Ireland is concerned, the history of the one cannot well be dissociated from the history of the other. The bards of the most ancient times, and indeed the bards of times comparatively modern, not only reached the highest excellence in the performance of instrumental music, but their own genius supplied them with words and ideas, and facility of musical composition, requisite for attaining thorough perfection in the cultivation of the sister art. It is, therefore, impossible for him who professes to trace the history of Irish music not to interweave with his theme the history of Irish poetry also. In the performance of this task, the historian or lecturer must expose himself to the ridicule of the unlearned sceptic, and to the incredulity of many of his own un-Irish fellow-countrymen when he claims for the poetry and music of his native land an antiquity scarcely attained by those arts in any region of the universal world. But scepticism and unpatriotism must yield to the adamantine sternness of truth; and it is truth to say that the history of Irish poetry and music can be traced back to the earliest dawnings of the history of mankind. Music is as old as the world, and the world was yet young when Ireland was colonized by wanderers from Oriental climes, where poetry and music appear to have been coeval with the very formation of society. Music is inherent in the very nature of man — it is the language specially adapted for expressing the joyous affections of an innocent mind. As the whispering of forest leaves, the rippling of the mountain stream, and the roar

* Delivered before the Cork Literary and Scientific Society, December 12, 1868.

of the angry storm, are the homage-giving music of inanimate creation, so vocal melody is the prescribed music in which nature dictates
to man to sound the praises of his God. No tribe or nation has been
ever known that was not susceptible of the influence of music; and
the more primitive the state of man, the more prevalent appears to
have been its cultivation. Hence the idea of pastoral life is always
associated with the idea of musical tastes. According to the fourth
chapter of Genesis, Jubal, the seventh descendant of Adam, with
whom he was contemporary, was "the father of them that play upon
the harp and the organs," that is, of all stringed and wind or pulsa-
tile instruments; and, appropriately enough, we find in the same
passage that he was the brother of Jabel, who was "the father of
such as dwell in tents and of herdsmen." Thus we find, at one of
the earliest periods of human history, that the nomad life was associated in one family with the cultivation of the art of music — a
circumstance which is illustrated in heathen mythology by the pipes
of the sylvan Pan and the lyre of the pastoral Apollo. Jubal was
also a contemporary of Noah, and doubtless transmitted through
the saved of the ark the secrets of his art to his postdiluvian descendants. The branches of the human family were soon after separated
from the parent stock, and migrating from the plain of Senaar,
brought with them their customs and traditions to every quarter of
the globe on which they settled. All truthful history assures us
that the earliest colonists of Ireland came from the East — that land
where the genial warmth of the climate, the surpassing beauty of
Nature, and the vivacious temperament of the people, together with
that simplicity and impressibility characteristic of the infancy of
society, made almost every man a poet. From that pure and generous source the poetry and music of Ireland have flown, and, after
the lapse of ages, to this day close affinity may be discerned between
the strains of several Oriental nations and the strains of our native
land. These similarities have been discovered in Persia and India.
Marsden, in his history of Sumatra, says that "the Sumatran tunes
much resemble to his ear those of the native Irish, having usually,
like them, a flat third." Modern travellers, or residents in India,
will tell you that there is a marvellous resemblance between the
Hindoo melodies and those of Ireland and Scotland. The same may
be said of the melodies of the Siamese. From these Eastern sources

FATHER BURKE.

FIRST LECTURE.

DELIVERED IN THE ACADEMY OF MUSIC, NEW YORK, NOVEMBER 12, 1872.

———

LADIES AND GENTLEMEN, — It is a strange fact that the old battle, which has been raging for seven hundred years, should continue so far away from the old land. The question on which I am come to speak to you this evening is one that has been disputed at many a council board, one that has been disputed in many a parliament, one that has been disputed on many a well-fought field, and is not yet decided — the question between England and Ireland. Amongst the visitors to America who came over this year there was one gentleman distinguished in Europe for his style of writing and for his historical knowledge, the author of several works which have created a profound sensation, at least for their originality. Mr. Froude has frankly stated that he came over to this country to deal with the English and with the Irish question, viewing it from the English standpoint; that, like a true man, he came to America to make the best case that he could for his own country; that he came to state that case to an American public as to a grand jury, and to demand a verdict from them the most extraordinary that was ever yet demanded from any people — namely, the declaration that England was right in the manner in which she has treated my native land for seven hundred years. It seems, according to this learned gentleman, that we Irish have been badly treated; that he confesses, but he put in as a plea *that we only got what we deserved.* It is true, he says, that we have governed them badly; the reason is, because it was impossible to govern them rightly. It is true that we have robbed them; the reason is, because it was a pity to leave them

their own, they made such a bad use of it. It is true we have persecuted them; the reason is, persecution was a fashion of the time and
the order of the day. On those pleas there is not a criminal in prison
to-day in the United States that should not instantly get his freedom
by acknowledging his crime and pleading some extenuating circumstance. Our ideas about Ireland have been all wrong, it seems.
Seven hundred years ago the exigencies of the time demanded the
foundation of a strong British empire; in order to do this, Ireland
had to be conquered, and Ireland was conquered. Since that time
the one ruling idea in the English mind has been to do all the good
that they could for the Irish. Their legislation and their action has
not always been tender, but it has been always beneficent. They
sometimes were severe; but they were severe to us for our own
good, and the difficulty of England has been the Irish during these
long hundreds of years; they never understood their own interests or
knew what was for their own good. Now, the American mind is
enlightened, and henceforth no Irishman must complain of the past
in this new light in which Mr. Froude puts it before us. Now, the
amiable gentlemen tells us, what has been our fate in the past he
greatly fears we must reconcile ourselves to in the future. He comes
to tell us his version of the history of Ireland, and also to solve Ireland's difficulty, and to lead us out of all the miseries that have been
our lot for hundreds of years. When he came, many persons questioned what was the motive or the reason of his coming. I have
heard people speaking all round me, and assigning to the learned
gentleman this motive or that. Some people said he was an emissary of the English government, that they sent him here because they
were beginning to be afraid of the rising power of Ireland in this
great nation; that they saw here eight millions of Irishmen by birth,
and perhaps fourteen millions by descent; and that they knew
enough of the Irish to realize that the Almighty God blessed them
always with an extraordinary power, not only to preserve themselves, but to spread themselves, until in a few years not fourteen,
but fifty millions of descendants of Irish blood and of Irish race will
be in this land. According to those who thus surmise, England
wants to check the sympathy of the American people for their Irish
fellow-citizens; and it was considered that the best way to effect this
was to send a learned man with a plausible story to this country, a

man with a singular power of viewing facts in the light which he wishes himself to view them and put them before others, a man with the extraordinary power of so mixing up these facts that many simple-minded people will look upon them as he puts them before them as true, and whose mission it was to alienate the mind of America from Ireland to-day by showing what an impracticable, obstinate, accursed race we are.

Others, again, surmise that the learned gentleman came for another purpose. They said, England is in the hour of her weakness; she is tottering fast and visibly to her ruin; the disruption of that old empire is visibly approaching; she is to-day cast off without an ally in Europe, her army a cipher, her fleet nothing — according to Mr. Reade, a great authority on this question — nothing to be compared to the rival fleet of the great Russian power now growing up. When France was paralyzed by her late defeat, England lost her best ally. The three emperors, in their meeting the other day, contemptuously ignored her, and they settled the affairs of the world without as much as mentioning the name of that kingdom, which was once so powerful. Her resources of coal and iron are failing, her people are discontented, and she is showing every sign of decay. Thus did some people argue that England was anxious for an American alliance; for, they said, "What would be more natural than that the old tottering empire should seek to lean on the strong, mighty, vigorous young arm of America?"

I have heard others say that the gentleman came over to this country on the invitation of a little *clique* of sectarian bigots in this country. Men who, feeling that the night of religious bigotry and sectarian bitterness is fast coming to a close before the increasing light of American intelligence and education, would fain prolong the darkness for an hour or two by whatever help Mr. Froude could lend them.

But I protest to you, gentlemen, here to-night that I have heard all these motives assigned to this learned man without giving them the least attention. I believe Mr. Froude's motives to be simple, straightforward, honorable and patriotic. I am willing to give him credit for the highest motives, and I consider him perfectly incapable of lending himself to any base or sordid proceedings from a base or sordid motive. But as the learned gentleman's motives have been so freely canvassed and criticised, and, I believe, indeed, in many cases misinterpreted, so my own motives in coming here to-night may be perhaps also misinterpreted and misunderstood, unless I state them clearly and plainly. As he is said to come as an emissary of the English Government, so I may be said, perhaps, to appear as an emissary of rebellion or of revolution. As he is supposed by some to have the sinister motive of alienating the American mind from the Irish citizenship of the States, so I may be suspected of endeavoring to excite religious or political hatred.

Now, I protest these are not my motives; I come here to-night simply to vindicate the honor of Ireland in her history. I come here to-night lest any man should think that in this our day, or in any day, Ireland is to be left without a son, who will speak for the mother that bore him.

And first of all I hold that Mr. Froude is unfit for the task he has undertaken for three great reasons : First, because I find in the writings of this learned gentleman that he solemnly and emphatically declares that he despairs of ever finding a remedy for Ireland, and he gives it up as a bad job. Here are the words, written in one of his essays a few years ago : "The present hope," he says, "is that by assiduous justice" (that is to say, by conceding everything that the Irish please to ask) "we shall disarm that enmity, and convince them of our good will." It may be so; there are persons sanguine enough to hope that the Irish will be so moderate in what they demand, and the English so liberal in what they grant, that at last we shall fling ourselves into each other's arms in tears of mutual forgiveness. I do not share that expectation; it is more likely they will push their importunities until at last we turn upon them and refuse to yield further. And there will be a struggle once more; and either emigration to America will increase in volume until it has carried the entire race beyond our reach, or in some shape or other they will again have to be coerced into submission. "Banish them or coerce them" : there is the true English speech. "My only remedy," he emphatically says, "my only hope, my only prospect for the future for Ireland is, let them all go to America; have done with the race; give to them a land at least that we have endeavored to make for seven hundred years a desert and a solitude; or, if they remain at home, they will have to be coerced into submission." I hold that

SECOND LECTURE.

DELIVERED IN THE ACADEMY OF MUSIC, NEW YORK, NOVEMBER
14, 1872.

LADIES AND GENTLEMEN, — We come now to consider
the second lecture of the eminent English historian who has
come among us. It covers one of the most interesting and
terrible passages in our history, and takes in three reigns —
the reign of Henry VIII., the reign of Elizabeth, and the reign of
James I. I scarcely consider the reign of Edward VI., or of Philip
and Mary, worth counting. Mr. Froude began his second lecture
with a rather startling paradox. He asserted that Henry VIII. was
a hater of disorder. Now, my friends, every man in this world has
his hero ; and, consciously or unconsciously, every man selects some
character out of history that he admires, until at length, by continually dwelling on the virtues and excellences of his hero, he comes
to almost worship him. From among the grand historic names
written in the world's annals every man is free to select whom he
likes best, and using this privilege, Mr. Froude has made the most
singular selection of which you or I ever heard. His hero is Henry
VIII. It speaks volumes for the integrity of Mr. Froude's own
mind. It is a strong argument that he possesses a charity most sublime that he is enabled to discover virtues in the historical character
of one of the greatest monsters that ever cursed the earth. But he
has succeeded in this, to us, apparent impossibility, and discovered,
among other shining virtues, in the character of the English Nero a
great love for order and hatred of disorder. Well, we must stop at
the very first sentence of the learned gentlemen and enquire how
much truth there is in it, and how much only a figment of imagina-

tion. All order in the state is based on three grand principles, **my** friends : first, the supremacy of the law ; second, respect for liberty of conscience ; and, third, a tender regard for that which lies at the foundation of all human society — namely, the sanctity of the marriage tie.

The first element of order in every state is the supremacy of the law, for in this lies the very quintessence of human freedom and **of** order. The law is supposed to be, according to the definition of Aquinas, "the judgment pronounced by profound reason and intellect, thinking and legislating for the public good." The law is therefore the expression of reason — reason backed by authority, reason influenced by the noble motive of the public good. This being the nature of law, the very first thing that is demanded for the law is that every man shall bow down to it and obey it. No man in any community has any right to claim exemption from obedience to the law, least of all the man at the head of the community, because he is supposed to represent the nation and nation's spirit, and to give to the people an example of virtue and of obedience to the law. Was Henry VIII. an upholder of the law? was he obedient to England's law? I deny it, and I have the evidence of history to back me in that denial, and to prove that Henry VIII. was one of the greatest enemies of freedom and law that ever lived in this world, and consequently one of the greatest tyrants. I shall only give one example out of ten thousand which might be taken from the history of the time. When Henry VIII. broke with the Pope, he called upon his subjects to acknowledge him (bless the mark!) as the spiritual head of the Church. There were three abbots of three Charter-houses in London — the Abbot of London, the Abbot of Asciolum, and the Abbot Belaval. These three abbots refused to acknowledge Henry as the supreme spiritual head of the Church. They were arrested and held for trial, and a jury of twelve citizens was impanelled to try them. The first principle of English law, the grand palladium of English legislation and freedom, is the perfect liberty of a jury. A jury must be free, not only from coercion, but from prejudice and prejudgment. A jury must be impartial, and free to record the verdict at which their impartial judgment has arrived. Those twelve men refused to convict the three abbots of high treason. Their decision was grounded on this, it has never

THIRD LECTURE.

DELIVERED IN THE ACADEMY OF MUSIC, NEW YORK, NOVEMBER 19, 1872.

LADIES AND GENTLEMEN, — I now approach, in answering Mr. Froude, some of the most awful periods of our history, and I confess that I approach this terrible ground with hesitancy, and with an extreme regret that Mr. Froude should have opened up questions which oblige an Irishman to undergo the pain of heart and anguish of spirit which a revision of those periods of our history must occasion. The learned gentleman began his third lecture by reminding his audience that he had closed his second lecture with a reference to the rise, progress, and collapse of a great rebellion which took place in Ireland in 1641 — that is to say, somewhat more than two hundred years ago. He made but a passing allusion to that great event in our history, and in that allusion — if he has been reported correctly — he said simply that the Irish rebelled in 1641. This was his first statement, that it was a rebellion; secondly, that this rebellion began in massacre and ended in ruin; thirdly, that for nine years the Irish leaders had the destinies of their country in their hands; and, fourthly, that those nine years were years of anarchy and mutual slaughter. Nothing, therefore, can be imagined more melancholy than the picture drawn by that learned gentleman of these nine sad years. And yet I will venture to say, and I hope I shall be able to prove, that each of these four statements is without sufficient historical foundation. My first position is that the movement of 1641 was not a rebellion; second, that it did not begin with massacre, although it ended in ruin; thirdly, that the Irish leaders had not the destiny of their country in their hands during these years; and, fourth, whether they had or not, that these years were not a period of anarchy and mutual slaughter. They were but the opening to a far more terrific period. We must discuss these questions, my friends, calmly and historically. We must look upon them rather like the antiquarian prying into the past than with the living, warm feelings of men whose blood boils up with the burnings of so much injustice and so much bloodshed.

In order to understand this question fully and fairly, it is necessary for us to go back to the historical events of the time. I find, then, that James I., the man who planted Ulster — that is to say, confiscated utterly and entirely six of the finest counties in Ireland, an entire province, rooting out the aboriginal Irish and Catholic inhabitants, even to a man, giving the whole country to Scotch and English settlers of the Protestant religion, under the condition that they were not to employ even as much as an Irish laborer on their grounds, that they were to banish them all — this man died in 1625 and was succeeded by his unfortunate son, Charles I. When Charles came to the throne, bred up as he was in the traditions of a monarchy which Henry VIII. had rendered almost absolute, as we know — whose absolute power was still continued in Elizabeth under forms the most tyrannical, whose absolute power was continued by his own father, James I. — Charles came to the throne with the most exaggerated ideas of royal privileges and supremacy. But during the days of his father a new spirit had grown up in Scotland and in England. The form which Protestantism took in Scotland was the hard, uncompromising, and highly cruel form of Calvinism in its most repellant aspect. The men who rose in Scotland in defence of their Presbyterian religion rose not against Catholic people, but against the Episcopalian Protestants of England. They defended what they called the kirk or covenant. They fought bravely, I acknowledge, for it, and they ended in establishing it as the religion of Scotland.

Now, Charles I. was an Episcopalian Protestant of the most sincere and devoted kind. The Parliament of England, in the very first years of Charles, admitted persons who were strongly tinged with Scottish Calvinism. The king demanded of them certain subsidies and they refused him; he asserted certain sovereign rights and they denied them. While this was going on in England from 1630 to

Fourth Lecture.

LADIES AND GENTLEMEN, — I have perceived in the public newspapers that Mr. Froude seems to be somewhat irritated by the remarks made as to his accuracy as a historian. Lest any word of mine might hurt in the least degree the just susceptibilities of an honorable man, I beg beforehand to say that nothing is further from my thoughts than the slightest word either of personality or disrespect for one who has won for himself so high a name as the English historian. Therefore I merely hope that it is not any word which may have fallen from me, even in the heat of our amicable controversy, that has given the least offence to that gentleman. Just as I would expect to receive from him, or from any other learned and educated man, the treatment which one gentleman is supposed to show to another, so do I also wish to give him that treatment.

Now, my friends, we come to the matter in hand. The last thing I did was to traverse a great portion of our previous history in reviewing the statements of the English historian, and one portion I was obliged to leave almost untouched. One portion of that sad history is included in the reign of Queen Anne, that estimable lady of whom history records the unwomanly vice of an overfondness for eating. Anne ascended the English throne in 1702, after the demise of William of Orange, and she sat upon that throne until 1711. As I before remarked, there was, perhaps, sufficient reason that the Roman Catholics of Ireland, trodden as they were in the very dust, should expect some quarter from the daughter of the man for whom they had shed their blood, and the granddaughter of the other Stuart king for whose cause they had fought with so much bravery in 1649. But the Irish Catholics got from this good Lady

Anne a return quite of another kind from what they might with reason have expected. Not content with the breach of the articles of Limerick of which her royal brother-in-law, William, had been guilty — not content with the atrocious penal laws which kept the Catholics of Ireland in grovelling misery, Anne went further. She appointed a new Lord Lieutenant, the Duke of Ormond, and no sooner did he assume his powers than the Irish Protestants fell on their knees before him and begged him to save them from their foes, the desperate Catholics. Great God! A people who had been robbed, persecuted, decimated, until there was hardly a miserable remnant left, without a vote in the election of the humblest board, without a voice in the transaction of the humblest business, without power, influence, or recognized existence — and of this people the strong Protestant body in Ireland complained as being dangerous. And so well were these complaints heard, my friends, that we find edict after edict coming out, declaring that no Papist shall be allowed to inherit land or possess land, or even have it under a lease ; declaring that if a Catholic child wished to become a Protestant, that moment that child became the owner and the master of his father's estate, and his father remained only a pensioner or tenant for life upon the bounty of his own apostate son ; declaring that if a child, however young, even an infant, became a Protestant, that moment that child was to be removed from the guardianship and custody of the father, and was to be handed over to some Protestant relation. Every enactment that the misguided ingenuity of the tyrannical mind of man could suggest was put in force. "One might be inclined," says Mr. Mitchell, "to suppose that Popery had already been sufficiently discouraged, seeing that the clergy had been banished, the Catholics were excluded by law from all honorable and lucrative employments, carefully disarmed and plundered of almost every acre of their ancient inheritance. But enough was not already done to make the Protestant interest feel secure. Consequently laws were sanctioned by Her Majesty Queen Anne that no Catholic could go near a walled town, especially Limerick or Galway. In order that they might be sure not to go near a walled town, they were to remain several miles away, as if they were lepers whose presence would contaminate their select and pampered Protestant fellow-citizens."

FIFTH LECTURE.

LADIES AND GENTLEMEN, — On this day a paragraph in a
a newspaper, the "New York Tribune," was brought under my
notice, and the reading of it caused me much pain and anguish
of mind. It recorded an act of discourtesy to my learned
antagonist, Mr. Froude, supposed to have been offered by Irishmen
in Boston. In the name of the Irishmen in America I tender to the
learned gentlemen my best apologies. I beg to assure him for my
Irish fellow-countrymen in this country that we are only too happy
to offer to him the courtesy and hospitality which Ireland has never
refused, even to her enemies. Mr. Froude does not come amongst
us as an enemy of Ireland, but he professes that he loves the Irish
people, and I believe him. When I read in the report of his last
lecture, which I am about to answer to-night, that he would yield to
no man in his love for the Irish people, I was reminded of what
O'Connell said to Lord Derby on a similar occasion. When the
noble lord stated in the House of Lords that he would yield to no
man in his great love for Ireland, the "Tribune" arose and said:
"Any man that loves Ireland cannot be my enemy; let our hearts
shake hands." I am sure, therefore, that I speak the sentiments of
every true Irishman in America when I assure this learned English
gentleman that as long as he is in this country he will receive from
the hands of the Irish citizens of America nothing but the same courtesy, the same polite hospitality and attention which he boasts he has
received from the Irish people in their native land. We Irishmen
in America know well that it is not by discourtesy, or anything approaching to rudeness or violence, that we expect to make our appeal to this great nation. If ever the reign of intellect and of mind
was practically established in this world, it is in glorious America.

Every man who seeks the truth, every man who preaches the truth, whether it be a religious or a historical truth, will find an audience in America; and I hope that he never will find an Irishman to stand up and offer him discourtesy or violence because he speaks what he imagines to be the truth.

So much being said in reference to the paragraph to which I have alluded, I come to the last of Mr. Froude's lectures and to the last of my own. First, the learned gentleman, in his fourth lecture, told the people of America his views of the rebellion of 1782 and the subsequent Irish rebellion of '98. According to Mr. Froude, the Irish made a great mistake in 1782 by asserting the independence of the Irish Parliament. "They abandoned," says this learned gentleman, "the paths of political reform, and they clamored for political agitation." Now, political agitation is one thing and political reform is another. Political reform, my friends, means the correction of great abuses, the repealing of bad laws, and the passing of good measures for the welfare and well-being of a people. According to this learned gentlemen, the English were taught by their bitter American experience that coercion would not answer with the people, and that it was impossible to thrust unjust laws upon a people or nation. According to Mr. Froude, England was only too willing, too happy, in the year 1780 to repeal all the bad laws that had been passed in the blindness and bigotry of bygone ages, and to grant to Ireland real redress of all her grievances. "But the Irish people," says Mr. Froude, "instead of demanding from England a redress for their grievances, insisted upon their national and parliamentary independence. And they were fools in this," he says, "for that very independence led to internal contention, from contention to conspiracy, from conspiracy to rebellion, and from rebellion to tyranny." Now, I am as great an enemy of political agitation as Mr. Froude or any other man. I hold, and I hold it by experience, that political agitation distracts men's minds from more serious and more necessary avocations of life; that political agitation distracts men's minds away from their business and from the safer pursuits of industry, while it creates animosity and bad blood between citizens; that it affords an easy and profitable employment to worthless demagogues, and that it brings very often to the surface the vilest and meanest element of society. All this I grant. But at the same time

JOHN PHILPOT CURRAN.

SPEECHES.

BY

JOHN PHILPOT CURRAN.

[313]

On Attachments.

February 24, 1785.

Renewed efforts were made in 1784 for Reform. In consequence of a requisition, Henry Reilly, Esq., Sheriff of the county of Dublin, summoned his bailiwick to the court-house of Kilmainham, for the 15th of October, 1784, to elect members to a national congress. For this Mr. Reilly was attached by the King's Bench, on a crown motion, and, on the 24th of February, 1785, the Right Hon. William Brownlow moved a vote of censure on the judges of that court for the attachment.

HOPE I may say a few words on this great subject, without disturbing the sleep of any right honorable member [the Attortorney-General * had fallen asleep on his seat]: and yet perhaps, I ought rather to envy than blame the tranquility of the right honorable gentleman. I do not feel myself so happily tempered, as to be lulled to repose by the storms that shake the land. If they invite rest to any, that rest ought not to be lavished on the guilty spirit. I never more strongly felt the necessity of a perfect union with Britain, of standing or falling with her in fortune and constitution, than on this occasion. She is the parent, the archetype of Irish liberty, which she has preserved inviolate in its grand points, while among us it has been violated and debased. I now call upon the house to consider the trust reposed in them as the Great Inquest of the people.

I respect judges highly; they ought to be respected, and feel their dignity and freedom from reprehension, while they do what judges ought to do; but their stations should not screen them, when they pass the limit of their duty. Whether they did or not,

* John Fitzgibbon. He was made Solicitor-General on the 9th of November, 1783, and on the 20th of December, 1783, succeeded Yelverton as Attorney-General. This latter office he retained till he was raised to the Chancellorship, on the 12th of August, 1789, thus making way for Arthur Wolfe, afterwards Lord Kilwarden.

is the question. This house is the judge of those judges; and it
would betray the people to tyranny, and abdicate their representation, if it do not act with probity and firmness.

In their proceedings against Reilly, I think they have trans-
gressed the law, and made a precedent, which while it remains, is
subversive of the trial by jury, and, of course, of liberty. I regard
the constitution, I regard the judges, three of that court at least;
and, for their sakes, I shall endeavor to undo what they have done.

The question is whether the court has really punished its own
officer for a real contempt; or whether it has abused that power, for
the illegal end of punishing a supposed offence against the state, by
a summary proceeding, without a trial by jury.

The question is plain, whether as a point of constitution, or as of
law; but I shall first consider it in the former view. When I feel
the constitution rocking over my head, my first anxiety is to
explore the foundation, to see if the great arches that support the
fabric have fallen in; but I find them firm, on the solid and massy
principle of Common Law. The principle of legal liberty is, that
offence, and trial, and punishment, should be fixed; it is sense, it is
Magna Charta — a trial by jury, as to fact, an appeal to judges as
to law.

I admit Attachment an exception to the general rule, as founded
in necessity, for the support of courts, in administering justice, by
a summary control over their officers acting under them; but the
necessity that gave rise to it is also the limit. If it were extended
farther, it would reach to all criminal cases not capital; and in the
room of a jury, crimes would be created by a judge, the party
accused by him, found guilty by him, punished by the utter loss of
his liberty and property for life, by indefinite fine and imprison-
ment without remedy or appeal. If he did not answer he was
guilty; even if he did, the court might think or say it thought, the
answer evasive, and so convict him for imputed prevarication.

The power of Attachment is wisely confined by the British laws,
and practised within that limit. The crown lawyers have not produced a single case where the King's Bench in England have gone
beyond it. They have ranged through the annals of history·
through every reign of folly and of blood; through the proud domi-

PENSIONS.

MARCH 13TH, 1786.

THE endeavour to regain by corruption what was surrendered to force, began in 1782, and increased greatly after the defeat of Orde's Propositions. To restrain this, Mr. Forbes, on the 13th of March, 1786, moved for leave to bring in a bill to limit the amount of pensions. It was read a first time, and he then moved that it "be read a second time to-morrow." Sir Hercules Langrishe moved the adjournment of the question to August (*i. e.* altogether), in a speech full of Hanoverian doctrines, and was supported by (amongst others) Sir Boyle Roche, in an absurd speech, which, as a specimen of his *celebrated* style, we insert :—

"Sir Boyle Roche — I opposed this bill at its first rising in this house, in the shape of a motion. [The house called to Sir Boyle to speak up.] Indeed I think it necessary that I should overcome my bashfulness and I lament that I was not brought up to the learned profession of the law, for that is the best remedy for bashfulness of all sorts.

"The just prerogative of the crown and the rights of parliament are the main pillars that support the ponderous pile of our constitution. I never will consent to meddle with either, lest I should bring the whole building about my ears.

"I would not stop the fountain of royal favor, but let it flow freely, spontaneously and abundantly as Holywell in Wales, that turns so many mills. Indeed some of the best men have drank of this fountain, which gives honor as well as vigor. This is my way of thinking ; at the same time I feel as much integrity and principle as any man that hears me. Principle is the fair ground to act upon, and that any man should doubt the principle of another, because he happens to differ with him in opinion, is so bad an act that I do not choose to give it a name. —*Debates*, Vol. VI., pp. 280, 81.

MR. CURRAN said — I object to adjourning this bill to the first of August, because I perceive in the present disposition of the house, that a proper decision will be made upon it this night. We have set out upon our enquiry in a manner so honorable, and so consistent, that we have reason to expect the happiest success, which I would not wish to see baffled by delay.

We began with giving the full affirmative of this house, that no grievance exists at all ; we considered a simple matter of fact, and adjourned our opinion ; or rather, we gave sentence on the conclusion, after having adjourned the premises. But I do begin to see a great deal of argument in what the learned Baronet has said ; and I beg gentlemen will acquit me of apostacy, if I offer some reasons why the bill should not be admitted to a second reading.

I am surprised that gentlemen have taken up such a foolish opinion, as that our constitution is maintained by its different component parts, mutually checking and controlling each other ; they seem to think, with Hobbes, that a state of nature is a state of warfare ; and that, like Mahomet's coffin, the constitution is suspended between the attraction of different powers. My friends seem to think that the crown should be restrained from doing wrong by a physical necessity ; forgetting that if you take away from man all power to do wrong, you, at the same time, take away from him all merit of doing right ; and, by making it impossible for men to run into slavery, you enslave them most effectually. But if, instead of the three different parts of our constitution drawing forcibly in right lines, in different directions, they were to unite their power, and draw all one way, in one right line, how great would be the effect of their force, how happy the direction of this union ! The present system is not only contrary to mathematical rectitude, but to public harmony ; but if, instead of privilege setting up his back to oppose prerogative, he were to saddle his back, and invite prerogative to ride, how comfortably they might both jog along ! and therefore it delights me to hear the advocates for the royal bounty flowing freely, and spontaneously, and abundantly, as Holywell in Wales. If the crown grant double the amount of the revenue in pensions, they approve of their royal master, for he is the breath of their nostrils.

But we shall find that this complaisance, this gentleness between the crown and its true servants, is not confined at home ; it extends its influence to foreign powers. Our merchants have been insulted in Portugal, our commerce interdicted ; what did the British lion do ? Did he whet his tusks? did he bristle up, and shake his mane ? did he roar? No ; no such thing ; the gentle creature wagged his tail for six years at the court of Lisbon ; and now we hear from the Delphic Oracle on the treasury bench, that he is wagging his tail in

London to Chevalier Pinto, who, he hopes soon to be able to tell us, will allow his lady to entertain him as a lap-dog; and when she does, no doubt the British factory will furnish some of their softest woollens, to make a cushion for him to lie upon. But though the gentle beast has continued so long fawning and couching, I believe his vengeance will be great as it is slow; and that posterity, whose ancestors are yet unborn, will be surprised at the vengeance he will take!

This polyglot of wealth, this museum of curiosities, the pension list, embraces every link in the human chain, every description of men, women, and children, from the exalted excellence of a Hawke or a Rodney, to the debased situation of the lady who humbleth herself that she may be exalted. But the lessons it inculcates form its greatest perfection; it teacheth, that slowth and vice may eat that bread which virtue and honesty may starve for after they have earned it. It teaches the idle and dissolute to look up for that support which they are too proud to stoop and earn. It directs the minds of men to an entire reliance on the ruling power of the state, who feed the ravens of the royal aviary, that cry continually for food. It teaches them to imitate those saints on the pension list that are like the lilies of the field, they toil not, neither do they spin, and yet are arrayed like Solomon in his glory. In fine, it teaches a lesson, which, indeed, they might have learned from Epictetus, that it is sometimes good not to be over virtuous; it shows, that in proportion as our distresses increase, the munificence of the crown increases also; in proportion as our clothes are rent, the royal mantle is extended over us.

Notwithstanding that the pension list, like charity, covers a multitude of sins, give me leave to consider it as coming home to the members of this house — give me leave to say, that the crown, in extending its charity, its liberality, its profusion, is laying a foundation for the independence of parliament; for hereafter, instead of orators or patriots accounting for their conduct to such mean and unworthy persons as freeholders, they will learn to despise them, and look to the first man in the state; and they will, by so doing, have this security for their independence, that while any man in the kingdom has a shilling, they will not want one.

Suppose at any future period of time the boroughs of Ireland

should decline from their present flourishing and prosperous state —
suppose they should fall into the hands of men who would wish to
drive a profitable commerce, by having members of parliament to
hire or let; in such a case a secretary would find great difficulty, if
the proprietors of members should enter into a combination to form
a monopoly: to prevent which, in time, the wisest way is to purchase up the raw material, young members of parliament, just rough
from the grass; and when they are a little bitted, and he has got a
pretty stud, perhaps of seventy, he may laugh at the slave merchant;
some of them he may teach to sound through the nose, like a barrel
organ; some, in the course of a few months, might be taught to cry,
"Hear! hear!" some "Chair! chair!" upon occasion — though
those latter might create a little confusion, if they were to forget
whether they were calling inside or outside of those doors.   Again
he might have some so trained that he need only pull a string, and
up gets a repeating member: and if they were so dull that they
could neither speak nor make orations (for they are different things),
he might have them taught to dance, *pedibus ire in sententia*.   This
improvement might be extended: he might have them dressed in
coats and shirts all of one color; and, of a Sunday, he might march
them to church two by two, to the great edification of the people,
and the honor of the Christian religion; afterwards, like ancient
Spartans, or the fraternity of Kilmainham, they might dine all together in a large hall.   Good heaven! what a sight to see them feeding
in public, upon public viands, and talking of public subjects, for the
benefit of the public!   It is a pity they are not immortal; but I hope
they will flourish as a corporation, and that pensioners will beget
pensioners, to the end of the chapter.—*Debates*, Vol. VI., pp. 281-4.

The adjournment was, however, carried. We shall presently find that the bill
was renewed, and supported by Curran, in the next year.

STAMP OFFICERS' SALARIES.

FEBRUARY 4TH, 1790.*

On this day Curran spoke and proposed as follows:—

I RISE with that deep concern and melancholy hesitation, which a man must feel who does not know whether he is addressing an independent parliament, the representatives of the people of Ireland, or whether he is addressing the representatives of corruption. I rise to make the experiment; and I approach the question with all the awful feelings of a man who finds a dear friend prostrate and wounded on the ground, and who dreads lest the means he should use to recover him may only serve to show that he is dead and gone forever. I rise to make an experiment upon the representatives of the people — whether they have abdicated their trust, and have become the paltry representatives of castle influence; it is to make an experiment on the feelings and probity of gentlemen, as was done on a great personage, when it was said "Thou art the man." It is not a question respecting a paltry viceroy; no, it is a question between the body of the country and the administration; it is a charge against the government, for opening the batteries of corruption against the liberties of the people. The grand inquest of the nation are called on to decide this charge; they are called on to declare whether they would appear as the prosecutors or the accomplices of corruption; for though the question relative to the division of the Boards of Stamps and Accounts is in itself of little importance, yet it will develop a system of corruption tending

* It is right to mention here that on the 5th of January, 1790, John Fane, Earl of Westmoreland, succeeded the *Marquis of Buckingham* as Viceroy, and Mr. R. Hobart (afterwards *Earl of Buckinghamshire*), became Secretary to the Lord Lieutenant.

to the utter destruction of Irish liberty, and to the separation of the connexion with England.

I bring forward an act of the meanest administration that ever disgraced this country. I bring it forward as one of the threads by which, united with others of similar texture, vermin of the meanest kind have been able to tie down a body of strength and importance. Let me not be supposed to rest here; when the murderer left the mark of his bloody hand upon the wall, it was not the trace of one finger, but the whole impression which convicted him. *

The Board of Accounts was instituted in Lord Townshend's administration;† it came forward in a manner rather inauspicious; it was questioned in parliament, and decided for by the majority of the five members who had received places under it. Born in corruption, it could only succeed by venality. It continued a useless board until the granting of the stamp duties, in Lord Harcourt's time;‡ the management of the stamps was then committed to it, and a solemn compact was made that the taxes should not be jobbed, but that both departments should be executed by one board. So it continued till it was thought necessary to increase the salaries of the commissioners, in the Marquis of Buckingham's famous admintration.§

Then nothing was held secret; the increase of the Revenue Board, the increase of the Ordnance, thirteen thousand pounds a year added to the infamous Pension List — these were not sufficient, but a compact which should have been held sacred was violated, in order to make places for members of parliament. How indecent! two county members prying into stamps! What could have provoked this insult? I will tell you. You remember when the sceptre was trembling in the hand of an almost expiring monarch; when a factious and desperate English minister attempted to grasp it, you stood up against the profanation of the English and the insult offered to the Irish crown; and had you not done it, the union of the empire would have been dissolved. You remember this; remember, then,

* Alluding to a notable conviction by circumstantial evidence.
† From 1767 to 1772.
‡ Lord Harcourt succeeded Lord Townshend.
§ The Marquis of Buckingham was Lord Lieutenant from the 15th of September, 1782, to the 3d of June, 1783, as Earl Temple. and from the 16th of December, 1787, to the 6th of January, 1790, as Marquis of Buckingham.

GOVERNMENT CORRUPTION.

FEBRUARY 12TH, 1791.

On this day Curran made another attempt to probe the impurities of government.

MR. CURRAN observing the house thin, and the gallery crowded, began by lamenting that curiosity seemed to act more powerfully on the public than a sense of duty on the members of the house. After saying a few words on his motives in making the intended motion, he stated its importance as going to induce enquiry into a crime which must, if not punished and prevented, ultimately effect the destruction of the society in which it was suffered; it was raising men to the peerage for money, which was disposed of to purchase the liberties of the people.

A man who stands forth an accuser in a case like this ought to be received by the house as its best friend, or, if his accusation should prove unfounded and malicious, then the heaviest indignation of the house should fall on him. When a motion of similar import was proposed on a former day, I could not suppose that it would have met with opposition; but finding it has been opposed, I think the house must have objected to its form, and that they were unwilling to enter into an enquiry wherein the honor and privileges of the Lords, as well as those of this house, are concerned, without their lordships' concurrence.

I am not inclined, after what has passed so recently on this subject, to expatiate on the enormity of the act, nor on the wretched situation of those miserable men who are, by it, introduced into this house, like beasts of burden, to drudge for their employers — the humble instruments and pliant tools of power. Still less am I inclined to depict the situation of those who are introduced into the other, clothed in the robes of justice, to frame laws, and dispose of the property of the kingdom, under the direction of that corruption by which they have been raised. It would be more useful to consider what should be done at such a crisis, and what is the duty of the house : and this duty is not difficult to be ascertained — it is not to be cited from volumes of law; we are the grand inquest of the nation — it is, therefore, our duty to enquire into the alleged offence. Every man capable of sitting on a Grand Jury is adequate to the enquiry ; the oath of the Grand Juror suggests their duty — *not to suppress from malice, nor find from favor.*

I have heard it affirmed that common fame is not sufficient ground to institute this enquiry ; but, on the principle of the constitution, I do assert that common fame is a full and sufficient ground of enquiry ; and I appeal to the house — to the kingdom — whether any report can be more prevalent, or more credited, than that such corrupt contract as I have mentioned, was entered into by administration.

But I rest not on common fame — I have PROOF, and I stake my character on producing such evidence to a committee as shall fully and incontrovertibly establish the fact, that a contract has been entered into by the present ministers to raise to the peerage certain persons, on condition of their purchasing a certain number of seats in this house. This evidence, however, I will not produce, till a committee shall be appointed ; for no man can suppose that a man who is rich enough to purchase a peerage is not rich enough to corrupt the witnesses, if I should produce them at the bar, before an inquiry is instituted.

I call on any lawyer to say, whether a man professing himself ready to prosecute, and staking himself to convict, would not, in any court, be admitted to go into trial ? I call on lawyers to answer this question, for on this it depends, not whether the culprits shall be tried, but whether the Commons of Ireland shall be acquitted. I call on you to be cautious in your decision of this question, for you are in the hearing of a great number of the people of Ireland.

The Speaker called to order, and informed him it was unparliamentary to allude to strangers — that there was a standing order, which excluded strangers, and if any allusions are made by a member, he must enforce the order. Sir H. Cavendish also spoke to order, and censured Mr. Curran's language as highly disorderly.

CATHOLIC EMANCIPATION.

—

FEBRUARY 18TH, 1792.

CURRAN was the unchanging friend of religious liberty. The Catholics had vainly prayed for a relaxation of the Penal Code, till the destruction of the British armies n America — then they succeeded. Again they prayed for further relaxation; their prayer was supported by Grattan and Curran and failed, till, in 1792-3, when Wolfe . one had worked up a Catholic organization, and the French armies began to conquer, when they gained fresh privileges.

The proceedings on the 18th of February, on the Roman Catholic Relief Bill are most remarkable. They began by the presentation of a petition from the Protestants of the County Antrim for the bill. A conversation on their admission to Trinity College then occurred, which is so important as to deserve quotation : —

Mr. Grattan gave notice, that in addition to the privileges now about to be granted to the Roman Catholics, the power of becoming Professors of Botany, Anatomy, and Chemistry, should be given.*

Hon. Mr. Knox said he also intended to propose that they should be permitted to take the academic degrees in the University of Dublin.

Hon. Denis Browne rose to say, he would second both these intentions.

The Attorney-General said, under the present laws of the University, Roman Catholics could not be admitted to take degrees without taking the oaths usually taken by Protestants. As the University is a corporation deriving by charter under the crown, and governed by the laws prescribed by its founder, it would not be very decorous for parliament to break through those laws; but the king might, if such was his pleasure, direct the College to dispense with these oaths; and in his opinion it would be wise to do so.

Mr. Knox said it was not his intention to infringe upon any prerogative of the crown, but he could not see how this proposal was an infringement, as the bill must in its ultimate stage, pass under the inspection of the crown, and receive the royal assent. Nevertheless, if any gentleman of the University would rise and say the wish of the University was to have these impediments removed, he would then not think it necessary to make the motion.

Sir Hercules Langrishe — The bill is intended to remove certain disabilities which the Catholics (by law) labor under. Now there is no law as to this point: When it became necessary for me, in framing the bill, to search through the laws relative to education, I found there was no law to prohibit Roman Catholics from taking degrees, but the rules of the University itself; these rules can be changed whenever the crown will think proper, but it would be very unbecoming for the parliament to interfere. As to the principle there can be no difference of opinion; we differ only as to the mode of carrying it into effect.

Doctor Browne (of the College) — I am unable to say what the sentiments of the heads of the College are upon this subject, as they have not informed me; but the reason the right honorable gentleman has stated is certainly the true reason why Roman Catholics are not admitted to degrees. If it shall be deemed expedient to admit them, the college must be much enlarged, and a greater number of governors must be appointed. My own sentiment is, that such a measure would tend much to remove prejudices, and to make them coalesce with Protestants. This is my own sentiment, and the sentiment of several persons of the University; but I cannot say whether it be the sentiment of the majority. If the house shall think the measure expedient, they may address his Majesty to remove the oath which bars them from taking degrees.

After the presentation of a petition by Mr. Egan, for the restoration of the elective franchise, the discussion on the bill proceeded. The speeches of Michael Smith, Hutchinson, Grattan, and Curran, gave the bill most powerful support. One of the boldest and finest speeches was that of the Hon. George Knox — a man too little remembered

MR. CURRAN said — I would have yielded to the lateness of the hour, my own indisposition, and the fatigue of the house, and have let the motion pass without a word from me on the subject, if I had not heard some principles advanced which could not pass without animadversion, I know that a trivial subject of the day would naturally engage you more deeply than any more distant object, of however greater importance, but I beg you will recollect, that the petty interest of party must expire with yourselves, and that your heirs must be not statesmen, nor placemen, nor pensioners, but the future people of the country at large. I know of no so awful call upon the justice and wisdom of an assembly, as the reflection that they are deliberating on the interests of posterity. On this subject, I cannot but lament, that the conduct of the administration is so unhappily calculated to disturb and divide the public mind, to prevent the nation from receiving so great a question with the coolness it requires.

At Cork, the present viceroy was pleased to reject a most moderate and modest petition from the Catholics of that city. The next step was to create a division among the Catholics themselves; the next was to hold them up as a body formidable to the English government, and to their Protestant fellow-subjects; for how else could any man account for the scandalous publication which was hawked about this city, in which his Majesty was made to give his royal fourth. I am sorry to think it is so very easy to conceive, that in case of such an event, the inevitable consequence would be an union with Great Britain. And if any one desires to know what that would be, I will tell him. It would be the emigration of every man of consequence from Ireland; it would be the participation of British taxes, without British trade; it would be the extinction of the Irish name as a people. We should become a wretched colony, perhaps leased out to a company of Jews, as was formerly in contemplation, and governed by a few tax-gatherers and excisemen, unless, possibly, you may add fifteen or twenty couple of Irish members, who may be found every session sleeping in their collars under the manger of the British minister. — *Debates*, Vol. XII., pp. 174 – 178.

Rev. William Jackson.

April 23d, 1795.

Mr. W. H. Curran, in the Memoirs of his Father, thus describes Jackson: —

"Mr. Jackson was a clergyman of the Established Church; he was a native of Ireland, but he had for several years resided out of that country. He spent a part of his life in the family of the noted Duchess of Kingston, and is said to have been the person who conducted that lady's controversy with the celebrated Foote. At the period of the French Revolution he passed over to Paris, where he formed political connections with the constituted authorities. From France he returned to London, in 1794, for the purpose of procuring information as to the practicability of an invasion of England, and was thence to proceed to Ireland on a similar mission. Upon his arrival in London, he renewed an intimacy with a person named Cockayne, who had formerly been his friend and confidential attorney. The extent of his communications, in the first instance, to Cockayne, did not exactly appear. The latter, however, was prevailed upon to write the directions of several of Jackson's letters, containing treasonable matters, to his correspondents abroad; but in a little time, either suspecting or repenting that he had been furnishing evidence of treason against himself, he revealed to the British Minister, Mr. Pitt, all that he knew or conjectured relative to Jackson's objects. By the desire of Mr. Pitt, Cockayne accompanied Jackson to Ireland, to watch and defeat his designs; and as soon as the evidence of his treason was mature, announced himself as a witness for the crown. Mr. Jackson was accordingly arrested, and committed to stand his trial for high treason.

"Mr. Jackson was committed to prison in April, 1794, but his trial was delayed, by successive adjournments, till the same month in the following year. In the interval he wrote and published a refutation of Paine's Age of Reason, probably in the hope that it might be accepted as an atonement. He was convicted, and brought up for judgment on the 30th of April, 1795."

He was indicted for treason in the Summer of 1794; but, sometimes for the crown, and others for the prisoner, the trial was postponed till the 23d of April, 1795.

Court — Right Hon. the Earl of Clonmel, Chief Justice; * Hon. Mr. Justice Downes, Hon. Mr. Justice Chamberlaine.

Counsel for the Crown — Mr. Attorney-General, Mr. Prime-Sergeant, Mr. Solicitor-General, Mr. Frankland and Mr. Trench. Agent — Thomas Kemmis, Esq., Crown Solicitor.

* Hon Mr. Justice Boyd was prevented from attending by indisposition.

what the idea of the statute is; it is that it must be an overt act brought home to the prisoner by each of the two witnesses swearing to it. If De Joncourt's evidence stood single, it could not have brought anything home to Jackson. Cockayne swore the superscription was his writing; he put the letters into the office. De Joncourt said nothing but that he found in the office a letter which he produced, and which Cockayne said was the one he had put into it. This observation appears to collect additional strength from this circumstance. Why did they not produce Tone? It is said they could not. I say they could. It was as easy to pardon him as to pardon Cockayne. But whether he was guilty or not, is no objection. Shall it be said that the argument turns about and affects Jackson as much as it does the prosecutor? I think certainly not. Jackson, I believe it has appeared in the course of the evidence, and is matter of judicial knowledge to the court, has lain in prison for twelve months past, from the moment of his arrest to the moment of his trial. If he is conscious that the charge is false, it is impossible for him to prove that falsehood; he was so circumstanced as that he could not procure the attendance of witnesses; a stranger in the country, he could not tell whether some of the persons named were in existence or not.

I have before apologized to you for trespassing upon your patience, and I have again trespassed — let me not repeat it. I shall only take the liberty of reminding you, that if you have any doubt, in a criminal case doubt should be acquittal; that you are trying a case which if tried in England would preclude the jury from the possibility of finding a verdict of condemnation. It is for you to put it into the power of mankind to say, that that which should pass harmlessly over the head of a man in Great Britain shall blast him here; — whether life is more valuable in that country than in this, or whether a verdict may more easily be obtained here in a case tending to establish pains and penalties of this severe nature.

SUSPENSION OF THE HABEAS CORPUS.

—

OCTOBER 14TH, 1796.

In Committee Ponsonby opposed the bill; so did Curran:—

I CONJURE the house to reflect seriously upon the moment that has been chosen by administration for the bringing in of this bill; I think it a melancholy proof of their want of temper and their want of judgment. My right honorable friend moved an amendment to the address in favor of the Roman Catholics; it was a motion of the very utmost importance; in the debates upon that motion the rights of the Roman Catholics were strongly urged, and as strongly opposed; the disposition of the administration towards them was fully manifested, and the motion was rejected. Of the propriety of that rejection I will not speak —I cannot but lament it; I lament still more the effect that I am sure the making of the present bill the immediate sequel to that rejection, will have on the public mind. [He dwelt strongly upon the indiscretion of ministers, in thus appearing to make the bill be an attack and an insult upon the Catholics; and then replied to the arguments that had been used in support of the measure; he adverted to the bills of the last session.] The Habeas Corpus act is almost the only remaining guardian of our liberties; and the ministry have stabbed the guardian upon its post and in the dark. The house was exhausted by a long debate upon a subject of the last importance to the union and to the peace of the country; those members of parliament who were likely to defend this last privilege of the people were withdrawn, and it was not till the next morning that they were told in their beds, that the Habeas Corpus act was repealed. That sacred palladium of our liberties which was never suffered to sleep, ought not to have been stolen

LAST SPEECH IN THE IRISH COMMONS,

MAY 15TH, 1797.

THE reader has seen the decreasing minorities of the party who gallantly struggled to maintain the parliamentary constitution of Ireland. But they grew daily more powerless. The people looked to the United Irish Executive, to France, to arms, to revolution. The government persisted in refusing Reform and Emancipation, continued the suspension of the constitution, and incessantly augmented the despotism of their laws, the profligacy of their administration, and the violence of their soldiery — they trusted to intimidation. Under these circumstances, the opposition determined to abandon the contest. They did unwisely. They might have embarrassed ministers seriously in the following year, and they did not so, nor did they join the military organization of the patriots.

The pre-determined secession took place on the 15th May, 1797. As the proceedings are of peculiar interest, I copy them from the *Debates:* —

The expectation of the very important business which was announced for this evening, the Reform in the Representation, had filled the galleries at three o'clock. The speaker took the chair at four, and proceeded to business. Two debates followed — the one on the Lords' address, the other on the Reform. The house continued to sit until past five next morning.

Lord Castlereagh pre-occupied the attention of the house by moving, that the address of the Lords on the subject of the treasonable papers, be now taken into consideration. The address contained strong expressions of the loyalty and affection of the house — alluded in very strong terms to the enormity and extent of this traitorous conspiracy — thanked his Majesty for the measures which had been already taken for restoring the due observation of the laws, and recommended to his adoption the most severe measures for the complete suppression of these dangerous disorders. His lordship animadverted on the danger of the conspiracy which had given occasion to this address — stated its object to be the overthrow of our most excellent constitution, and the separation of this country from Great Britain — that the evidence in proof of these assertions had been so full that even the most sceptic could not doubt, and so plain that no man could question the inferences which had been made by their lordships. His lordship then entered into a long and minute history of the society of United Irishman, repeating nearly what had been said on that subject in the report of the Secret Committee. He deprecated, in any debate which might arise on this question, the admixture of any foreign matter with this particular subject, which was simply an inquiry into the most extraordinary mass of treason which had ever appeared in the country; to introduce any other matter into the debate would be construed by the ignorance of the country as a proof that treason and traitors had abettors even within those walls. A speech of much vehemence against the United Irishmen &c., was concluded by a motion — " that the Commons should agree with their Lordships in this address."

Mr. Grattan declared that he did not on this subject wish to bring on a debate, as he would reserve the opinion which he meant to give at large on the state of the country, for the debate on the question of Reform. He could not help, however, declaring, that to that part of the address which expressed approbation of the measures of government, he was bound in consistency not to give any approbation, neither could he do so of that part which prayed for a continuance of coercion, because he believed in his conscience that such measures could be productive of no good.

Mr. Smith, after a short preface, moved an amendment, which alone could reconcile him to the address. His amendment was in substance a request that his Majesty would use conciliatory measures to remove every pretext of discontent from the well-disposed, as well as measures of coercion for the prevention and punishment of conspiracy and treason—urging the necessity of correcting abuses, as well as adopting strong laws to repress disaffection, &c.

This amendment introduced much very animated conversation from Mr. George Ponsonby, Mr. Fletcher, Mr. Jephson, Mr. Grattan, and Mr. Hoare, who supported the amendment, which was opposed by the Attorney-General, Denis Browne, Mr. Egan, Sir B. Roche, Mr. Alexander, Messrs. J. and M. Beresford, Mr. Ogle, Mr. Toler, and Mr. Annesley.

The most contentious topic in the debate was an expression which fell from Mr. Fletcher in the course of his speech, in which he said, that if coercive measures were to be pursued, the whole country must be coerced, for the *spirit of insurrection had pervaded every part of it.*

Mr. M. Beresford ordered the clerk to take down these words, and the gallery was instantly cleared. When strangers were again admitted, the debate on the address still continued, and in the course of it Mr. J. C. Beresford thought himself called on to defend the Secret Committee against an assertion which had fallen from Mr. Fletcher in the course of his speech. The assertion was in substance that he feared the people would be led to look on the report of the committee as fabricated rather to justify the past measures of Government, than to state facts!

Mr. Fletcher contended that he had a right to animadvert on the report, but disclaimed any design of imputing anything unfair to the members of that committee individually.

In the course of the altercation which followed on this subject, Mr. Toler threatened, and actually did move an abstract resolution, declaring that the imputation conveyed in these words (of Mr. Fletcher) was an unfounded calumny on the report. He was at length, however persuaded to withdraw his motion. The house then divided on Mr. Smith's amendment which was lost without a division.

PARLIAMENTARY REFORM.

Mr. W. Ponsonby, in a short prefatory speech, proposed his Resolutions on Parliamentary Reform. Before he moved any of them specifically, he read them all to the house. They are in substance as follow : —

" Resolved, that it is indispensably necessary to a fundamental reform of the representation, that all disabilities on account of religion be forever abolished, and out asperity — I speak without resentment; I speak, perhaps, my delusion, but it is my heart-felt conviction — I speak my apprehension for the immediate state of our liberty, and for the ultimate state of the empire. I see, or I imagine I see, in this system, everything which is dangerous to both. I hope I am mistaken — at least, I hope I exaggerate; possibly I may. If so, I shall acknowledge my error with more satisfaction than is usual in the acknowledgment of error. I cannot, however, banish from my memory the lesson of the American war; and yet at that time the English government was at the head of Europe, and was possessed of resources comparatively unbroken. If that lesson has no effect on ministers, surely I can suggest nothing that will. We have offered you our measure — you will reject it; we deprecate yours — you will persevere. Having no hopes left to persuade or dissuade, and having discharged our duty, we shall trouble you no more, and, AFTER THIS DAY, SHALL NOT ATTEND THE HOUSE OF COMMONS! — *Debates,* Vol. XVII., pp. 569–70.

The question being put on the adjournment it was carried : — for it, 170; against it, 30.

The opposition ceased to attend, and the parliament, after a few sittings, was adjourned, in a speech from the Lord Lieutenant, of unusual length, on the 3rd of July, 1797. Thus, in the twilight of his country, ended Curran's parliamentary career; but in the awful night which followed, he was a beacon.

FOR PETER FINNERTY, PUBLISHER OF "THE PRESS."

[LIBEL.]

DECEMBER 22ND, 1797.

THE Government and the United Irishmen were now face to face, the former armed with a full code of coercion, and a large army and unscrupulous agents to support it; — the latter with a good cause, the organization given by Tone, and the prospect of French aid. Each party tried to strengthen itself by conciliation and intimidation. Among the government instruments were spies (such as Maguane and others, chronicled in Dr. Madden's work), "the battalion of testimony" (Bird, Newell, O'Brien, &c.), free quarters, prosecutions, bribery, patronage and calumny.

One of the best auxiliaries summoned by the United Irishmen was "The Press" newspaper.

The first number of it was published in Dublin, on Thursday, the 28th of September, 1797, and was thence continued on Tuesdays, Thursdays and Saturdays, until Tuesday, the 13th of March, 1798, when the 69th and last number was seized by the government. It was not, like the "Northern Star," a chronicle of French politics. It was a true propagandist organ of Liberal and National opinions, filled with essays, letters and addresses of great ability. Arthur O'Connor mainly originated it, and he, Thomas Emmet, Drennan, Sampson, &c., wrote it.

Government naturally longed to crush such a paper, as it had done the "Northern Star," but raw force was premature for Dublin, so they waited for a libel, and, as they gave plenty of provocation, they waited not long. They found one, which irritated them deeply, while it gave them a good opening, in a letter published on Thursday, the 26th of October, 1797, addressed to the Lord Lieutenant, signed "Marcus." Most of the letter is set out in the indictment; so are the legal facts which were the text of it, but it is right to say something more of them.

William Orr was a Presbyterian farmer, resident at Farranshane, in the County of Antrim — a man of pious, gentle and gallant character; a tall, athletic and hearty fellow, too, and popular exceedingly. He was arrested in 1796, under the Insurrection Act (passed in the February of that year), for having, in April, 1796, administered the United Irish oath to Hugh Wheatly, a private in the Fifeshire Fencibles. He was indicted at Carrickfergus, on the 17th of April, 1797, and tried on Saturday, 16th of September, 1797, before Chief Baron Lord Yelverton. The chief witness was Wheatly, who deposed that Orr acted as chairman or secretary of a Baronial Committee in Antrim, where Wheatly was induced to go, and was there forced to

RICHARD LALOR SHIEL.

SPEECHES.

BY

RICHARD LALOR SHEIL.

[421].

administration. Mr. O'Connell has reason to rejoice at his failure in carrying this proposition; for if he had succeeded, no ground for opposing the return of Mr. Vesey Fitzgerald would have existed.

The promotion of that gentleman to a seat in the cabinet created a vacancy in the representation of the county of Clare; and an opportunity was afforded the Roman Catholic body of proving that the resolution which had been passed against the Duke of Wellington's government was not an idle vaunt, but that it could be carried in a striking instance into effect. It was determined that all the power of the people should be put forth. The Association looked round for a candidate, and without having previously consulted him, selected Major M'Namara. He is a Protestant in religion, a Catho.ic in politics, and a Milesian in descent. He was called upon to stand. Some days elapsed and no answer was returned by him. The public mind was thrown into suspense, and various conjectures went abroad as to the cause of this singular omission. Some alleged that he was gone to an island off the coast of Clare, where the proceedings of the Association had not reached him; while others suggested that he was only waiting until the clergy of the county should declare themselves more unequivocally favorable to him. The latter, it was said, had evinced much apathy, and it was rumored that Dean O'Shaughnessy, who is a distant relative of Mr. Fitzgerald, had intimated a determination not to support any anti-ministerial candidate. The major's silence, and the doubts which were entertained with regard to the allegiance of the priests, created a sort of panic at the Association. A meeting was called, and various opinions were delivered as to the propriety of engaging in a contest, the issue of which was considered exceedingly doubtful, and in which, failure would be attended with such disastrous consequences. Mr. O'Connell himself did not appear exceedingly sanguine: and Mr. Purcell O'Gorman, a native of Clare, and who had a minute knowledge of the feelings of the people, expressed apprehensions. There were, however, two gentlemen (O'Gorman Mahon and Mr. Steele), who strongly insisted that the people might be roused, and that the priests were not as lukewarm as was imagined. Upon the zeal of Dean O'Shaughnessy, however, a good deal of question was thrown. By a singular coincidence, just as his name was uttered, a gentleman entered, who, but for the peculiar locality, might have been readily

REPEAL OF THE UNION.

SPEECH IN THE HOUSE OF COMMONS ON THE 25TH OF APRIL, 1834.

———

THE speech just spoken by the member for the county of Wexford has been received with acclamations, and if it were less able, the acclamation would not, perhaps, have been less enthusiastic, or less loud. Fortunate advocate, whose success depends as much at least on the predilections of the tribunal, as upon the merits of the cause! I have heard my honorable friend when he exhibited fully as much eloquence as upon this occasion, but never saw him received with such cordiality at the outset, or such rapture at the termination of any of his former harangues. With what clearness of exposition, with what irresistible force, for example, did he demand justice for the Irish people after the massacre of Newtownbarry? He presented a picture of that atrocious transaction, compared to which, his accounts of the fatal effects of agitation are weak and inefficient indeed. The incidents which he described, and the picturesque diction in which his narrative was conveyed, ought to have produced a great impression upon his auditory, yet how coldly did all that he then urged fall upon his hearers. You were then frigid and apathetic; you are now, in the highest degree, susceptible and alive to the accomplishments of the member for the county of Wexford. My honorable friend is now a devoted and unqualified antagonist of repeal. Was it always thus? Did he not say — that if justice was not done to Ireland on the tithe question, he should, however reluctantly, become an advocate for repeal?

Mr. Lambert — I do not recollect having ever said so.

Mr. Sheil — At all events, he declared that the denial of justice with respect to the Irish Church, would have the effect of inducing the great mass of the population to embrace repeal. Whether he spoke of himself, or of the country, putting personal considerations out of view, the inference is nearly the same. He expressed a desire when he began, that the member for Dublin should be in attendance while he reviewed his conduct. The wish was gratified. The member for Dublin entered the house (which the honorable member for the county of Wexford never would have entered but for the member for Dublin), and I own that I did not think that he had any cause to wince under the chastisement applied to him by the hon. member. But how, after all, are the real merits of this great question affected by these resentful references to incidents which have taken place outside this house? Is this the proper field for encounter between two honorable gentlemen? The member for the county of Wexford may have been wronged ;—language may have been applied to him by the member for Dublin with regard to his conduct on the Coercion Bill, which deserves condemnation. I regret it; but let him bear in mind that the obligation conferred upon him by the member for Dublin, ought to outweigh every injury. Though he has been smitten in the face, let him remember that the hand that struck him, struck his fetters off. The honorable member for Wexford has adverted to the remuneration, which the people of Ireland have bestowed upon the member for Dublin. He should have considered the extent of the service, before he derided the reward. For thirty years the member for Dublin has toiled in the cause of Ireland; he has been mainly instrumental in achieving the liberty of his fellow-countrymen; he has relinquished great emoluments by abstracting himself from his profession, and by making a dedication of his faculties to the interests of his country : — Ireland felt that it behove her to prove her gratitude for that freedom, which is above all price.

I turn from these painful topics to the subject presented to our deliberation. Not a word has yet been said upon the amendment. Many may conceive that the original proposition ought to be rejected, and yet will, I hope, pause before they adopt the sentiments contained in the address. The question before the house is, not merely whether a committee should be granted for the purpose of investigating a question on which the Secretary for the Treasury thought it not inexpedient to deliver an harangue, of which the length must be admitted to be unsurpassed, but whether we shall

Orange Lodges.

Speech in the House of Commons, August 11, 1835.

—

IT is remarkable that the gallant colonel (Verner), the Deputy Grand Master of Ireland and Viceroy to the Duke of Cumberland, has not stated that he was ignorant of the existence of Orange lodges in the army. This omission is the more deserving of notice, because he was colonel of the 7th dragoons — because he was examined twice before the committee — and because the several other functionaries of the Orange body have declared their utter ignorance of that which they ought to have known so well. Independently of these considerations, it appears by a report of the proceedings of the English Grand Lodge, that the gallant colonel was present when (the Duke of Cumberland being in the chair) a resolution respecting the establishment of Orange lodges in the army was moved. Is it true that he was present?

Colonel Verner. — I was never asked, in the committee, whether I knew of the existence of Orange lodges in the army. I now declare that I was utterly ignorant of the fact; and I do not remember whether I was or was not present when the resolution, to which the honorable gentleman adverts, was carried in the English Grand Lodge.

Mr. Sheil. — How far the answer fits the question let the house judge. It appears that the gallant colonel did attend the English Grand Lodge, on what occasion he does not distinctly recollect — his memory is misty — but it would be important that he should state how far the impression is correct, that Orange lodges have been established in the army with the sanction of the Duke of Cumberland, and by virtue of resolutions, passed when the Orange Grand Lodge was graced by the presence of his Royal Highness! I turn from the

gallant colonel to the general question. At the commencement of
the session I charged the Conservative government with having
advanced Orangemen to places of high station, and having given to
Orange lodges answers amounting to a recognition of their public
usefulness. This motion was not unattended with a salutary effect;
immediately after the member, for Kilkenny,* to whom the country
is greatly indebted for the disclosures which he has been instrumental
in producing, moved the appointment of the committee. On that
committee the leading functionaries of the Orange body were placed.
And yet it is said that the committee was packed; but let us see who
were the members of it:—the honorable members for Sligo and
for Cavan were upon it; and there were also Mr. Jackson, Mr.
Wilson Patten—I suppose that he is a Conservative—Colonel
Wood, Lord Castlereagh, Mr. Nicholl, Sir James Graham—(I really
do not know with which party to class him)—Colonel Conolly and
Colonel Perceval. I do not think that this selection can be said
to be an unfair one, but it is alleged that the mode in which the
witnesses were examined was unjust. The Grand Master, and the
Grand Treasurer, and the Grand Secretary were examined—(they
are all Grand)—the order of investigation was altogether inverted,
and the Orange party were allowed to open the case themselves, and
for a number of days none but Orange witnesses were examined.
Colonel Verner was twice examined—first on the 7th of April, 1835,
and again on the 9th of April. Then came the Reverend Mortimer
O'Sullivan—certainly a very competent witness to give evidence
with respect to both religions, for with regard to one he could indulge in the "Pleasures of Memory," and to the other, he, doubtless,
looked with the "Pleasures of Hope;" Mr. M. O'Sullivan, the
Grand Chaplain, was produced, and was examined on the 13th of
April, on the 21st and 26th of May, and again on the 27th of May:
so many days expended upon theology and the Reverend Mortimer
O'Sullivan. Then came Mr. Swan, the Deputy Grand Secretary;
next came Mr. Stewart Blacker, the Assistant Grand Treasurer, who
was examined on the 8th, 10th, 12th, and 13th, of June; next Mr. W.
Ward, the solicitor of the Orange body, who was produced to show
that they never in any way interfered with the administration of justice; then again, on the 15th of June came Mr. Mortimer O'Sullivan

* Mr. Finn.

IRISH MUNICIPAL BILL.

SPEECH IN THE HOUSE OF COMMONS, FEBRUARY 22, 1837.

THE right honorable baronet (Sir James Graham) began the speech, in many particulars remarkable, which he has just concluded amidst the applauses of those, whose approbation, at one period of his political life, he would have blushed to incur, by intimating that he was regarded as a "bigot" on this side of the house. Whether he deserves the appellation by which he has informed us that he is designated, his speech to-night affords some means of determining. I will not call him a bigot, I am not disposed to use an expression in any degree offensive to the right honorable baronet, but I will presume to call him a convert, who exhibits all the zeal for which conversion is proverbially conspicuous. Of that zeal we have manifestations in his references to pamphlets about Spain, in his allusions to the mother of Cabrera, in his remarks on the Spanish clergy, and the practice of confession in the Catholic Church. I own that, when he takes in such bad part the strong expressions employed in reference to the Irish Church (expressions employed by Protestants, and not by Roman Catholics), I am surprised that he should not himself abstain from observations offensive to the religious feelings of Roman Catholic members of this house. The right honorable baronet has done me the honor to produce an extract from a speech of mine, delivered nearly two years ago at the Coburg Gardens; and at the same time expressed himself in terms of praise of the humble individual who now addresses you. I can assure the right honorable baronet that I feel at least as much pleasure in listening to him, as he has the goodness to say that he derives from hearing me. He has many of the accomplishments

attributed by Milton to a distinguished speaker in a celebrated council. He is "in act most graceful and humane, his tongue drops
manna." I cannot but feel pride that he should entertain so high an
opinion of me, as to induce him to peruse and collect all that I say
even beyond these walls. He has spent the recess, it appears, in
the diligent selection of such passages as he has read to-night, and
which I little thought, when they were uttered, that the right honorable baronet would think worthy of his comments. However, he
owes me the return of an obligation. The last time I spoke in this
house, I referred to a celebrated speech of his at Cockermouth, in
which he pronounced an eloquent invective against "a recreant
Whig;" and as he found that I was a diligent student of those
models of eloquence which the right honorable baronet used formerly
to supply, in advocating the popular rights, he thought himself
bound, I suppose, to repay me by the citation, which has, I believe,
produced less effect than he had anticipated. The right honorable
baronet also adverted to what he calls "the Lichfield House compact." It is not worth while to go over the same ground, after I
have already proved, by reading in the house the speech which has
been the subject of so much remark — how much I have been mis-
represented; I never said that there was a " compact;" I did say,
and I repeat it, that there was "a compact alliance." Was that the
first occasion on which an alliance was entered into? Was Lichfield
House the only spot ever dedicated to political reconciliations? Has
the right honorable baronet forgotten, or has the noble lord (Stanley)
who sits beside him, succeeded in dismissing from his recollection,
a meeting at Brookes's Club, at which the Irish and English reform-
ers assembled, and, in the emergency which had taken place, agreed
to relinquish their differences and make a united stand against the
common foe? Does the noble lord forget an admirable speech (it
was the best post-prandial oration it was ever my good fortune to
have heard) delivered by a right honorable gentleman who was not
then a noble lord, and was accompanied by a vehemence of gesture
and a force of intonation not a little illustrative of the emotions of
the orator, on his anticipated ejectment from office? That eloquent
individual, whom I now see on the Tory side of the house, got up on
a table, and with vehement and almost appalling gesture, pronounced
an invective against the Duke of Wellington, to which, in the

THE CATHOLICS OF IRELAND.

SPEECH AT PENENDEN HEATH, 24TH OCTOBER, 1828.

———

LET no man believe that I have come here, in order that I might enter the lists of religious controversy and engage with any of you in a scholastic disputation. In the year 1828, the Real Presence does not afford an appropriate subject for debate, and it is not by the shades of a mystery that the rights of a British citizen are to be determined. I do not know whether there are many here by whom I am regarded as an idolater, because I conscientiously adhere to the faith of your forefathers, and profess the doctrine in which I was born and bred; but if I am so accounted by you, you ought not to inflict a civil deprivation upon the accident of the cradle. You ought not to punish me for that for which I am not in reality to blame. If you do, you will make the misfortune of the Catholic the fault of the Protestant, and by inflicting a wrong upon my religion, cast a discredit upon your own. I am not the worse subject of my king, and the worse citizen of my country, because I concur in the belief of the great majority of the Christian world; and I will venture to add, with the frankness and something of the bluntness by which Englishmen are considered to be characterised, that if I am an idolater, I have a right to be one, if I choose; my idolatry is a branch of my prerogative, and is no business of yours. But you have been told by Lord Winchelsea that the Catholic religion is the adversary of freedom. It may occur to you, perhaps, that his lordship affords a proof in his own person, that a passion for Protestantism and a love of liberty are not inseparably associated; but without instituting too minute or embarrassing an inquiry into the services to freedom, which in the course of his political life have been conferred by my Lord Winchelsea, and putting aside all per-

sonal considerations connected with the accuser, let me proceed to
the accusation. Calumniators of Catholicism, have you read the
history of your country? Of the charges against the religion of
Ireland, the annals of England afford the confutation. The body of
your common laws was given by the Catholic Alfred. He gave you
your judges, your magistrates, your high sheriffs — (you, sir, hold
your office, and have called this great assembly, by virtue of his
institutions) — your courts of justice, your elective system, and, the
great bulwark of your liberties, the trial by jury. When Englishmen peruse the chronicles of their glory, their hearts beat high with
exultation, their emotions are profoundly stirred, and their souls are
ardently expanded. Where is the English boy, who reads the story
of his great island, whose pulse does not beat at the name of Runne-
mede, and whose nature is not deeply thrilled at the contemplation
of that great incident, when the mitred Langton, with his uplifted
crosier, confronted the tyrant, whose sceptre shook in his trembling
hand, and extorted what you have so justly called the Great, and
what, I trust in God, you will have cause to designate as your ever-
lasting Charter? It was by a Catholic Pontiff that the foundation-
stone in the temple of liberty was laid ; and it was at the altars of
that religion, which you are accustomed to consider as the handmaid
of oppression, that the architects of the constitution knelt down.
Who conferred upon the people the right of self-taxation, and fixed,
if he did not create, the representation of the people? The Catholic
Edward the First ; while, in the reign of Edward the Third, perfection was given to the representative system, parliaments were
annually called, and the statute against constructive treason was
enacted. It is false, foully, infamously false, that the Catholic religion, the religion of your forefathers, the religion of seven millions
of your fellow-subjects, has been the auxiliary of debasement, and
that to its influences the suppression of British freedom can, in a
single instance, be referred. I am loath to say that which can give
you cause to take offence ; but when the faith of my country is made
the object of imputation, I cannot help, I cannot refrain, from breaking into a retaliatory interrogation, and from asking whether the
overthrow of the old religion of England was not effected by a
tyrant, with a hand of iron and a heart of stone ; whether Henry
did not trample upon freedom, while upon Catholicism he set his

Speech in Reply to Mr. M'Clintock.

——

Mr. M'Clintock, a Protestant gentleman of rank and fortune in the county of Louth, having attended a Roman Catholic Meeting, held in the chapel of Dundalk, and delivered a speech containing strictures on the Catholic religion.

MR. SHEIL rose immediately after Mr. M'Clintock had concluded and said, The speech of Mr. M'Clintock (and a more singular exhibition of gratuitous eloquence I have never heard) calls for a prompt and immediate expression of gratitude. He has had the goodness to advise us (for he has our interests at heart) to depute certain emissaries from the new Order of Liberators to his Holiness at Rome, for the purpose of procuring a repeal of certain obnoxious canons of the Council of Lateran. If Mr. M'Clintock had not assured us that he was serious, and was not actuated by an anxiety to throw ridicule upon the religion and proceedings of those whom he has taken under his spiritual tutelage, I should have been disposed to consider him an insidious fanatic, who, under the hypocritical pretence of giving us a salutary admonition, had come here with no other end than to fling vilification upon our creed, and to throw contumely upon the persons who take the most active part in the conduct of our cause. But knowing him to be a person of high rank and large fortune, and believing him to possess the feelings as well as the station of a gentleman, I am willing to acquit him of any such unworthy purpose, and do not believe that his object in addressing us, was to offer a deliberate and premeditated insult. He did not, I am sure (for it would be inconsistent with the character which I have ascribed to him) enter this meeting for the purpose of venting his bile in our faces, and voiding upon his auditory the foul calumnies against the religion of his countrymen, which furnish the ordinary materials of rhetoric in the Bible Societies, of which he is so renowned a member. He did not come here to talk of the Pope's golden stirrups to a mass of ignorant and unenlightened people, and to turn their belief into ridicule with his lugubrious derision. The topics which he selected were, indeed, singularly chosen, and when he talked of the Order of Liberators, I was disposed to take him for a wag. — But I raised my eyes and looked him in the face, and perceiving a person, whose countenance would furnish Cruikshank with a frontispiece to the Spiritual Quixote, I at once acquitted him of all propensities to humour, and could not bring myself to believe it possible that Mr. M'Clintock had ever intended to be droll. At one moment I confess I was in pain for him, for I was apprehensive that the language in which he expressed himself in regard to our clergy, and the forms and habitudes of Popery, would be apt to excite the indignation of a portion of this immense auditory, but the spirit of courtesy prevailed over the feelings of the people, and so far from having been treated with disrespect, he was listened to with more than ordinary indulgence. He excited less of our anger than of our commiseration. I am upon this account rejoiced that he should have undertaken an exploit of this kind. We have given him evidence, at all events, that however intolerant the theory of our religion may appear to him, we are practically forbearing and indulgent. We allowed him to inveigh against the bridle and saddle of the Pope, without a remonstrance; we permitted him to indulge in his dismal merriment, and his melancholy ridicule, without a murmur; he will therefore have derived a useful lesson from his experiment upon the public patience, and when he shall recount to his confederates of the Bible Society his achievements amongst us, he will have an opportunity of telling them that we are far more tolerant of a difference of opinion than the pious auditory which Mr. M'Clintock is in the habit of addressing. I have occasionally attended meetings of the Bible Society, and observed that whoever ventured to remonstrate against the use of the Apocalypse as a Spelling Book, incurred the indignation of the assembly. I remember to have heard it suggested, that the amatory pictures which are offered to the imagination in the Canticle of Canticles, were not exactly fitted to the private meditation of young ladies, when the countenances of the fair auditors immediately assumed an expression

SPEECH ON THE DUKE OF YORK.

I HAVE waited until the chair had been left, and the meeting of the Association had terminated, in order to introduce a subject which, as it is of a purely political nature, I refrained from mentioning during the discussions of the Association, lest it should give them a character of illegality, and expose me to the imputation of having violated the law. I refer to the recent observations which have been made in the London papers upon the report of a speech of mine at a public dinner. I hope that I shall not be considered guilty of an overweening egotism, in drawing the attention of the individuals who happen to be assembled here to what may appear to relate to myself. But the topics on which I mean to address you are of public as well as of personal interest. The truculent jocularity and the spirit of savage jest which have been ascribed to me, in expatiating on the infirmities of an illustrious person, have been regarded as characteristic of the moral habitudes of the body to which I belong. Thus, my vindication (for I do not rise to make an apology) extends beyond myself. Yet let me be permitted to suggest, that it is most unfair to impute to a whole people the feelings or the sentiments of any single man. The Catholics of Ireland have been repeatedly held responsible for the unauthorised and unsanctioned language of individuals. Every ardent expression, every word that overflows with gall, every phrase uttered in the suddenness of unpremeditated emotion, are converted into charges against seven millions of the Irish people. It is dealing rather hardly with us, to make a loose after-dinner speech, (the mere bubble of the mind,) thrown off in the heedlessness of conviviality, a matter of serious accusation against a whole community. I am not endeavoring to excuse myself upon any such plea as the Bishop of Kilmore might resort to, in extenuating his late oration in

Cavan; on the contrary, I am prepared to show the circumstances which, in my mind, gave warrant to what I said. But I deprecate the notion that the language employed either by myself or by any other individual should be held to represent the opinions of the Irish Catholics. It has been stated that laughter was produced by an ebullition of disastrous merriment. I will suppose that some two or three dozen of individuals in an obscure country town, did not preserve the solemnity with which any allusion to the maladies of an illustrious person ought to have been received, yet it is wholly unjust to hold the Irish Catholics responsible for their lack of sensibility. Having said this much, in order to rescue my fellow-laborers in the cause of emancipation from any responsibility for individual demerit, I shall proceed to state what, in my judgment, affords a justification of the language employed upon the occasion to which I refer. I shall not deny that I entertain a solicitude upon this subject. It is affectation on the part of any man to say that he holds the censure of the press in no account. I cannot but be sensible that I am, from my comparative want of personal importance, more exposed to the injurious consequence of such a simultaneous assault. But I do not complain; whoever intermeddles in public proceedings must be prepared for occasional condemnation. It is one of the necessary results of notoriety, and I submit to it as a portion of my fate. I shall not, therefore, insinuate that there is any mock sentimentality in the amiable indignation with which the writers of the Whig journals have vented their censures upon what they call the barbarous hilarity of an after-dinner harangue. I will not say that it is easy to procure a character for high sentiment by indulging in a paroxysm of editorial anger. Nay, I will give the gentlemen who have put so much sentiment into type credit for sincerity, and without attempting to retaliate, without referring them to their own comments upon the illustrious immoralities of the distinguished person to whom I have alluded, I shall state the grounds of which I conceive that I have been unjustly assailed. It is right that I should at once proceed to mention exactly what took place. The chairman of the meeting in question deviated from the ordinary usage at Roman Catholic dinners, and, in compliance with what, from his inexperience, he considered to be a sort of formula of convivial loyalty, proposed the health of a man who is an object, to use the

HENRY GRATTAN.

SELECT SPEECHES

BY

RIGHT HON. HENRY GRATTAN.

[537]

DECLARATION OF IRISH RIGHTS.

APRIL 19, 1780.

On this day came on the most important subject that had ever been discussed in the Irish Parliament, — the question of independence — the recovery of that legislative power, of which, for centuries, Ireland had been so unjustly deprived.

Her right to make laws for herself, was first affected by the act of the 10th of Henry the Seventh, in a parliament, held at Drogheda, before the then Deputy, Sir Edward Poynings. It was there enacted that no parliament should be holden in Ireland, until the Lord-lieutenant and Privy Council should certify to the King under the great seal of Ireland, the causes, considerations, and acts that were to pass; that the same should be affirmed by the King and council in England, and his license to summon a parliament be obtained under the great seal of England. This was further explained by the 3d and 4th of Philip and Mary, whereby any change or alteration in the form or tenor of such acts to be passed after they were returned from England, was prohibited. Thus, by these laws the English privy council got the power to alter or suppress, and the Irish parliament were deprived of the power to originate, alter, or amend.

By these acts were the legislative rights of Ireland invaded: her judicial rights, however, remained untouched, till, in 1688, a petition and appeal was lodged with the House of Lords of England, from the English society of the new plantation of Ulster, complaining of the Irish House of Lords, who had decided in a case between them and the Bishop of Derry. Upon this the English House of Lords passed an order declaring, that this appeal was *coram non judice.* To this order fourteen reasons and answers were written by the celebrated Molyneux, and the appeal gave rise to his famous work, entitled "The Case of Ireland," which excited the hostility of the English House of Commons, and was burned by the hands of the common hangman! The Irish House of Lords then asserted their rights, passed resolutions, and protested against the English proceedings; thus matters remained until 1703, when came on the case of the Earl and Countess of Meath against the Lord Ward, who were dispossessed of their lands by a pretended order of the House of Lords in England, on which the Irish House of Peers adopted the former resolutions, asserting their rights, and restored possession to the Earl and Countess. In 1703, the appeal of Maurice Annesley was entertained in England, and the decree of the Irish House of Lords was reversed; and the English House of Lords had recourse to the authority of the Barons of the Exchequer in Ireland to enforce their order; the Sheriff refused obedience; the Irish House of Lords protected the Sheriff, and agreed to a representation to the King on the subject. This produced the arbitrary act of the 6th of George the First, which declared, that Ireland was a subordinate and dependent kingdom; that the King, Lords, and Commons of England had power to make Laws to bind Ireland; that the House of Lords of Ireland had no jurisdiction, and that all proceedings before that Court were void. Under this act, and to such injustice, the Irish nation were compelled to submit, until the spirit of the present day arose, and that commanding power which the armed volunteers gave to the country, encouraged the people to rise unanimously against this usurped and tyrannical authority. The efforts of the nation to obtain a free trade, the compliance of the British Parliament with that claim; the British act passed in consequence thereof, which allowed the trade between Ireland and the British colonies and plantations in America and the West Indies, and the British settlements on the coast of Africa, had raised the hopes of the Irish people. The resolutions and proceedings of the volunteers, and the answers to their addresses by the patriotic members, had still further roused the people to a sense of their rights and their condition, and the hour was approaching which was to witness the restoration of their liberty. Mr. Grattan had, on a preceding day, given notice that he would bring forward a measure regarding the rights of Ireland; and in pursuance of that notice he rose and spoke as follows:

IR, I have entreated an attendance on this day, that you might, in the most public manner, deny the claim of the British Parliament to make law for Ireland, and with one voice lift up your hands against it.

If I had lived when the 9th of William took away the woollen manufacture, or when the 6th of George the First declared this country to be dependent, and subject to laws to be enacted by the Parliament of England, I should have made a covenant with my own conscience to seize the first moment of rescuing my country from the ignominy of such acts of power; or, if I had a son, I should have administered to him an oath that he would consider himself a person separate and set apart for the discharge of so important a duty; upon the same principle I am now come to move a declaration of right, the first moment occurring, since my time, in which such a declaration could be made with any chance of success, and without aggravation of oppression.

Sir, it must appear to every person, that, notwithstanding the import of sugar and export of woollens, the people of this country are not satisfied — something remains; the greater work is behind; the public heart is not well at ease. To promulgate our satisfaction; to stop the throats of millions with the votes of Parliament; to preach homilies to the volunteers; to utter invectives against the people, under pretence of affectionate advice, is an attempt, weak, suspicious and inflammatory.

erty. I do call upon you, by the laws of the land and their violation, by the instruction of eighteen counties, by the arms, inspiration, and providence of the present moment, tell us the rule by which we shall go, — assert the law of Ireland, — declare the liberty of the land.

I will not be answered by a public lie, in the shape of an amendment; neither, speaking for the subject's freedom, am I to hear of faction. I wish for nothing but to breathe, in this our island, in common with my fellow-subjects, the air of liberty. I have no ambition, unless it be the ambition to break your chain, and contemplate your glory. I never will be satisfied so long as the meanest cottager in Ireland has a link of the British chain clanking to his rags; he may be naked, he shall not be in iron; and I do see the time is at hand, the spirit is gone forth, the declaration is planted; and though great men shall apostatize, yet the cause will live; and though the public speaker should die, yet the immortal fire shall outlast the organ which conveyed it, and the breath of liberty, like the word of the holy man, will not die with the prophet, but survive him.

PHILIPPIC AGAINST FLOOD.

OCTOBER 28, 1783.

IT was said " that the pen would fall from the hand, and the fœtus of the mind would die unborn," * if men had not a privilege to maintain a right in the Parliament of England to make law for Ireland. The affectation of zeal, and a burst of forced and metaphorical conceits, aided by the acts of the press, gave an alarm which, I hope, was momentary, and which only exposed the artifice of those who were wicked, and the haste of those who were deceived.

But it is not the slander of an evil tongue that can defame me. I maintain my reputation in public and in private life. No man, who has not a bad character, can ever say that I deceived ; no country can call me a cheat. But I will suppose such a public character. I will suppose such a man to have existence ; I will begin with his character in his political cradle, and I will follow him to the last state of political dissolution.

I will suppose him, in the first stage of his life, to have been intemperate ; in the second, to have been corrupt ; and in the last, seditious ; that, after an envenomed attack on the persons and measures of a succession of viceroys, and after much declamation against their illegalities and their profusion, he took office, and became a supporter of Government, when the profusion of ministers had greatly increased, and their crimes multiplied beyond example : when your money bills were altered without reserve by the council ; when an embargo was laid on your export trade, and a war declared against the liberties of America. At such a critical moment I will suppose this gentleman to be corrupted by a great sinecure office to muzzle

* Mr. Flood's expression.

COMMERCIAL PROPOSITIONS.

—

AUGUST 12, 1785.

HOWEVER, lest certain glosses should seem to go unanswered, I shall, for the sake of argument, waive past settlements, and combat the reasoning of the English resolutions, the address, His Majesty's answer and the reasoning of this day. It is here said, that the laws respecting commerce and navigation should be similar, and inferred that Ireland should subscribe the laws of England on those subjects; that is the same law, the same legislature. But this argument goes a great deal too far: it goes to the army, for the mutiny bill should be the same; it was endeavored to be extended to the collection of your revenue, and is in train to be extended to your taxes; it goes to the extinction of the most invaluable part of your parliamentary capacity; it is a union, an incipient and creeping union; a virtual union, establishing one will in the general concerns of commerce and navigation, and reposing that will in the Parliament of Great Britain; a union where our Parliament preserves its existence after it has lost its authority, and our people are to pay for a parliamentary establishment, without any proportion of parliamentary representation. In opposing the right honorable gentleman's bill, I consider myself as opposing a union *in limine*, and that argument for union which makes similarity of law and community of interest (reason strong for the freedom of Ireland!) a pretence for a condition which would be dissimilarity of law, because extinction of constitution, and therefore hostility, not community of interest. I ask on what experience is this argument founded? Have you, ever since your redemption, refused to preserve a similarity of law in trade and navigation? Have you not followed Great Britain in all her changes of the act of navigation during the whole of that unpalatable business, the American war? Have you not excluded the cheap produce of other plantations, in order that Irish poverty might give a monopoly to the dear produce of the British colonies? Have you not made a better use of your liberty than Great Britain did of her power? But I have an objection to this argument, stronger even than its want of foundation in reason and experiment; I hold it to be nothing less than an intolerance of the parliamentary constitution of Ireland, a declaration that the full and free external legislation of the Irish Parliament is incompatible with the British empire. I do acknowledge that by your external power, you might discompose the harmony of the empire, and I add that by your power over the purse, you might dissolve the state: but to the latter you owe your existence in the constitution, and to the former, your authority and station in the empire: this argument, therefore, rests the connection upon a new and a false principle, goes directly against the root of Parliament, and is not a difficulty to be accommodated, but an error to be eradicated; and if any body of men can still think that the Irish constitution is incompatible with the British empire — doctrine which I abjure as sedition against the connection; but if any body of men are justified in thinking that the Irish constitution is incompatible with the British empire, perish the empire! live the constitution! Reduced by this false dilemma to take a part, my second wish is the British empire, my first wish and bounden duty is the liberty of Ireland.

But we are told this imperial power is not only necessary for England, but safe for Ireland. What is the present question? what but the abuse of this very power of regulating the trade of Ireland by the British Parliament, excluding you and including herself by virtue of the same words of the same act of navigation? And what was the promovent cause of this arrangement? what but the power you are going to surrender — the distinct and independent external authority of the Irish Parliament, competent to question that misconstruction? What is the remedy now proposed? — the evil. Go back to the Parliament of England. I ask again, what were the difficulties in the way of your eleven propositions? what but the jealousy of the British manufacturers on the subject of trade? And will you make them your parliament, and that too forever, and that too on the subject of their jealousy, and in the moment they displayed it! I will he makes you another offer, inconsistent with the former, which offer the English do not support, and the Irish deprecate.

We can go on; we have a growing prosperity, and as yet an exemption from intolerable taxes; we can from time to time regulate our own commerce, cherish our manufactures, keep down our taxes, and bring on our people, and brood over the growing prosperity of young Ireland. In the mean time we will guard our free trade and free constitution, as our only real resources; they were the struggles of great virtue, the result of much perseverance, and our broad base of public action! We should recollect that this House may now, with peculiar propriety, interpose, because you did, with great zeal and success, on this very subject of trade, bring on the people; and you did, with great prudence and moderation, on another occasion, check a certain description of the people, and you are now called upon by consistency to defend the people. Thus mediating between extremes, you will preserve this island long, and preserve her with a certain degree of renown. Thus faithful to the constitution of the country, you will command and insure her tranquility; for our best authority with the people is protection afforded against the ministers of the Crown. It is not public clamour, but public injury that should alarm you; your high ground of expostulation with your fellow-subjects has been your services; the free trade you have given the merchant, and the free constitution you have given the island! Make your third great effort — preserve them, and with them preserve unaltered your own calm sense of public right, the dignity of the parliament, the majesty of the people, and the powers of the island! Keep them unsullied, uncovenanted, uncircumscribed, and unstipendiary! These paths are the paths to glory, and, let me add, these ways are the ways of peace: so shall the prosperity of your country, though without a tongue to thank you, yet laden with the blessings of constitution and of commerce, bear attestation to your services, and wait on your progress with involuntary praise!

ANTI-UNION SPEECHES.

JANUARY 15, 1800.

MR. EGAN had just risen to speak, when Mr. Grattan entered the House, supported (in consequence of illness) by Mr. W. B. Ponsonby and Mr. Arthur Moore.* He took the oaths and his seat, and after Mr. Egan had concluded, in consequence of illness being obliged to speak sitting, he addressed the House as follows: —

SIR, The gentleman who spoke last but one (Mr. Fox) has spoken the pamphlet of the English minister — I answer that minister. He has published two celebrated productions, in both of which he declares his intolerance of the constitution of Ireland. He concurs with the men whom he has hanged, in thinking the constitution a grievance, and differs from them in the remedy only; they proposing to substitute a republic, and he proposing to substitute the yoke of the British Parliament; the one turns rebel to the King, the minister a rebel to the constitution.

We have seen him inveigh against their projects, let us hear him in defence of his own. He denies in the face of the two nations a public fact registered and recorded; he disclaims the final adjustment of 1782, and he tells you that this final adjustment was no more than an incipient train of negotiation. The settlement of which I speak consists of several parts, every part a record, establishing on the whole two grand positions. First, the admission of Ireland's claim to be legislated for by no other parliament but that of Ireland. Secondly, the finality imposed upon the two nations, regarding all constitutional projects affecting each other. On the admission of

* The reporters who have transmitted the account of the debates of the day, state, "Never was beheld a scene more solemn; an indescribable emotion seized the House and gallery, and every heart heaved in tributary pulsation to the name, virtues, and the return to parliament of the founder of the constitution of 1782; the existence of which was then the subject of debate."

INVECTIVE AGAINST CORRY.

FEBRUARY 14TH, 1800.

HAS the gentleman done? Has he completely done? He was unparliamentary from the beginning to the end of his speech. There was scarce a word he uttered that was not a violation of the privileges of the House; but I did not call him to order — why? because the limited talents of some men render it impossible for them to be severe without being unparliamentary. But before I sit down I shall show him how to be severe and parliamentary at the same time. On any other occasion I should think myself justifiable in treating with silent contempt anything which might fall from that honorable member; but there are times when the insignificance of the accuser is lost in the magnitude of the accusation. I know the difficulty the honorable gentleman labored under when he attacked me, conscious that, on a comparative view of our characters, public and private, there is nothing he could say which would injure me. The public would not believe the charge. I despise the falsehood. If such a charge were made by an honest man, I would answer it in the manner I shall do before I sit down. But I shall first reply to it when not made by an honest man.

The right honorable gentleman has called me "an unimpeached traitor." I ask, why not "traitor," unqualified by any epithet? I will tell him; it was because he dare not. It was the act of a coward, who raises his aim to strike, but has not courage to give the blow. I will not call him villain, because it would be unparliamentary, and he is a privy counsellor. I will not call him fool, because he happens to be Chancellor of the Exchequer. But I say he is one who has abused the privilege of parliament and freedom of debate to the uttering language, which, if spoken out of the House, I should answer only with a blow. I care not how high his situation, how low his character, how contemptible his speech; whether a privy counsellor or a parasite, my answer would be a blow. He has charged me with being connected with the rebels: the charge is utterly, totally, and meanly false. Does the honorable gentleman rely on the report of the House of Lords for the foundation of his assertion? If he does, I can prove to the committee there was a physical impossibility of that report being true. But I scorn to answer any man for my conduct, whether he be a political coxcomb, or whether he brought himself into power by a false glare of courage or not. I scorn to answer any wizard of the Castle throwing himself into fantastical airs. But if an honorable and independent man were to make a charge against me, I would say : "You charge me with having an intercourse with the rebels, and you found your charge upon what is said to have appeared before a committee of the Lords. Sir, the report of that committee is totally and egregiously irregular." I will read a letter from Mr. Nelson, who had been examined before that committee; it states that what the report represents him as having spoken, is *not what he said.* [Mr. Grattan here read a letter from Mr. Nelson, denying that he had any connection with Mr. Grattan as charged in the report; and concluding by saying, "*never was misrepresentation more vile than that put into my mouth by the report.*"]

From the situation that I held, and from the connections I had in the city of Dublin, it was necessary for me to hold intercourse with various descriptions of persons. The right honorable member might as well have been charged with a participation in the guilt of those traitors; for he had communicated with some of those very persons on the subject of parliamentary reform. The Irish government, too, were in communication with some of them.

The right honorable member has told me I deserted a profession where wealth and station were the reward of industry and talent. If I mistake not, that gentleman endeavored to obtain those rewards by the same means; but he soon deserted the occupation of a barrister for those of a parasite and pander. He fled from the labor of study to flatter at the table of the great. He found the lord's parlor a better sphere for his exertions than the hall of the Four Courts; the house of a great man a more convenient way to power and to

DANIEL O'CONNELL.

SPEECHES.

BY

DANIEL O'CONNELL, M. P.

[615]

Speech at Limerick, 1812

I FEEL it my duty, as a professed agitator, to address the meeting. It is merely in the exercise of my office of agitation, that I think it necessary to say a few words. For any purpose of illustration or argument, further discourse is useless: all the topics which the present period suggested, have been treated of with sound judgment, and a rare felicity of diction, by my respected and talented friend (Mr. Roche); all I shall do is, to add a few observations to what has fallen from that gentleman; and whilst I sincerely admire the happy style in which he has treated those subjects, I feel deep regret at being unable to imitate his excellent discourse.

And, first, let me concur with him in congratulating the Catholics of Limerick on the progress our great cause has made since we were last assembled. Since that period our cause has not rested for support on the efforts of those alone who were immediately interested; no, our Protestant brethren throughout the land have added their zealous exertions for our emancipation. They have, with admirable patriotism, evinced their desire to conciliate by serving us, and I am sure I do but justice to the Catholics, when I proclaim our gratitude, as written on our hearts, and to be extinguished only with our lives.

Nor has the support and the zeal of our Protestant brethren been vain and barren. No, it has been productive of great and solid advantages; it has procured, for the cause of religious liberty, the respect even of the most bigoted of our opponents; it has struck down English prejudice; it has convinced the mistaken honest; it has terrified the hypocritical knaves: and finally, it has pronounced for us, by a great and triumphant majority, from one of the branches of the legislature, the distinct recognition of the propriety and the necessity of conceding justice to the great body of the Irish people.

Let us, therefore, rejoice in our mutual success; let us rejoice in the near approach of freedom; let us rejoice in the prospect of soon shaking off our chains, and of the speedy extinction of our grievances. But above all, let us rejoice at the means by which these happy effects have been produced; let us doubly rejoice, because they afford no triumph to any part of the Irish nation over the other — that they are not the result of any contention among ourselves; but constitute a victory, obtained for the Catholics by the Protestants — that they prove the liberality of the one, and require the eternal gratitude of the other — that they prove and promise the eternal dissolution of ancient animosities and domestic feuds, and afford to every Christian and to every patriot, the cheering certainty of seeing peace, harmony, and benevolence prevail in that country, where a wicked and perverted policy has so long and so fatally propagated and encouraged dissension, discord, and rancor.

We owe it to the liberality of the Irish Protestants — to the zeal of the Irish Presbyterians — to the friendly exertion of the Irish Quakers; we owe, to the cordial re-union of every sect and denomination of Irish Christians, the progress of our cause. They have procured for us the solemn and distinct promise and pledge of the House of Commons — they almost obtained for us a similar declaration from the House of Lords. It was lost by the petty majority of one — it was lost by a majority, not of those who listened to the absurd prosings of Lord Eldon, to the bigoted and turbid declamation of that English Chief Justice, whose sentiments so forcibly recall the memory of the star-chamber; not of those who were able to compare the vapid or violent folly of the one party, with the statesman-like sentiments, the profound arguments, the splendid eloquence of the Marquis Wellesley. Not of those who heard the reasonings of our other illustrious advocates; but by a majority of men who acted upon preconceived opinions, or, from a distance, carried into effect their bigotry, or, perhaps, worse propensities — who availed themselves of that absurd privilege of the peerage, which enables those to decide who have not heard — which permits men to pronounce upon subjects they have not discussed — and allows a final determination to precede argument.

It was not, however, to this privilege alone, that our want of success was to be attributed. The very principle upon which the present

Erin, and my beloved friend, whose delightful muse has the sound of the ancient minstrelsy —

> "Still shalt thou be my midnight dream —
> Thy glory still my waking theme;
> And ev'ry thought and wish of mine,
> Unconquered Erin, shall be thine!"

· SPEECH

IN THE BRITISH CATHOLIC ASSOCIATION, ON THE DEFEAT OF THE
EMANCIPATION BILL.

MAY 26TH, 1825.

THE measure of which we complained is of too recent a date,
the injury which we have sustained is yet too fresh, too gall-
ing in its effects, to allow my reason to assume the ascendant
over my feelings, and to give my judgment time to operate
on, and influence the tenor of my reflections. I shall nevertheless
be as respectful in my allusions, and as moderate in the remarks I
have to offer, as the overboiling fervency of my Irish blood will
permit. By rejecting that bill which the Commons had sent up to
them for their concurrence and approval, the House of Lords has
inflicted a vital injury on the stability of English power, and on
Irish feelings and Irish honesty. They, however, would not be cast
down by that injury. The Catholics were sometimes in derision
termed "Roman." I am a Catholic, and proud am I to say that in
one thing at least I am a Roman — I never will despair. But on
what is this boastful assertion founded? Why should I say that
which I feel has not reason or sound policy to support it? Where
now, I would ask, is there a rational hope for a Catholic? Where
shall I look for consolation under the present great and serious dis-
appointment? Am I to look back? Alas! there is nothing cheering in the events which have for some time past met us on the way
to success and dashed our hopes to the earth. Does history furnish
any grounds for the supposition that those who have been found
incapable of maintaining their plighted faith, and preserving the
terms of a great national contract, will now, in the hour of success,
be induced to yield any reason, any inducement to us to proceed in
the course we have adopted? Is this, I would ask, the example

all the expenses; there should be no hireling advocacy. Prosecutors never see one another until they are brought into court, and their case comes on in the shape of a record. In every case of litigation, the contending parties should previously see one another, the judge explain the laws, and I have no doubt that under those circumstances a mutual compromise and arrangement would take place before the parties would leave the court. There is one subject more to which I shall advert. I am the respecter of authority. If calumny assail the Throne, then private life cannot be secure. I have read with horror some details of a distinguished individual in the London newspapers. The story of Captain Garth, however, must come to light, and the Duke of Cumberland, I have no doubt, will be freed from the foul calumny with which he has been assailed. No — I shall not see the brother of my King attacked. I am no respecter of persons, but I will call for and demand investigation into this transaction. There is a moral progress at present in the world. There is no true basis for liberty but religion.

Speech

At Mullaghmast Monster Meeting.

——

September, 1843.

ACCEPT, with the greatest alacrity, the high honor you have done me in calling me to the chair of this majestic meeting. I feel more honored than I ever did in my life, with one single exception, and that related to, if possible, an equally majestic meeting at Tara. But I must say that if a comparison were instituted between them, it would take a more discriminating eye than mine to discover any difference between them. There are the same incalculable numbers; there is the same firmness; there is the same determination; there is the same exhibition of love to old Ireland; there is the same resolution not to violate the peace; not to be guilty of the slightest outrage; not to give the enemy power by committing a crime, but peacefully and manfully to stand together in the open day, to protest before man and in the presence of God against the iniquity of continuing the Union.

At Tara, I protested against the Union — I repeat the protest at Mullaghmast. I declare solemnly my thorough conviction as a constitutional lawyer, that the Union is totally void in point of principle and of constitutional force. I tell you that no portion of the empire had the power to traffic on the rights and liberties of the Irish people. The Irish people nominated them to make laws, and not legislatures. They were appointed to act under the constitution and not annihilate it. Their delegation from the people was confined within the limits of the constitution, and the moment the Irish parliament went beyond those limits and destroyed the constitution, that moment it annihilated its own power, but could not annihilate the immortal spirit of liberty, which belongs, as a rightful inheritance, to the people of Ireland. Take it then from me that the Union is void. I admit there is the

SPEECHES.

BY

CHARLES PHILLIPS, ESQ.

[475]

A SPEECH

DELIVERED AT A PUBLIC DINNER GIVEN TO MR. FINLAY BY THE
ROMAN CATHOLICS OF THE TOWN AND COUNTY OF SLIGO.

———— .

THINK, Sir, you will agree with me, that the most experienced
speaker might justly tremble in addressing you, after the
display you have just witnessed. What then, must I feel,
who never before addressed a public audience? However, it
would be but an unworthy affectation in me, were I to conceal from
you the emotions with which I am agitated by this kindness. The
exaggerated estimate which other countries have made of the few
services so young a man could render, has I hope, inspired me with
the sentiments it ought; but *here*, I do confess to you, I feel no
ordinary sensation — here, where every object springs some new
association, and the loveliest objects, mellowed as they are by time,
rise painted on the eye of memory — here, where the light of
heaven first blessed my infant view, and nature breathed into my
infant heart, that ardor for my country which nothing but death
can chill — here, where the scenes of my childhood remind me how
innocent I was, and the graves of my fathers admonish me how
pure I should continue — here, standing as I do amongst my fairest,
fondest, earliest sympathies — such a welcome, operating, not
merely as an affectionate tribute, but as a moral testimony, does
indeed quite oppress and overwhelm me.

Oh! believe me, warm is the heart that feels, and willing is the
tongue that speaks; and still, I cannot, by shaping it to my rudely
inexpressive phrase, shock the sensibility of a gratitude too full to
be suppressed, and yet (how far!) too eloquent for language.

If any circumstance could add to the pleasure of this day, it is
that which I feel in introducing to the friends of my youth the friend
of my adoption; though perhaps I am committing one of our im-

puted blunders, when I speak of introducing one whose patriotism
has already rendered him familiar to every heart in Ireland; a man,
who, conquering every disadvantage, and spurning every difficulty,
has poured around our misfortunes the splendor of an intellect,
that at once irradiates and consumes them.   For the services he has
rendered to his country, from my heart I thank him; and, for
myself, I offer him a personal, it may be selfish tribute, for saving me,
by his presence this night, from an impotent attempt at his pane-
gyric.   Indeed, gentlemen, you can have little idea of what he has to
endure, who in these times, advocates your cause.   Every calumny
which the venal and the vulgar, and the vile, are lavishing upon you,
is visited with exaggeration upon us.   We are called traitors,
because we would rally round the crown an unanimous people.   We
are called apostates, because we will not persecute Christianity.
We are branded as separatists, because of our endeavors to annihilate the fetters that, instead of binding,. clog the connection.   To
these may be added, the frowns of power, the envy of dulness, the
mean malice of exposed self-interest, and, it may be, in despite of
all natural affection, even the discountenance of kindred!—Well, be
it so, —

> For thee, fair Freedom, welcome all the past,
> For thee, my country, welcome, even the last!

I am not ashamed to confess to you, that there was a day when I was
bigoted as the blackest; but I thank the Being who gifted me with
a mind not quite impervious to conviction, and I thank you, who
afforded such convincing testimonies of my error.   I saw you
enduring with patience the most unmerited assaults, bowing before
the insults of revived anniversaries; in private life, exemplary; in
public, unoffending; in the hour of peace, asserting your loyalty; in the hour of danger, proving it.   Even when an invading
enemy victoriously penetrated into the very heart of our country, I
saw the banner of your allegiance beaming refutation on your slan-
derers; was it a wonder, then that I seized my prejudices, and with
a blush burned them on the altar of my country!

The great question of Catholic, shall I not rather say, of Irish
emancipation, has now assumed that national aspect which imperi-
ously challenges the scrutiny of every one.   While it was shrouded
in the mantle of religious mystery, with the temple for its sanctuary,

with the energies and stamped with the patent of the Deity, which, under proper culture might perhaps bless, adorn, immortalize, or ennoble empires; some Cincinnatus, in whose breast the destinies of a nation may lie dormant; some Milton, "pregnant with celestial fire;" some Curran, who, when thrones were crumbled and dynasties forgotten, might stand the landmark of his country's genius, rearing himself amid regal ruins and national dissolution, a mental pyramid in the solitude of time, beneath whose shade things might moulder, and round whose summit eternity must play. Even in such a circle the young Demosthenes might have once been found, and Homer, the disgrace and glory of his age, have sung neglected! Have not other nations witnessed those things, and who shall say that nature has peculiarly degraded the intellect of Ireland? Oh, my countrymen, let us hope that under better auspices and a sounder policy, the ignorance that thinks so may meet its refutation. Let us turn from the blight and ruin of this wintry day to the fond anticipation of a happier period, when our prostrate land shall stand erect among the nations, fearless and unfettered; her brow blooming with the wreath of science, and her path strewed with the offerings of art; the breath of heaven blessing her flag, the extremities of earth acknowledging her name, her fields waving with the fruits of agriculture, her ports alive with the contributions of commerce, and her temples vocal with unrestricted piety. Such is the ambition of the true patriot; such are the views for which we are calumniated! Oh, divine ambition! Oh, delightful calumny! Happy he who shall see thee accomplished! Happy he who through every peril toils for thy attainment! Proceed, friend of Ireland and partaker of her wrongs, proceed undaunted to this glorious consummation. Fortune will not gild, power will not ennoble thee : but thou shalt be rich in the love and titled by the blessings of thy country; thy path shall be illumined by the public eye, thy labors enlightened by the public gratitude; and oh, remember — amid the impediments with which corruption will oppose, and the dejection with which disappointments may depress you — remember you are acquiring a name to be cherished by the future generations of earth, long after it has been enrolled amongst the inheritors of heaven.

A SPEECH

DELIVERED AT AN AGGREGATE MEETING OF THE ROMAN CATHOLICS OF CORK.

IT is with no small degree of self-congratulation that I at length find myself in a province which every glance of the eye, and every throb of the heart, tells me is truly Irish; and that congratulation is not a little enhanced by finding that you receive me not quite as a stranger. Indeed, if to respect the Christian without regard to his creed, if to love the country but the more for its calamities, if to hate oppression though it be robed in power, if to venerate integrity though it pine under persecution, gives a man any claim to your recognition, then, indeed, I am not a stranger amongst you. There is a bond of union between brethren, however distant; there is a sympathy between the virtuous, however sepparated; there is a heaven-born instinct by which the associates of the heart become at once acquainted, and kindred natures, as it were by magic, see in the face of a stranger, the features of a friend. Thus it is, that, though we never met, you hail in me the sweet association, and I feel myself amongst you even as if I were in the home of my nativity. But this my knowledge of you was not left to chance; nor was it left to the records of your charity, the memorials of your patriotism, your municipal magnificence, or your commercial splendor; it came to me hallowed by the accents of that tongue on which Ireland has so often hung with ecstasy, heightened by the eloquence and endeared by the sincerity of, I hope, our mutual friend. Let me congratulate him on having become in some degree, naturalized in a province, where the spirit of the elder day seems to have lingered; and let me congratulate you on the acquisition of a man who is at once the zealous advocate of your cause, and a practical instance of the injustice of your oppressions. Surely,

A Speech

Delivered at a Dinner given on Dinas Island, in the Lake of Killarney, on Mr. Phillips' Health being given, together with that of Mr. Payne, a young American.

———

IT is not with the vain hope of returning by words the kindnesses which have been literally showered on me during the short period of our acquaintance, that I now interrupt, for a moment, the flow of your festivity. Indeed, it is not necessary; an Irishman needs no requital for his hospitality; its generous impulse is the instinct of his nature, and the very consciousness of the act carries its recompense along with it. But, sir, there are sensations excited by an allusion in your toast, under the influence of which silence would be impossible. To be associated with Mr. Payne must be, to any one who regards private virtues and personal accomplishments, a source of peculiar pride; and that feeling is not a little enhanced in me by a recollection of the country to which we are indebted for his qualifications. Indeed, the mention of America has never failed to fill me with the most lively emotions. In my earliest infancy, that tender season when impressions, at once the most permanent and the most powerful, are likely to be excited, the story of her then recent struggle raised a throb in every heart that loved liberty, and wrung a reluctant tribute even from discomfited oppression. I saw her spurning alike the luxuries that would enervate, and the legions that would intimidate; dashing from her lips the poisoned cup of European servitude, and, through all the vicissitudes of her protracted conflict, displaying a magnanimity that defied misfortune, and a moderation that gave new grace to victory. It was the first vision of my childhood; it will descend with me to the grave. But if as a man, I venerate the mention of America, what

must be my feelings towards her as an Irishman. Never, oh never,
while memory remains, can Ireland forget the home of her emigrant
and the asylum of her exile. No matter whether their sorrows
sprung from the errors of enthusiasm, or the realities of suffering —
from fancy or infliction; that must be reserved for the scrutiny of
those whom the lapse of time shall acquit of partiality. It is for the
men of other ages to investigate and record it; but surely it is for
the men of every age to hail the hospitality that received the shel-
terless, and love the feeling that befriended the unfortunate. Search
creation round, where can you find a country that presents so sublime a view, so interesting an anticipation? What noble institutions!
What a comprehensive policy! What a wise equalization of every
political advantage! The oppressed of all countries, the martyrs of
every creed, the innocent victim of despotic arrogance or supersti-
tious phrenzy, may there find refuge; his industry encouraged, his
piety respected, his ambition animated; with no restraint but those
laws which are the same to all, and no distinction but that which his
merit may originate. Who can deny that the existence of such a
country presents a subject for human congratulation! Who can
deny that its gigantic advancement offers a field for the most rational
conjecture! At the end of the very next century, if she proceeds
as she seems to promise, what a wondrous spectacle may she not
exhibit! Who shall say for what purpose a mysterious Providence
may not have designed her! Who shall say that when in its follies
or its crimes, the old world may have interred all the pride of its
power, and all the pomp of its civilization, human nature may not
find its destined renovation in the new! For myself, I have no
doubt of it. I have not the least doubt that when our temples and
our trophies shall have mouldered into dust; when the glories of
our name shall be but the legend of tradition, and the light of our
achievements only live in song; philosophy will rise again in the
sky of her Franklin, and glory rekindle at the urn of her Washington. Is this the vision of romantic fancy? Is it even improbable?
Is it half so improbable as the events, which, for the last twenty
years have rolled like successive tides over the surface of the European world, each erasing the impressions that preceded it? Thousands upon thousands, sir, I know there are, who will consider this
supposition as wild and whimsical; but they have dwelt with little

the contest, and his country called him to the command.   Liberty
unsheathed his sword, necessity stained, victory returned it.   If he
had paused here, history might have doubted what station to assign
him, whether at the head of her citizens or her soldiers, her heroes,
or her patriots.   But the last glorious act crowns his career, and banishes all hesitation.   Who, like Washington, after having emanci-
pated a hemisphere, resigned its crown, and preferred the retirement
of domestic life to the adoration of a land he might be almost said
to have created?

> "How shall we rank thee upon glory's page,
> Thou more than soldier, and just less than sage;
> All thou hast been reflects less fame on thee,
> Far less than all thou hast forborne to be!"

Such, Sir, is the testimony of one not to be accused of partiality
in his estimate of America.   Happy, proud America! the lightnings
of heaven yielded to your philosophy!   The temptations of earth
could not seduce your patriotism!

I have the honor, Sir, of proposing to you as a toast, THE IMMORTAL
MEMORY OF GEORGE WASHINGTON.

A SPEECH

DELIVERED AT AN AGGREGATE MEETING OF THE ROMAN CATHOLICS OF THE COUNTY AND CITY OF DUBLIN.

HAVING taken, in the discussions on your question, such humble share as was allotted to my station and capacity, I may be permitted to offer my ardent congratulations at the proud pinnacle on which it this day reposes. After having combated calumnies the most atrocious, sophistries the most plausible, and perils the most appalling that slander could invent or ingenuity could devise or power array against you, I at length behold the assembled rank and wealth and talent of the Catholic body offering to the legislature that appeal which cannot be rejected, if there be a Power in heaven to redress injury, or a spirit on earth to administer justice. No matter what may be the depreciations of faction or of bigotry; this earth never presented a more ennobling spectacle than that of a Christian country suffering for her religion with the patience of a martyr, and suing for her liberties with the expostulations of a philosopher; reclaiming the bad by her piety; refuting the bigoted by her practice; wielding the Apostle's weapons in the patriot's cause, and at length, laden with chains and with laurels, seeking from the country she had saved, the constitution she had shielded! Little did I imagine, that in such a state of your cause, we should be called together to counteract the impediments to its success, created not by its enemies, but by those supposed to be its friends. It is a melancholy occasion; but melancholy as it is, it must be met, and met with the fortitude of men struggling in the sacred cause of liberty. I do not allude to the proclamation of your Board; of that Board I never was a member, so I can speak impartially. It contained much talent, some learning, many virtues. It was valuable on that account: but it was doubly valuable as being a vehicle for

EDMUND BURKE.

SPEECHES.

BY

RIGHT HON. EDMUND BURKE.

[721]

Speech on American Taxation.

On the 19th April, 1774, Mr. Rose Fuller, member for Rye, proposed in the House of Commons that the House should proceed to take into consideration the duty of 3d. per lb., imposed under the Act of 1767, on tea imported into America. It was on this occasion that Burke, then member for the borough of Wendover, delivered the following speech — an oration which contains some of the most splendid passages in the English language. It was marked with such energy, that it roused the attention of the House, though spoken at a very late period in the debate. It is said that Lord John Townshend, struck by the remarkable beauty of one passage, cried aloud, "What a man is this! how could he acquire such transcendent powers?" The speech was published under the orator's supervision, in compliance with the public wish. Few literary efforts have given evidence of the possession of so much power of sarcasm, as the description of the coalition ministry of Lord Grafton. The character of Lord Chatham is most exquisitely portrayed. For elegance of diction, and beauty of illustration, it has, perhaps, never been surpassed.

SIR, — I agree with the honorable gentleman who spoke last, that this subject is not new in this house. Very disagreeably to this house, very unfortunately to this nation, and to the peace and prosperity of this whole empire, no topic has been more familiar to us. For nine long years, session after session, we have been lashed round and round this miserable circle of occasional arguments and temporary expedients. I am sure our heads must turn, and our stomachs nauseate with them. We have had them in every shape; we have looked at them in every point of view. Invention is exhausted; reason is fatigued; experience has given judgment; but obstinacy is not yet conquered.

The honorable gentleman has made one endeavor more to diversify the form of this disgusting argument. He has thrown out a speech composed almost entirely of challenges. Challenges are serious things; and as he is a man of prudence as well as resolution, I dare say he has very well weighed those challenges before he delivered them. I had long the happiness to sit at the same side of the house, and to agree with the honorable gentleman on all the American questions. My sentiments, I am sure, are well known to him; and I thought I had been perfectly acquainted with his. Though I find myself mistaken, he will still permit me to use the privilege of an old friendship, he will permit me to apply myself to the house under the sanction of his authority; and, on the various grounds he has measured out, to submit to you the poor opinions which I have formed, upon a matter of importance enough to demand the fullest consideration I could bestow upon it.

He has stated to the house two grounds of deliberation; one narrow and simple, and merely confined to the question on your paper: the other more large and more complicated; comprehending the whole series of the parliamentary proceedings with regard to America, their causes, and their consequences. With regard to the latter ground, he states it as useless, and thinks it may be even dangerous, to enter into so extensive a field of inquiry. Yet, to my surprise, he had hardly laid down this restrictive proposition, to which his authority would have given so much weight, when directly, and with the same authority, he condemns it, and declares it absolutely necessary to enter into the most ample historical detail. His zeal has thrown him a little out of his usual accuracy. In this perplexity what shall we do, Sir, who are willing to submit to the law he gives us? He has reprobated in one part of his speech the rule he had laid down for debate in the other; and, after narrowing the ground for all those who are to speak after him, he takes an excursion himself, as unbounded as the subject and the extent of his great abilities.

Sir, when I cannot obey all his laws, I will do the best I can. I will endeavor to obey such of them as have the sanction of his example, and to stick to that rule, which, though not inconsistent with the other, is the most rational. He was certainly in the right when he took the matter largely. I cannot prevail on myself to agree with him in his censure of his own conduct. It is not, he will give me leave to say, either useless or dangerous. He asserts, that retrospect is not wise; and the proper, the only proper, subject of inquiry is, " not how we got into this difficulty, but how we are to get out of it." In other words, we are, according to him, to consult our invention, and to reject our experience. The mode of deliberation he recommends is diametrically opposite to every rule of reason, and every principle of

SPEECH

ON TAKING LEAVE OF THE ELECTORS OF BRISTOL.

———

Although Burke entered on his canvass of the Bristol electors in September, 1780, with the support of the Mayor and several other leading citizens, he found the tide of bigotry and prejudice too strong against him, and accordingly, on the morning on which the polling was to commence, he resigned. On this occasion he delivered the following graceful speech, perhaps the *best-tempered* any unsuccessful canvasser ever spoke.

GENTLEMEN, — I decline the election. It has ever been my rule through life to observe a proportion between my efforts and my objects. I have never been remarkable for a bold, active and sanguine pursuit of advantages that are personal to myself.

I have not canvassed the whole of this city in form. But I have taken such a view of it, as satisfies my own mind, that your choice will not ultimately fall upon me. Your city, gentleman, is in a state of miserable distraction : and I am resolved to withdraw whatever share my pretensions may have had in its unhappy divisions. I have not been in haste ; I have tried all prudent means ; I have waited for the effects of all contingencies. If I were fond of a contest, by the partiality of my numerous friends (whom you know to be among the most weighty and respectable people of the city) I have the means of a sharp one in my hands. But I thought it far better, with my strength unspent, and my reputation unimpaired, to do, early and from foresight, that which I might be obliged to do from necessity at last.

[NOTE. — Burke left Bristol immediately and proceeded to Malton (where he had been elected in 1774), for which borough he was immediately returned. He sat for Malton during the remainder of his parliamentary career.]

I am not in the least surprised, nor in the least angry at this view of things. I have read the book of life for a long time, and I have read other books a little. Nothing has happened to me, but what has happened to men much better than I, and in times and in nations full as good as the age and country that we live in. To say that I am no way concerned, would be neither decent nor true. The representation of Bristol was an object on many accounts dear to me; and I certainly should very far prefer it to any other in the kingdom. My habits are made to it; and it is in general more unpleasant to be rejected after long trial, than not to be chosen at all.

But, gentlemen, I will see nothing except your former kindness, and I will give way to no other sentiments than those of gratitude. From the bottom of my heart I thank you for what you have done for me. You have given me a long term, which is now expired. I have performed the conditions, and enjoyed all the profits to the full; and I now surrender your estate into your hands without being in a single tile, or a single stone, impaired or wasted by my use. I have served the public for fifteen years. I have served you in particular for six. What is passed is well stored. It is safe and out of the power of fortune. What is to come, is in wiser hands than ours; and He, in whose hands it is, best knows whether it is best for you and me, that I should be in parliament or even in the world.

Gentlemen, the melancholy event of yesterday reads to us an awful lesson against being too much troubled about any of the objects of ordinary ambition. The worthy gentleman, Mr. Coombe, the candidate who has died suddenly, and who has been snatched from us at the moment of the election, and in the middle of the contest, whilst his desires were as warm, and his hopes as eager as ours, has feelingly told us what shadows we are, and what shadows we pursue.

It has been usual for a candidate who declines to take his leave by a letter to the sheriffs, but I received your trust in the face of day; and in the face of day I accept your dismission. I am not, — I am not at all ashamed to look upon you; nor can my presence discompose the order of business here. I humbly and respectfully take my leave of the sheriffs, the candidates and the electors; wishing heartily that the choice may be for the best, at a time which calls, if ever time did call, for service that is not nominal. It is no plaything you are about. I tremble when I consider the trust I have presumed to ask. I confided perhaps too much in my intentions. They were really fair and upright; and I am bold to say, that I ask no ill thing for you, when on parting from this place I pray that whomsoever you choose to succeed me, he may resemble me exactly in all things, except in my abilities to serve, and my fortune to please you.

SELECT PASSAGES

FROM BURKE'S SPEECHES ON THE IMPEACHMENT OF WARREN HASTINGS.

Burke spoke three times during the trial of Hastings. He opened the impeachment in February, 1788, in a speech which lasted for several days, containing several passages of surpassing power. He also spoke to one of the charges in 1789, and replied to the defence in 1794. Our limits do not permit us to give to the reader these orations, but we cannot refrain from presenting to his notice some of the most striking passages.

The following passage in reply to Hastings' statement, that to govern Hindostan properly it was necessary to make use of arbitrary power, is very fine.

HASTINGS, the lieutenant of a British monarch, claiming absolute dominion! From whom, in the name of all that was strange, could he derive, or how had he the audacity to claim, such authority? He could not have derived it from the East India Company, for they had it not to confer. He could not have received it from his sovereign, for the sovereign had it not to bestow. It could not have been given by either house of parliament, for it was unknown to the British constitution! Yet Mr. Hastings, acting under the assumption of this power, had avowed his rejection of British acts of parliament, had gloried in the success which he pretended to derive from their violation, and had on every occasion attempted to justify the exercise of arbitrary power in its greatest extent. Having thus avowedly acted in opposition to the laws of Great Britain, he sought a shield in vain, in other laws and other usages. Would he appeal to the Mahomedan law for his justification? In the whole Koran there was not a single text which could justify the power he had assumed. Would he appeal to the Gentoo code? Vain there the effort also; a system of stricter justice, or more pure morality, did not exist. It was, therefore, equal whether he fled for shelter to a British court of justice or a Gentoo pagoda;

LETTERS

OF

His Grace the Most Rev. Dr. McHale,

ARCHBISHOP OF TUAM.

[789]

To the Most Rev. Dr. Manners,

———

The Question of the Divorce between George IV. and his Queen.

MAYNOOTH COLLEGE, Dec. 2, 1820.

> *Fœcunda culpæ secula, nuptias*
> *Primum inquinavere, et genus, et domus,*
>   *Hoc fonte derivata clades*
>   *In patriam populumque fluxit.* — HORACE.

Fruitful of crimes, this age first stained
Their hapless offspring, and profaned
The nuptial bed; from whence the woes,
Which various and unnumbered rose;
From this polluted fountain head
O'er Rome, and o'er the nation spread. — FRANCIS.

MY LORD — During the late portentous proceedings which have awed public curiosity, your Grace and episcopal colleagues stood out in too prominent an attitude, not to attract and fix observation. As the question of divorce embraced much of ecclesiastical polity, it was naturally expected that the faithful would be enlightened by the wisdom and confirmed by the accordance of the hierarchy. But, alas! these anticipations have been sadly frustrated, and the surprise and disedification that were feebly murmured among the Lords have been long since loudly re-echoed through the empire.* It has been a subject of regret to some, of triumph to others, and of wonder to all, to see the heads of a religion which hinges on the principle of the universal intel-

---

* Witness among others the speech of my Lord King, who sported a good deal of mirth and raillery at the expense of the premier, until his seriousness was restored by the shock which his faith had sustained in the collision of the prelacy.

ligibility of the Scripture, arrayed in adverse ranks on a momentous question, involving in its general tendency the best interests of mankind, and in this particular instance, the safety and the honor of the empire; disputing every inch of ground with Scripture authority, and thereby demonstrating to the world the obscurity of the sacred volume. For I will not — I cannot, my lord, suppose that any unworthy bias or flexibility to power could warp the judgment of men of such exalted station and sanctity. And hence, one cannot sufficiently express his indignation against those rash advocates of the Bible, who cannot defend its perspicuity without impeaching the integrity of its expounders. Hitherto, whatever might be the opinion of the prelates, they uniformly affected the language of orthodoxy and concord, and like the ancient philosophers, though they might inwardly disbelieve, they exteriorly reverenced the doctrines of the Church. But on this occasion they scandalized the faithful, and edified the sectary, by sincerely revealing the mysteries of their own disunion.

I have heard, my lord, of the distinction of essentials, by which the lovers of subtlety, more than of truth, have thought to elude the arguments of their adversaries. It will not, doubtless, be recurred to on this occasion, nor will it be deemed presumption to assert, that there is nothing essential in Scripture, if the doctrine of marriage does not form an essential point of Christian morality. It is not a speculative article, on which one could be supposed to err without danger, and propagate his errors, without affecting the public repose. It is a duty of every day's occurrence, connected with the happiness of almost every individual; nor have the ministers of the establishment themselves aspired to such unearthly sanctity, as to be exempt from its obligations. It is, therefore, of vast importance to know whether the marriage contract lasts for life, or only during the discretion of the parties; and whether we are to believe, with his lordship of Chester, that its ties are indissoluble, or, with your Grace of Canterbury, that adultery annuls its engagements.

On reading the report of your Grace's speech, I was not a little surprised to find a minister of Christ principally resting on the obsolete laws of Moses. However, it may appear consistent enough, that they who have abjured the living authority of the intended to be made the instrument of every blasphemer, who would fain conceal his extravagance and impiety under the mask of respect for religion. The indecent levity with which the awful concerns of religion are often treated by polemics, and the flippancy with which they abuse the Scripture, would almost make one think that the Scriptures were written for the vain and irreligious as a matter of idle disputation. But the Scriptures are too sacred for familiarity; nor ought the mysteries of heaven be profanely agitated between the vain contentions of men. Placed in the sanctuary of the Catholic Church, the Scripture is the monument of God's covenant with his people; it affords a proof of his presence, and a pledge of his protection. But when it is dragged out of that sanctuary by the impiety of the sectaries, and sacrilegiously carried out to battle, it becomes like the same ark of the covenant in the hands of the hypocritical sons of Heli: it provokes the vengeance of heaven — it becomes the signal of their shame — and the instrument of their discomfiture. *

HIEROPHILOS.

* And the ark of God was taken; and the two sons of Heli, Ophni and Phinees, were slain. — I. *Kings*, iv. 11.

DR. MCHALE'S LETTER TO LORD BEXLEY.

BALLINA, November, 1828

MY LORD — These are strange times; nor is it the least strange of the features which characterize them to see with what recklessness of their dignity the peers of the realm are rushing into print, and becoming ambitious candidates of ridicule. Heretofore they seemed to have adopted the Persian maxim of investing themselves with reverence, by keeping aloof from the ranks of the people. If they were not great men, the secret of their littleness was only known to their *valet de chambre;* nor did they rashly exhibit themselves abroad, if they did not possess those hardy qualities which are proof against public collisions. Rely on it, my lord, the people take delight in those exhibitions of aristocratic intellect, as it gives them an opportunity of measuring the relative distance between it and their own. "The Morning Chronicle," which conveyed to me Lord Bexley's letter, contained another of William Cobbett's on the opposite side, and surely no reader has failed to remark how the puny production of the peer shrinks before the strong and simple energy of the man of the people. With the Duke of Newcastle and Lord Kenyon, your lordship fills up the triumvirate of literature. Lords Farnham, and Lorton, and Winchilsea, are doubtless panting for the honor of digesting in plates of brass, the laws of the Constitution. Lords Wicklow and Roden must contribute their share to the labor, nor shall they cease to associate to their body all the writing peers of the land, until they complete the number of Decemvirs — a combination equally ominous to the liberties of the country.

It is difficult to compress within appropriate limits the refutation of your address, since, with a lofty disregard of all the unities of time, and place, and persons, your lordship's excursive fancy ranged over every topic that could minister to the prejudices of the public mind

tempts on the religion of either.   The Catholic religion can be made
a useful ally to the state; but it is only when its profession is un-
shackled, and its ministers are beyond the reach of any sinister
political control.

I have the honor to be, your lordship's obedient servant.

✠ JOHN, BISHOP OF MARONIA.

To the Protestant Archbishop of Tuam.

BALLINA, February 10, 1830.

MY LORD—It appears from the public prints that your Grace has been lately exercising your pastoral zeal, in writing to your clergy, to carry on a mission among the Roman Catholics; and if the copy of the circular be genuine, it is a production that evinces no ordinary spirit. It was fondly imagined that a benevolent legislature had succeeded in stilling the angry spirit of controversy by which the land was so long shaken, and the appearance of the olive branch was hailed as a presage of mutual conciliation. But, whilst the Government brings peace, your Grace seems to imagine that the sword is a more befitting badge for the ministers of religion; and hence you seize once more your theological trumpet, to arouse the sentinels of Israel to vigilance and war.

At any time the letter to which I allude would be considered the production of a mind under the most potent preternatural influences. At present, and with all the difficulties that stare the Establishment in the face, it exhibits the calmest indifference to all earthly consideration. There is no alloy of worldly prudence about your zeal; no cold calculations of the dangers to which the Church is exposed can chill the ardor of your charity. No; whilst the Establishment is now deliberately weighed in the balance, and the other prelates are watching the legislature with trembling anxiety for what may come to pass; — whilst Lord Mountcashel, with a warning voice, is turning the public attention to the decayed state of the walls, and wishes to exchange some vain and gilded decorations for Doric pillars, to sustain the tottering edifice; — whilst Sir John Newport is giving notice that he will submit this important subject to the wisdom of the assembled senate of the empire; — whilst the pressure of tithes and church-rates is the theme of every theorist, of whatever creed, repose on cushions and their devotions may be warmed by the comfortable effusions of a stove. But, my lord, the parsons will not thus expose themselves to the bitter irony of a people perhaps more famed than any other for an exhaustless strain of sarcastic intelligence; they will not, for their own sakes, be marked exceptions to the good sense that is pervading all classes of society. There is now no further controversy about the purity of the Protestant Church; it is all turning on the permanence of its temporalities. All are now agreed that the Establishment is a political machine originally framed by political artificers, since kept together for political motives, and which, like every other machine, as soon as the expense of keeping it in repair shall overbalance its benefits, must be abandoned to a quiet and natural decay.

On this topic there is no room for further disputation, now that a controversy altogether of a different kind has started up in the country; which is the most effectual method of promoting the prosperity of Ireland, and of uniting more closely all classes of the long-distracted people. Who shall be foremost in exploring its resources? in giving vigor to its trade? in opening new avenues of industry, and consigning to merited contempt all the leaden lore of malignant bigotry by which the minds of the people were so long poisoned? Yes; the apostles of discord must at length retire. There is now a rivalry of benevolence—an emulation in laboring for the public good —a contention for advancing a nation's happiness, which all the arts of narrow-minded individuals will not be able to suspend. There is, in short, a great anxiety to bury, by recent acts of kindness, the memory of ancient strife; and a flow of mutual good feeling, silently working through the country, which all the *odium theologicum* poured forth from your Grace's episcopal vial shall not be able to embitter.

I am your Grace's obedient servant,

✠ JOHN, BISHOP OF MARONIA.

CHRISTMAS DAY AT THE VATICAN.

FEAST OF ST. STEPHEN, ROME, 1831.

NWILLING to interrupt the series of observations suggested by the contemplation of the seven hills of the ancient city, I have not as yet made any reference to the Vatican. Yet no part of Rome possesses stronger claims on the affections of the Christian. It was not one of the seven hills on which the city was seated, yet it is the object which generally challenges the first visit from the piety of the pilgrim or the curiosity of the mere traveller. I was scarcely an hour arrived, when I hastened to Saint Peter's, to offer up my cold and imperfect prayers in unison with the incense of prayer and sacrifice that is daily ascending from that magnificent and holy temple, to the throne of the Almighty. Its precincts were worthy of the majesty of the temple. The obelisk in front proclaimed the homage of the conquered arts and wealth of Paganism to the spirit of Catholicity ; its refreshing fountains, continually playing in the sunbeams, were an emblem of its pure and perennial doctrine flowing from the shrine of the apostles ; and its curved colonnades, stretching out on either side, most significantly represented the ardent and affectionate eagerness with which the Catholic Church greets her children and cherishes them in her bosom. No sooner did I cross the threshold of the church than I felt, what others are said to feel, the illusion of its folded perspective. As I advanced, it appeared to be gradually unrolled, adjusting the harmonious position and size of the surrounding objects, until I stood under the stupendous dome, of which I had just seen the original model in the Pantheon : the one reposing on the earth, the masterpiece of Pagan temples, and the other resting on lofty pillars, penetrating to the heavens — the wondrous trophy of the Christian artist by whose skill and energy it was raised.

guages, inviting Greek and Hebrew, you are struck with the hidden and mysterious immensity of the place — an emblem of Him to whom it is dedicated — and forced silently to exclaim that this is no "other but the house of God," into which "the nations should be continually flowing from the four winds of heaven."

✠ JOHN, BISHOP OF MARONIA.

LETTER FROM ROME.

MY VISIT TO THE POPE. — A MANUSCRIPT LETTER OF MARY QUEEN
OF SCOTS. — THE TOMBS OF O'NEIL AND O'DONNELL, ETC.

––––––

ROME, March 27, 1832.

THE first of my visits to manifest the homage of my dutiful reverence to the Holy Father, was a few days after my arrival.
It was to a Catholic bishop from Ireland a visit fraught with
consolation. Notwithstanding all the efforts, which an impi-
ous policy had recourse to, to sever our connexion with the chair of
Peter, efforts far more ingenious in their cruelty than those of the
earlier persecutions that hunted the Christians into the catacombs, it
was a gladsome introduction to be presented to the good Father of
the Faithful, and to receive at his feet the Apostolical benediction.
He is worthy of the elevation to which he has been raised. Benevolence! — it is too weak a word; — affectionate charity beams in
every feature of the good Pontiff, nor is there wanting that visible
indication of a stern and unbending intrepidity* of character, which
will not fail, whenever it may be necessary, to vindicate the dearest
interests of religion.

The interval between Christmas and Easter was occupied in visit-
ing the most conspicuous churches, galleries, colleges, and libraries
of Rome, together with occasional excursions to the remarkable
places in the vicinity, which history and fable have so much associated with the early fortunes of Rome. On the feast of the
Epiphany, it was a rare and interesting spectacle to see priests
from the different Eastern Churches, Armenians, Greeks, and Mar-
onites, celebrating mass in their own peculiar rites, and in their own

––––––

* His fortitude in supporting the illustrious Archbishop of Cologne against the
persecuting policy of the King of Prussia, as well as his Apostolical rebuke of the
atrocious tyranny of the Russian autocrat, justify this view of his character

ALEXANDER M. SULLIVAN, M. P.

ADDRESS IN HIS OWN DEFENCE.

BY

A. M. SULLIVAN, M.P.

[831]

ADDRESS

DELIVERED BY A. M. SULLIVAN, M. P., IN HIS OWN DEFENCE,
IN GREEN STREET COURT HOUSE, DUBLIN, FEB. 20, 1868.

———

MY LORDS AND GENTLEMEN OF THE JURY,—I rise to address you under circumstances of embarrassment which will, I hope, secure for me a little consideration and indulgence at your hands. I have to ask you at the outset to banish any prejudice that might arise in your minds against a man who adopts the singular course—who undertakes the serious responsibility—of pleading his own defence. Such a proceeding might be thought to be dictated either by disparagement of the ordinary legal advocacy, by some poor idea of personal vanity, or by way of reflection on the tribunal before which the defence is made. My conduct is dictated by neither of these considerations or influences. Last of all men living should I reflect upon the ability, zeal, and fidelity of the Bar of Ireland, represented as it has been in my own behalf, within the past two days, by a man whose heart and genius are, thank God, still left to the service of our country, and represented, too, as it has been here this day by that gifted young advocate, the echoes of whose eloquence still resound in this court, and place me at disadvantage in immediately following him. And, assuredly, I design no disrespect to this court; either to tribunal in the abstract or to the individual judges who preside, from one of whom I heard two days ago, delivered in my own case, a charge of which I shall say—though followed by a verdict which already consigns me to prison—that it was, judging it as a whole, the fairest, the clearest, the most just and impartial ever given, to my knowledge, in a political case of this kind in Ireland between the subject and the Crown. No; I stand here in my own defence to-day, because long since I formed the opinion that on many grounds, in such a prosecution as this, such a course would be the most fair and most consistent for a man like me. That resolution I was, for the sake of others, induced to depart from on Saturday last, in the first prosecution against me. When it came to be seen that I was the first to be tried out of two journalists prosecuted, it was strongly urged on me that my course and the result of my trial might largely affect the case of the other journalists to be tried after me; and that I ought to waive my individual views and feelings, and have the utmost legal ability brought to bear in behalf of the case of the national press at the first point of conflict. I did so. I was defended by a bar not to be surpassed in the kingdom for ability and earnest zeal; yet the result was what I anticipated. For I knew, as I had held all along, that in a case like this, where law and fact are left to the jury, legal ability is of no avail if the Crown comes in with its arbitrary power of moulding the jury. In that case, as in this one, I openly, publicly, and distinctly announced that I for my part would challenge no one, whether with cause or without cause. Yet the Crown, in the face of this fact, and in a case where they knew that, at least, the accused had no like power of peremptory challenge, did not venture to meet me on equal footing; did not venture to abstain from their practice of absolute challenge; in fine, did not dare to trust their case to twelve men "indifferently chosen," as the constitution supposes a jury to be. Now, gentlemen, before I enter further upon this jury question, let me say that with me this is no complaint merely against "the Tories." On this, as well as on numerous other subjects, it is well known that it has been my unfortunate lot to arraign both Whigs and Tories. I say further, that I care not a jot whether the twelve men selected or permitted by the Crown to try me, or rather to convict me, be twelve of my own co-religionists and political compatriots, or twelve Protestants, Conservatives, Tories or "Orangemen." Understand me clearly on this. My objection is not to the individuals comprising the jury. You may be all Catholics, or you may be all Protestants, for aught that affects my protest, which is against the mode by which you are selected—selected by the Crown—their choice for their own ends—and not "indifferently chosen" between the Crown and the accused. You may disappoint or you may justify the calculations of the Crown official who has picked you out from the panel, by negative or posi-

RICHARD BRINSLEY SHERIDAN.

SPEECH.

RICHARD BRINSLEY SHERIDAN.

[857]

SPEECH

IN THE HOUSE OF COMMONS, IN OPPOSITION TO PITT'S FIRST INCOME TAX.

A WISE man, sir, it is said, should doubt of everything. It was this maxim, probably, that dictated the amiable diffidence of the learned gentleman,* who addressed himself to the chair in these remarkable words: "I rise, Mr. Speaker, if I have risen." Now, to remove all doubts, I can assure the learned gentleman† that he actually did rise; and not only rose, but pronounced an able, long, and elaborate discourse, a considerable portion of which was employed in an erudite dissertation on the histories of Rome and Carthage. He further informed the House, upon the authority of Scipio, that we could never conquer the enemy until we were first conquered ourselves. It was when Hannibal was at the gates of Rome, that Scipio had thought the proper moment for the invasion of Carthage, — what a pity it is that the learned gentleman does not go with this consolation and the authority of Scipio to the lord mayor and aldermen of the city of London! Let him say, "Rejoice, my friends! Bonaparte is encamped at Blackheath! What happy tidings!" For here Scipio tells us, you may every moment expect to hear of Lord Hawkesbury making his triumphal entry into Paris. ‡ It would be whimsical to observe how they would receive such joyful news. I should like to see such faces as they would make on that occasion. Though

---

* Dr. Lawrence.
† Mr. Perceval, afterwards Chancellor of the Exchequer, and, in 1809, Prime Minister. He was assassinated in the lobby of the House of Commons, May 11, 1812, by a man named Bellingham.
‡ Alludes to a boast of his lordship, at an early period of the war against France.

I doubt not of the erudition of the learned gentleman, he seems to me to have somehow confounded the stories of Hanno and Hannibal, of Scipio and the Romans. He told us that Carthage was lost by the parsimony or envy of Hanno, in preventing the necessary supplies for the war being sent to Hannibal; but he neglected to go a little further, and to relate that Hanno accused the latter of having been ambitious —

" Juvenum furentem cupidine regni ; "

and assured the senate that Hannibal, though at the gates of Rome, was no less dangerous to Hanno. Be this, however, as it may, is there any Hanno in the British senate? If there is, nothing can be more certain than that all the efforts and remonstrances of the British Hanno could not prevent a single man, or a single guinea, being sent for the supply of any Hannibal our ministers might choose. The learned gentleman added, after the defeat of Hannibal, Hanno laughed at the senate; but he did not tell us what he laughed at. The advice of Hannibal has all the appearance of being a good one : —

" Carthaginis mœnia Romæ munerata."

If they did not follow his advice, they had themselves to blame for it.

From the strain of declamation in which the learned gentleman launched out, it seems as if he came to this House as executor to a man whose genius was scarcely equalled by the eccentricities he sometimes indulged. He appears to come as executor, and in the House of Commons, to administer to Mr. Burke's fury without any of his fire. It is, however, in vain for him to attempt any imitation of those declamatory harangues and writings of the transcendent author, which, towards the latter part of his life, were, as I think, unfortunately too much applauded. When not embellished with those ornaments which Mr. Burke was so capable of adding to all he either spoke or wrote, the subject of such declamations could only claim the admiration of a school-boy. The circumstance of a great, extensive and victorious republic, breathing nothing but war in the long exercise of its most successful operations, surrounded with triumphs, and panting for fresh laurels, to be compared, much

A D D R E S S.

BY

ROBERT EMMET.

1867

ROBERT EMMETT.

POWERFUL ADDRESS OF ROBERT EMMET,

DELIVERED AT HIS TRIAL BEFORE LORD NORBURY, SEPT. 19, 1803.

———

MY LORDS—I am asked what have I to say why sentence of death should not be pronounced on me, according to law. I have nothing to say that can alter your predetermination, nor that it will become me to say, with any view to the mitigation of that sentence which you are to pronounce, and I must abide by. But I have that to say which interests me more than life, and which you have labored to destroy. I have much to say why my reputation should be rescued from the load of false accusation and calumny which has been cast upon it. I do not imagine that, seated where you are, your mind can be so free from prejudice as to receive the least impression from what I am going to utter. I have no hopes that I can anchor my character in the breast of a court constituted and trammelled as this is. I only wish, and that is the utmost that I expect, that your lordships may suffer it to float down your memories untainted by the foul breath of prejudice, until it finds some more hospitable harbor to shelter it from the storms by which it is buffeted. Was I only to suffer death, after being adjudged guilty by your tribunal, I should bow in silence, and meet the fate that awaits me without a murmur; but the sentence of the law which delivers my body to the executioner will, through the ministry of the law, labor in its own vindication to consign my character to obloquy; for there must be guilt somewhere; whether in the sentence of the court, or in the catastrophe, time must determine. A man in my situation has not only to encounter the difficulties of fortune, and the force of power over minds which it has corrupted or subjugated, but the difficulties of established prejudice.

The man dies, but his memory lives. That mine may not perish, that it may live in the respect of my countrymen, I seize upon this opportunity to vindicate myself from some of the charges alleged against me. When my spirit shall be wafted to a more friendly port —when my shade shall have joined the bands of those martyred heroes who have shed their blood on the scaffold and in the field in the defence of their country and of virtue, this is my hope—I wish that my memory and my name may animate those who survive me, while I look down with complacency on the destruction of that perfidious government which upholds its domination by blasphemy of the Most High — which displays its power over man, as over the beasts of the forest — which sets man upon his brother, and lifts his hand, in the name of God, against the throat of his fellow who believes or doubts a little more or a little less than the government standard — a government which is steeled to barbarity by the cries of the orphans and the tears of the widows it has made.

Here Lord Norbury interrupted Mr. Emmet, saying, " that the mean and wicked enthusiasts who felt as he did, were not equal to the accomplishment of their wild designs."

I appeal to the immaculate God — I swear by the throne of Heaven, before which I must shortly appear — by the blood of the murdered patriots who have gone before me — that my conduct has been, through all this peril, and through all my purposes, governed only by the conviction which I have uttered, and by no other view than that of the emancipation of my country from the superinhuman oppression under which she has so long and too patiently travailed ; and I confidently hope that, wild and chimerical as it may appear, there is still union and strength in Ireland to accomplish this noblest of enterprises. Of this I speak with confidence of intimate knowledge, and with the consolation that appertains to that confidence. Think not, my lords, I say this for the petty gratification of giving you a transitory uneasiness. A man who never yet raised his voice to assert a lie, will not hazard his character with posterity by asserting a falsehood on a subject so important to his country, and on an occasion like this. Yes, my lords, a man who does not wish to have his epitaph written until his country is liberated, will not leave a weapon in the power of envy, or a pretence to impeach the probity

Sincerely yours
Michael Davitt

ADDRESS.

BY

MICHAEL DAVITT.

[877]

FUTURE POLICY OF IRISH NATIONALISTS,

The following masterly address on the "Future Policy of Irish Nationalists," which he delivered in Mechanic's Hall, Boston, on December 8, 1878, before his departure for Ireland, being his first great effort in oratory, and a clear exposition of the reasons for unity of action amongst all classes of Irishmen, we give in full : —

IT would be difficult to conceive a position more unenviable than that in which an Irish Nationalist places himself when he attempts to review the past of his party in order to point out what he believes to have been rash or impolitic in its career. A criticism of the wisdom of an action that has failed or a line of conduct which has been injudicious, is at once construed into disloyalty to the principles or party which may have prompted such action by a sincere but imprudent resolve. But when he expresses himself dissatisfied with the narrow sphere of a policy which tends to exclude from National labor every one but a pronounced Separatist, and adds his belief that a change of tactics would turn the exertions of sincere Irishmen, though now pronounced Separatists, into the National cause, he is at once assumed to have "forfeited his principles," and to be on the high road to West-Britonism.

In consequence of this proneness of the Irish mind to hasty and uncharitable deductions, men (who *think* while working in Ireland's cause) are deterred from condemning what they know to be injudicious, lest they should find themselves ostracized from its ranks for their anxiety to see it directed the surest way to success. In my humble opinion, a want of moral courage belittles a man far more than a deficiency in the physical article, and that real cowardice consists in dreading the sentimental consequences of an upright, honest action. It has ever been the practice to pander to the popular prejudices of our country, by hyperbolical eulogies on everything

Irish, and we have thus become the spoiled children of struggling nationalities, and, as a necessary consequence, backward in our political education as a people, as well as behind the progressive march of the age. Holding these opinions, I will endeavor to-night to show you how we ourselves are to blame for past failures, and how essential it is, that the causes which led to such failures be guarded against in the future. The indestructibility of Irish nationality is no more its distinguishing characteristic, than is its past inapplicability to the working out of its own success, or the winning of an advanced social and political position for the people who profess it. We can boast that hundreds of years of the worst rule that ever cursed a country has failed to crush it; but can we say that Ireland is to-day in a condition commensurate with the struggles and sacrifices of her sons on her behalf during the past seven centuries? I think not; and the "why and wherefore" of this fact is what should focus upon it the thought and studies of practical Nationalists of the present. That there has been an unmethodical application of energies, or rather, a reckless waste of national strength in this long contest, is but too patent from a comparison between the position, social and political, of our country to-day, and that of other peoples who have struggled successfully against the same enemy. The very strength of our purpose and determination of our resolves were the means which invited defeat. We grasped at liberty in the intoxication of sincerity, and blindly discarded every other practical consideration. We "resolved," and "swore," and "determined" to *avenge Ireland's wrongs!* but took no essential method to win her liberty. We were actuated as much by *revenge* as by patriotism, and received the penalty which follows the obeying of a passion instead of the dictates of a virtue. While recognizing that it was a war of races, Saxon against Celtic, we refused to shelter ourselves behind the ramparts of expediency or employ any of the many justifiable means by which a weak people might utilize their strength; and we therefore marched into the open plain inviting destruction. Instead of watching our enemy from behind the Torres Vedras of Ireland's imperishable national principles, and determining our action by his weakness or strength according to the powers arrayed against him, we left our position exposed in order to challenge him to single combat, and we never

GENL. THOS. F. MEAGHER.

S P E E C H.

BY

Thomas Francis Meagher,

[895]

as the costliest legacy a true citizen could bequeath to the land that gave him birth.

What said this aged orator?

"National independence does not necessarily lead to national virtue and happiness; but reason and experience demonstrate that public spirit and general happiness are looked for in vain under the withering influence of provincial subjection. The very consciousness of being dependent on another power for advancement in the scale of national being, weighs down the spirit of a people, manacles the efforts of genius, depresses the energies of virtue, blunts the sense of common glory and common good, and produces an insulated selfishness of character, the surest mark of debasement in the individual, and mortality in the state."

My lord, it was once said by an eminent citizen of Rome, the elder Pliny, that "we owe our youth and manhood to our country, but our declining age to ourselves." This may have been the maxim of the Roman—it is not the maxim of the Irish patriot. One might have thought that the anxieties, the labors, the vicissitudes of a long career, had dimmed the fire which burned in the heart of the illustrious Roman whose words I have cited ; but now, almost from the shadow of death, he comes forth with the vigor of youth, and the authority of age, to serve the country in the defence of which he once bore arms, by an example, my lord, that must shame the coward, rouse the sluggard, and stimulate the bold. These sentiments have sunk deep into the public mind ; they are recited as the national creed. Whilst these sentiments inspire the people, I have no fear for the national cause. I do not dread the venal influence of the Whigs.

Inspired by such sentiments, the people of this country will look beyond the mere redress of existing wrong, and strive for the attainment of future power.

A good government may, indeed, redress the grievances of an injured people, but a strong people alone can build up a great nation. To be strong, a people must be self-reliant, self-ruled, self-sustained. The dependence of one people upon another, even for the benefits of legislation, is the deepest source of national weakness. By an unnatural law it exempts a people from their just duties — their just responsibilities. When you exempt a people from these duties, from these responsibilities, you generate in them a distrust in their own powers. Thus you enervate, if you do not

SPEECH.

BY

THOMAS D'ARCY McGEE.

[905]

www.ingramcontent.com/pod-product-compliance
Lightning Source LLC
Chambersburg PA
CBHW030644030726
47497CB00006B/1947